THEM WITHOUT PAIN

THEM WITHOUT PAIN

Chris Nickson

**SEVERN
HOUSE**

First world edition published in Great Britain and the USA in 2024
by Severn House, an imprint of Canongate Books Ltd,
14 High Street, Edinburgh EH1 1TE.

severnhouse.com

British Library Cataloguing-in-Publication Data
A CIP catalogue record for this title is available from the British Library.

ISBN-13: 978-1-4483-1440-9 (cased)
ISBN-13: 978-1-4483-1483-6 (e-book)

All Severn House titles are printed on acid-free paper.

Typeset by Palimpsest Book Production Ltd., Falkirk,
Stirlingshire, Scotland.
Printed and bound in Great Britain by TJ Books,
Padstow, Cornwall.

Praise for the Simon Westow mysteries

"A dark and complex mystery that contrasts genuine honor with the false tokens paraded by the upper classes"
Kirkus Reviews Starred Review of *The Scream of Sins*

"A dark, gritty page-turner . . . Multiple twists combined with realistic period ambience and vivid characters make this a riveting read"
Booklist on *The Scream of Sins*

"This gritty and surprise-filled mystery will enthrall both newcomers and series fans"
Publishers Weekly Starred Review of *The Dead Will Rise*

"Nickson's richly authentic descriptions of life in nineteenth-century Britain combine with a grisly plot and characters who jump off the page"
Booklist on *The Dead Will Rise*

"An action-packed mystery that provides interesting historical details about despicable crimes"
Kirkus Reviews on *The Dead Will Rise*

"Nickson does a superb job using the grim living and working conditions for the city's poor as a backdrop for a memorable and affecting plot. James Ellroy fans will be enthralled"
Publishers Weekly Starred Review of *The Blood Covenant*

"A gritty tale of perseverance, cruelty, rage, and redemption not for the faint of heart"
Kirkus Reviews on *The Blood Covenant*

"A fine choice for fans of British historical mysteries"
Booklist on *The Blood Covenant*

"Superior . . . The whodunit is enhanced by a grim portrait of life on the streets, embodied in a homeless child whom Jane befriends. Nickson again demonstrates mastery of the historical mystery"
Publishers Weekly Starred Review of *To The Dark*

About the author

Chris Nickson is the author of eleven Tom Harper mysteries, seven highly acclaimed novels in the Richard Nottingham series and seven Simon Westow books. Born and raised in Leeds, he returned to live there a decade ago.

www.chrisnickson.co.uk

Leeds, May 1825

The clamour of people at the market rose in her ears. Women shopping, servants on errands. All pressing around the stall to buy apples just arrived from the country. The first of autumn, green, blushed with red. Plump. Filling.

She could feel the hunger rippling through her belly. Nothing to eat since yesterday, and that had been the scrapings of a pie that someone had tossed away on Briggate. Stretching, she reached between the bodies. Touched the fruit. Cool, firm, smooth. She took a breath, grabbed it and pulled her hand back before anyone could catch her.

Darted away, holding the apple close to her chest. She wouldn't starve today. The first thing she'd ever stolen. Three days out here and she knew she'd need to learn if she was going to stay alive.

Before she could move any further, the hand came down hard on her shoulder—

Jane woke. She couldn't breathe. She was still caught, twisting, trying to fight free. Slowly, very, very slowly, she began to realize she was in her own bed, with the room, the house, safety, around her. She was safe. Gasping, gulping down air. Not eight years old, thrown out by her mother, fresh on the streets and terrified but determined to survive. Those days had long passed.

She was grown, she had a home, a proper home, with Mrs Shields.

Jane sat up and placed a hand over her heart. It fluttered and raced like a captured bird. Her face was clammy with sweat. Fear. She took quiet, shallow breaths, keeping still as her body grew calmer. A drink from the glass on the table.

That made three times in less than two weeks the bad dreams had come to torment her. Different on each occasion, but every one of them took her back to the time she lived on the streets.

In one she was fighting a man, knowing inside that killing him was the only way she'd stay alive. In another she'd been cutting a purse and trying to run, too terrified even to look around.

She'd left that life years before. Both that and the one that came after it, working for Simon Westow, the thief-taker. He'd valued her skills, the way she could follow without being seen, become the invisible girl who was deadly when it was necessary.

Jane had made good money with him. Then, finally, she'd needed to shed that skin. She found Simon a replacement, someone better at the work than she could ever be, promised she'd help if he ever needed it, and walked away.

No backward glance. No longing, only relief. She was content in her life now. She'd saved ample from her share of Simon's fees, enough to last her for years. In Mrs Shields, she had someone who needed her.

Jane had believed she was free. Looking to the future.

But the past was coming back to try and claim her.

ONE

Still early in the morning, but the sun was already warm, the way it had been for almost two weeks now, as if summer had arrived early. The machines were busy in the factories and mills, filling the air with noise as their chimneys belched smoke into the sky.

Simon Westow stood by the coffee cart on Briggate, listening to the gossip, most of it about the Moot Hall up the street. The old building had finally been demolished the week before, a teetering wreck that had needed to come down for years.

Now it was no more than a day or two until Middle Row, the shops and workshops that had stood behind the Hall in the centre of the street, would become a pile of rubble, too.

The voices were a murmur, a background to the welcome warmth on his face. From the corner of his eye, he saw Sally begin to move. She was the girl who worked for him, the one who'd taken over from Jane. Young, somewhere close to twelve years old but learning quickly; another survivor of the streets with the skills and speed a thief-taker's trade required.

Most mornings she followed him, keeping her distance, but always ready. Twice since the start of the year, men had tried to attack him; that came with the job. Sally had taken it on herself to be his bodyguard.

His hand slid towards his knife. For days now, he'd carried a vague feeling with him, a nagging little fear of danger at the back of his mind. No reason at all for it; he wasn't even working at the moment. Simon let the hand fall once he saw it was only George Mudie, the failed newspaperman who owned a printing shop on the far side of the Head Row. Someone he'd known for years. A friend of sorts; certainly a man he trusted.

'Don't often see you down here, George.'

'Never, you mean.' He snorted and paid his money for a tin mug of coffee, then stood staring at it.

'Changing your habits?'

'Here, I have this for you.' He reached inside a shabby coat and pulled out a crisp, folded piece of paper with a wax seal.

'From someone important?' Simon weighed it in his hand. So light it might blow away.

'A man asked me to do it.' Mudie took a sip of the coffee and spat. 'God Almighty, you drink this every day? The mud from the river probably tastes better.'

Simon laughed. 'It's an acquired taste.'

'I won't take the time to develop it.' He tipped the liquid into the road and placed the cup back on the trestle. 'Go and see him, Simon.'

'Who sent it?'

'You'll have to take a look and see. Now I'd better go and try to make an honest living.' He shambled away, hands thrust in the pockets of his trousers. Simon glanced at the seal: plain wax. He tucked the letter out of sight; time to read it once they were home.

'What did he want?' Sally asked as they walked.

'Bringing us some work. Looks like someone's keen to employ us but doesn't want the whole world to know.' Secrets and discretion were the lifeblood of his job, one he did very well. 'We'll find out soon enough.'

Simon placed the paper on the table. Rosie, his wife, picked it up.

'Old silver,' she said thoughtfully after she'd finished reading. 'Probably worth a fair bit of money.'

Their twin sons, Richard and Amos, were roughhousing upstairs. Sally moved to go and quieten them, but Simon gave a brief shake of his head. Let them have a few minutes of fun before the tutor arrived.

The note laid it out in a swift, flowing hand. Sir Robert Foley was the kind of man who'd always known wealth. It had passed through his family for generations, and he'd married a woman who brought her own healthy dowry. His life had been comfortable, perfectly cushioned against the world. Until yesterday morning, at least; he'd come down to breakfast to discover his valet gone, and four silver cups along with him. That was why he needed a thief-taker, someone who recovered stolen items for a fee.

The cups been made for one of Foley's ancestors more than a hundred years before. They were valuable in their own right, but that wasn't the only reason he wanted them found; they carried the thread of family. The man was clear. Find the cups and return them. No prosecution. As far as possible, he'd prefer everything out of the public eye, to avoid the humiliation of people knowing he'd been outfoxed by a servant. That was why he was using Mudie as an intermediary, a man he trusted could keep his mouth closed. At the end, the promise of a handsome fee.

'What's the valet's name?' Sally asked.

'He doesn't say.'

'Then you're going to need to go and talk to him,' Rosie said. 'Find out the details and come to a proper agreement.'

'I will,' he promised, and felt another twinge of fear in his belly. Strange.

Simon left his reply with Mudie and strolled back down Briggate. Thieving servants were common enough in his trade. He'd have to know all the details, but it sounded quite straightforward.

Sally remained his shadow, staying four or five paces behind, alert and keeping watch. She proved to be a natural at this; all he'd needed to do was refine her skills and teach her some subtleties of the business.

He'd never asked her real age. Maybe she didn't know. Not much older than his boys, that was certain. The girl had never spoken about her past and he'd let it lie; if she wanted him to know, she'd say. She was still small, easily able to stay hidden in a crowd, but he knew she'd kill to survive without any conscience or regret. That was how she'd lasted on the street. But now she had somewhere safe to live, with Simon and Rosie, up in the attic room. The twins loved her; she'd quickly become a part of the family, helping with the chores and errands, playing her part in the games.

With Jane no longer working, he'd been able to give Sally all

the small jobs, building to more responsibility and earning her
share of the fees he made for returning stolen goods. Two or
three times a week she would disappear for a few hours in the
evening. He never said a word, but Simon knew where she went:
the homeless camps where she'd once lived, giving money to
keep the children alive. Her business, not his.

The girl was an odd mix. Occasionally flashes of furious
darkness would explode, a dangerous, searing anger. At other
times she revealed a gentle compassion. She had a quick intel-
ligence and hard determination; deep under it all, usually carefully
hidden, the angry fire that seemed to constantly burn inside her.
Impossible to fathom. But he'd quickly come to trust her with
his life.

Simon watched the workmen carting away more of the rubble
from the Moot Hall and making their preparations to take down
Middle Row. Leeds was changing.

Constable Porter was standing at the side of Briggate, talking
to a man who gestured up at Middle Row with his cane. Simon
had seen the fellow's face around Leeds but never paid him much
attention. It was impossible to keep track of every soul when
Leeds kept growing by thousands each year. He was older, with
unruly grey hair and the stooped shoulders of someone who'd
spent many years bent over a desk. Definitely not a clerk, though.
Instead, a man who carried an air of genteel neglect with him;
his jacket was elegantly cut but fraying at the cuffs, the trousers
stylish ten years before, and his shoes were carelessly scuffed.
The silver at the head of his cane was cloudy and tarnished.

'Westow.' Porter raised his hand in greeting. 'You should come
and hear something interesting. This is Mr Armistead. He knows
a little about Middle Row.'

What was there to know? Simon wondered. It had stood empty
for months, decaying into a ruin of a building. The ground floor
had once been the Shambles, home to all the butchers' shops
until they'd been moved to new premises on Fleet Street and
Cheapside. Their ghosts lingered in the stink of dead meat that
had seeped into the wood and the stone. Above that, along a
wooden gallery, lay the old workshops, scarcely holding together
now. Good riddance to the whole damned thing.

'A pleasure, sir.' Simon lifted his hat.

'Mr Armistead claims there's something hidden inside one of those workshops.'

Hidden? What could be up there? Where?

'Your servant.' The man gave a small bow then pointed with his cane. 'That one, do you see it?' He turned to Sally. 'Miss. There's a secret room in there.'

Her eyes widened in astonishment. Simon glanced at the constable. His face showed nothing.

'It's all coming down on Thursday,' Porter said with relish. 'Can you imagine that, nothing standing in the middle of Briggate any longer?'

'I have permission to go and find this room before the demolition,' Armistead continued.

Sally frowned. 'If it's hidden, how do you know it's there?'

'Ah.' Armistead's face lit up. 'A fine question, miss. There's testimony, you see, from a trial. The room was part of a workshop that belonged to a silversmith named Arthur Mangey. In his day he was highly regarded here; he made the Leeds mace that they still use in the official processions. Then someone accused him of coin clipping. It came out about the room when he was in court.'

Tales, Simon thought. 'What happened to him?'

Armistead shifted his gaze down towards the ground. 'He was found guilty. Coin clipping is treason, you see. He was hanged in York. It all happened over a hundred years ago,' he added.

'You're saying that nobody's managed to find this room since then?' Simon asked. It sounded unlikely. People would have been scrambling to see it.

'No, sir, not that I've ever read,' the man replied. 'Thursday will be the final chance to look for it.'

'You should come along, Westow,' Porter said. An invitation. It didn't seem too long since they'd been wary around each other. Things had changed. They were hardly friends, but amiable enough. The constable seemed to have accepted that they both stood on the same side of the law. 'It'll be quite something to tell your boys.'

'Maybe so.' It could prove interesting, if he wasn't busy working for Foley. He nodded and raised his hat again. 'Good day to you, gentlemen.'

'Do you believe him?' Sally asked as they strode away. He could hear her doubt.

'Not a word,' he told her. 'Probably all in his imagination.'

Sir Robert Foley was a tall, nervous man in his late forties. Even in his own house, he seemed to start and turn at the smallest sound.

'I've been like this since Monday,' he explained with a distant smile. 'It's left me on edge.'

He was a wealthy man, living south of the river on Water Lane in a solid, well-kept house with a garden that ran down towards the river. He seemed to feel no need to impress, an unprepossessing figure in a worn, dowdy coat and shoes with plain buckles. A very ordinary face, the type that few would remember.

'George Mudie tells me you're good at your work,' he said. 'He recommended you.'

'I'm grateful to him. He probably told you that I've been doing this for a long time. Before we start, Sir Robert, it would help to know something from your letter: why would you rather nobody knew about the theft? That's going to make my job harder.'

'Honestly, it's nothing sinister.' Another fleeting smile. 'I'd simply prefer not to be the butt of gossip and jokes, if that's possible.'

If people found out, it would be nothing. They'd forget in a day; they always did, Simon had learned that. Still, it was his choice; he was paying the bills.

'I'll do what I can to keep it quiet. You wrote that you noticed the cups were missing on Monday morning.'

'Yes, the same time I learned that Kendall had gone.'

'Kendall?'

'Thomas Kendall,' Foley said. 'My valet. The one who stole them.' He reached into his pocket and produced several folded sheets of paper. 'I've written down everything I know about him. I described the cups.'

The man seemed like a rare one for putting pen to paper.

'You said they'd been in your family for a long time.'

He nodded. 'Well over a century. The details about them are all in there, too. My great-grandfather commissioned them from a local silversmith called Mangey.'

'Mangey?' Suddenly Sir Robert Foley had his full attention.

'Yes. He was supposed to be the best in Leeds.'

'Arthur Mangey. I've heard his name.'

'Really?' Foley narrowed his eyes, curious. 'Not many have. Do you know his story?'

'Only the barest of bones,' Simon answered. The same name, twice in a short time. That was very odd. A coincidence? Or an omen?

'I've put what I know in that letter. There's a fair description of Kendall, the name of his previous employer, all about the cups and their hallmark. Return them and I'll pay you well.' He named the fee. Very generous, Simon thought; a good incentive to take the job.

'Very well.'

'Are you going to do it?' Mudie asked as Simon settled by the desk of the printing shop. He was bent over a block of type, peering close as he checked the letters. Sally sat quietly, observing everything.

'He seems like an odd one.'

Mudie laughed. 'Always has been. I've known him for years.'

'Can you vouch for him?'

Not a moment's hesitation. 'Yes. Absolutely.'

That was good enough.

TWO

F oley had put plenty of detail in the document. A complete description of Thomas Kendall, with his single distinguishing mark: a pair of old scars, parallel lines, across the back of his left hand. Hard to hide those.

Simon read the whole thing out loud. Rosie listened as she kneaded dough for the next day's bread. Sally hung on the words, frowning with concentration. She couldn't read, saw no reason to learn. Not like Jane, who'd taken to words like a duck to water when Mrs Shields began to teach her. But Sally had a formidable memory. She noticed, and fitted the pieces together.

'He'd been with Foley for a year,' Simon said. 'Completely trusted, the man says. Nothing ever missing before the cups, not even any questions about items that were lost. He can't understand why it happened.'

'Who did he work for before that?' Rosie asked.

Simon leafed through the pages. 'A family called Richmond on Park Square.'

She brightened. 'Richmond the banker? I've met his wife a few times.' She covered the dough with a towel. 'I can pay a call on her while this rises. The boys will be busy with their tutor for hours yet. It won't take me long to put on a decent gown.'

'Evidently they gave Kendall a good reference.'

'Come on, Simon,' Rosie said. 'A good reference could mean anything at all. You know that.' Her eyes gleamed at the chance to work with him again.

'What do you want me to do?' Sally asked.

'Let's start by asking around. See if anyone knows this man Kendall. People will probably remember the scars.' He thought for a second. 'Go to the pawn shops.' Simon had introduced her to the men who owned them. It seemed unlikely that Kendall would try to sell anything so valuable there, but everything needed to be checked.

Sitting alone in the kitchen, he thought: Mangey. The name niggled at him. It had to be a coincidence. And yet . . .

He stood, gathered his hat off the peg and closed the front door behind himself.

Jane had finished her errands. An early stop at the market for vegetables and fruit, picking through to find the best of last year's crop and haggling over the prices like a housewife. Then to the circulating library, to return the book she'd finished and choose another: *The Scottish Chiefs*, by a woman named Jane Porter. She'd stood and read the first two pages, gripped enough to borrow it. A stop at the clothes stall, finding a muslin dress with a print of peacocks that seemed to fit when she held it against her body. The one she wore around the house had been ripped and mended so many times it was only fit for rags. This was a lucky find, in good condition, the seams strong, and no more than second- or third-hand. A fair price, too. As she handed over the coins, Jane was aware of the children darting back and forth, scavenging anything that dropped, trying to pick a pocket or cut a purse. Whatever they could do to keep themselves alive.

Finally, across Timble Bridge to the butcher's shop. On the way back, she stopped to talk to Kate the pie-seller.

'Look at you. You're still too thin,' the woman said as Jane gave her the money for a pie. 'How many years has it been and there's still not much to you but skin and bone.'

'I'm fine.' Kate was a large woman, growing stouter each year. Something close to a friend, who'd occasionally stopped her going hungry during her years on the streets. As she spoke, Jane felt a prickle up her spine and her body tensed. Someone was waiting for her. 'There's no need for you to worry.'

She began to walk up Briggate. Taking her time, glancing in the shop windows to see if anyone was following her. A minute or two listening to Davy Cassidy, the blind fiddler. For once, though, she couldn't soar with his music.

After months of nothing at all, so long that she'd believed she was free of a thief-taker's life, the feeling was here again, coming out of nowhere. This and the dreams, they had to mean something. She shifted the basket to her left hand, feeling the nub of her little finger rub against the willow handle. She'd exacted her revenge against the man who'd taken the rest of it, her very last act before she walked away from working for Simon Westow. Her right hand took hold of the knife in the pocket of her dress. It felt unfamiliar, awkward, but reassuring to keep it close.

The sense was real, growing stronger as she walked. Not her imagination, she was absolutely certain of that. But nobody she'd been able to spot. That didn't mean much. Jane had allowed her skills to grow rusty, happy that she didn't need them any longer.

Now the past was spreading its arms, reaching out to embrace her.

The suspicion remained, all the way along the Head Row. By the time she turned into Green Dragon Yard, her breath was tight in her chest. So close to the safety of home. But he was there, waiting for her.

'You'd better come in.'

'Oh, child, you have to go and see that,' Mrs Shields clapped her hands together like a child. Her eyes twinkled with excitement. 'A secret room right here in the middle of town. It seems impossible to believe. Go on, you can be my eyes and tell me what happens. Middle Row was already ancient when I was your age.'

It was the first time in months that Simon had been in the cottage. She'd see him in town and they'd exchange short, pleasant greetings, but nothing more than that. Easier to keep a wary distance, she'd decided.

He looked awkward, out of place. He wasn't sure how welcome he'd be, he told her as they stood outside the house. That was why he'd waited for her. Now he was sitting on a stool, the first man in a long time to enter this house of women. But inside a few minutes she felt stifled by his presence. He seemed to fill the room, to draw all the air from it. The dreams, him sitting in front of her: the world was tilting and leaving her unsure and off balance.

'I'm really not sure I believe this story about a secret room,' he warned. 'It sounds too fanciful to be true. But Mangey's name has come up twice now. That's strange enough.' He looked at Jane. 'I know you enjoy stories and history. I thought you might be interested to see it.'

The invitation was an offering. His gift. She glanced across at the old woman, seeing the hope and longing in her eyes; she'd go and see the spectacle herself if she were able.

'I'll come,' Jane told him. 'Thank you.'

As she stood at the door, watching him ease through the gap in the wall and out into Green Dragon Yard, away from her, she started to feel like she could breathe again.

THREE

'One of the children claimed he'd seen a man with scars on his hand,' Sally said as they sat at the kitchen table. The boys were gulping down their bread and dripping, paying no attention to the conversation. 'But he doesn't remember what they were like.'

Maybe that was something; maybe not. 'What about the pawnbrokers? Did you have any luck there?' They were always busy, people pledging whatever they had for money to survive the week.

She shook her head. 'Nobody's brought in a set of silver cups.' She paused and pursed her lips. 'I'm not sure if I believe them all, though.'

That wasn't much of a surprise; half the pawnbrokers in town skirted the law. 'Any particular one you think is lying?'

'Josiah Green,' Sally replied. 'You know the way he is, he kept looking away from me when he answered.'

Simon nodded. Green was slippery, one of nature's born liars. He'd visit and discover some truth. After he'd seen this secret room – if it actually existed.

'Banker Richmond and his wife are away until Friday,' Rosie said. 'Visiting relatives in Durham.'

'That'll have to wait, then.'

Jane had been reluctant to wear her best dress, a rich chocolate colour with a pattern of small raspberries across the fabric. She'd had it made in some fit of madness, but hardly worn it since. When did she ever need to dress up? Mrs Shields had persuaded her to put it on, then brushed her hair. She brought out an old, embroidered cotton shawl and draped it delicately around Jane's shoulders.

'That's lovely,' she said as her fingertips caressed the material. 'Is it yours?'

'I used to wear it a long time ago.' She took a step back and nodded. 'It suits you, child.'

'Thank you.'

'The weather is right for it, and you're attending an occasion,' Catherine Shields said. 'Clothes ought to be worn, not hidden away in a chest.'

Was this such a grand event? she wondered as she walked down Briggate, feeling the warmth on her face. Perhaps it was; a crowd had gathered in the heat to watch. Workmen stood off to the side, smoking their pipes and drinking as they awaited the order to begin the demolition. Jane was suddenly aware of the ladder of old scars on her arms. Faded almost to nothing now, but a reminder of the darkness in her past when using a knife on her own flesh had felt like an answer. She spotted Simon, dressed in a good suit, and Constable Porter in his best swallowtail coat, with a fresh, crisp stock tied around his neck. Mrs Shields had been right to insist that she wore her best dress; she fitted in. Another man stood with Simon and Porter, someone older, with a sprawl of grey hair and expensive, unfashionable clothes, an eager expression on his face. She touched the gold ring on her right hand that Mrs Shields had long ago given her for luck.

'This is Miss Jane Truscott', Simon introduced her. 'Mr Armistead.'

The man had fine manners, taking her hand and bowing.

'It's time,' the constable said as he glanced at his watch. He picked up a heavy hammer and started to lead the way up the creaking wooden stairs to the galley. Eagerly, Armistead skipped ahead of him.

Jane had been up here before; she knew every crevice of Leeds in her pores. Yet never inside any of the workshops. She watched as Porter selected a rusty old key from a heavy ring of them looped over his arm, and turned it in the lock.

Simon kept his eyes on Armistead. The man was full of anticipation, shifting from one foot to another as the constable opened the door, then scurrying to be first into the room.

He paused, feeling the tiny sliver of fear return at the edge of his mind. Stupid. It was a bright morning, an empty room with others around; there was no danger here.

The workshop was almost bare, only a scarred old wooden table under the dirty window that looked out over Briggate. A

thick layer of dust covered everything, cobwebs across the glass
and in all the corners. He breathed in the smell of neglect and
dereliction, years of scents piled on top of each other. Simon
watched Porter gaze around, unimpressed.

Armistead was running his hands across the dirty wooden panel-
ling on the far wall, his face so close to it that he looked to be
studying the grain. Very lightly, he tapped his fist against the wood.

Simon heard. So did the constable; he raised his head. Hollow.
There was space behind there.

'I can't see any catch to open it,' Armistead said.

'Doesn't matter. It's going to come down, anyway. Stand back.'
He was reluctant to move until Porter brought the hammer down
close to his hands and he slid away to safety.

The first blow fell like thunder, dry wood shattering as splinters
flew around the room. Simon realized his throat was dry. He was
holding his breath in anticipation. From the corner of his eye he
saw Jane, standing, silent, gaze fixed on the scene. He'd done
right to ask her. Neither Rosie nor Sally had seemed too interested, but she was rapt.

A second blow, then a third turned into a rhythm of booming.
By the fifth he'd made a small gap, enough for an arm. Finally,
sweating from the effort, the constable lowered the hammer.
Space for a man to wriggle through.

Armistead was the first. That was only fair; he was the one
who'd been so certain this hidden room existed. A small shout
of delight became a wail of horror. Simon looked at Porter, then
squeezed through the hole.

The secret workshop ran the width of the room. No windows.
No light beyond the little that came through the gap. Four feet
wide at most, hard rat droppings all over the floorboards. A small
wooden bench held two rusted pairs of shears and a tarnished
silver coin.

The body was sprawled face down across the floor.

Not an ancient wastage of bones and dry, leathery skin. This
one was fresh, barely the start of a high summer stink. The
rodents and insects had begun to feast on him, but he guessed
the corpse hadn't even been here a full day.

Simon squatted. In the gloom he could make out two pale
lines about an inch apart on the back of the corpse's left hand.

He knew of one man with scars like that. He'd read about them just the day before.

That little gnaw of fear grew stronger.

The tiny room hadn't been such a tight secret, after all.

Armistead was torn, head moving between the old treasures on the bench and the dead man on the floor.

'It's better if you leave,' Simon told him in a quiet voice. With a frightened nod, the man hurriedly gathered up the shears and the coin and scrambled away. Simon followed him out.

'Well?' Porter asked.

'You'd better go and see it for yourself.'

Ten seconds was enough. He came out wearing a strained frown.

'Do you know who he is?'

'His name's Thomas Kendall. He stole a set of silver cups.' Simon let the words hang in the air. 'They were made by Arthur Mangey.'

For a moment the room was silent, then Armistead and Porter both began speaking. He saw Jane slip through the opening and into the hidden room.

The dead had never scared her. She'd seen too many of them in her life, and this one held nothing for her. She wanted to look at this secret place. It was the entire reason she'd come. To breathe it in, to absorb a sense of it before it all came crashing to nothing. From the other end of Middle Row she could already make out the shouting and hammers of the workmen, the dull thump of stone as it tumbled to the ground.

In here, though, everything was different. She closed her eyes to feel the play of history around her. Jane moved her left hand over the surface of the bench. The silversmith must have made the gouges and scrapes in the wood. Committed his crimes here, out of sight, by the light of a candle.

The body lay on the floor. Nothing she could do to help him. But the question ran through her mind: how had he ended up in this place?

Simon was talking as she came out.

'There's no pool of blood under Kendall's body, so he might

have been murdered somewhere else. But—' he turned to
Armistead '—you're obviously not the only one who knew
about that place. Whoever did this understood how to get in
and out.'

'I . . .' the man begin. He clutched the shears close to his
chest, as if someone might drag them out of his grasp. A hunted
look froze on his face.

Porter calmed him. 'No one's accusing you. You'd never have
brought us here if you were guilty. But you seemed certain that
nobody else had heard of the place.'

'I am,' he replied, then corrected himself. 'I was.'

'How many people have you told about it?' Simon asked.

'A few over the years, I would suppose.' It came out as a
reluctant admission.

Jane saw Simon glance at the constable and raise his eyebrows.
A nod as a response.

'It's probably best if you go home now, Mr Armistead,' Porter
said. 'I'm sure it's been a shock and taken away your pleasure
in the moment.'

'Yes.' He dipped his head. 'It has.'

'I'll come and talk to you later.'

They waited until he'd gone, his feet hurrying down the stairs.

'Well, Westow, why were you looking for Kendall? Whose
silver had he stolen?'

'Sir Robert Foley.' He wasn't going to lie. Not with Kendall's
corpse a few feet away. 'He wants the cups back, that's all. I'll
have to talk to him, tell him what's happened.'

'You do that. Cups made by Mangey and the thief's body turns
up in his workshop, a place that's supposed to be secret, on the
one day it's almost certain to be found.' He snorted. 'That's
stretching the idea of coincidence, isn't it?'

'What does it mean, though?' Simon asked. 'If he was
murdered in any of the other rooms here, it's too late to find out
where it happened. Just listen: half of this place is probably
already rubble.'

'I'll have my men take the body to the infirmary. Dr Hey can
examine it. Anything you find . . .'

'Of course.'

He raised his hat to her as he left. 'Miss.'

Simon turned to her and she sensed what was coming. 'You said you'd be willing to help if I needed you.'

She dipped her head so he couldn't see her eyes. 'I did.'

'I'd value you on this.'

Jane took a breath. Maybe the dreams, Simon's appearance, all the events had been leading up to this. But until she opened her mouth to speak, she wasn't sure how she'd answer.

'Yes.'

FOUR

't's murder. I had to give the constable your name.'

Sir Robert remained silent for a long time, looking at the garden through the window without really seeing it. Then he nodded. 'Of course. You had no choice under the circumstances,' he said with weary acceptance, exhaling slowly and shook his head. 'Murder . . . that puts a very different complexion on everything. I'd hoped for privacy but . . . who could have anticipated this? God knows, I've cursed Kendall up and down since he vanished, but I never wished death on him.' A bitter sigh. 'I don't suppose there was any sign of the cups?'

'Nothing,' Simon told him. 'You can bet that word about the killing is all over town already. The constable will probably be coming to talk to you.'

'I daresay he will.' His eyes were full of sadness, but for what, Simon wondered. Kendall's death, the loss of something he treasured, or that people would know he'd been gulled by a servant? 'Keep on searching, Mr Westow. I want those cups back. They belong with my family.'

'I will.'

Friday morning, and Jane settled on the bench in Simon's kitchen. Everything was familiar, the smells, the furniture, the faces, but strange, too, after months away. She'd never expected to return; she didn't quite belong, visiting her past only to find she no longer quite fitted. Even as she sat here, she still wasn't certain she'd made the right decision when she agreed to help. Somehow it seemed to have been made for her, to be dragging her along.

'Foley wants us to carry on searching for the cups,' Simon announced. 'Dr Hey's examined Kendall's body. He was stabbed once. The knife went in under his ribs and up, straight into the heart. Instant death, probably very little blood, so I was wrong. It's very likely he was killed in that room.' He paused and she waited. 'At least one person apart from Armistead knew it existed,

and how to get in and out of it. He must have known about the
connection to Mangey and the cups, too.'

Rosie stared at the table as she followed the thread in her
mind. 'Someone hired Kendall to steal the cups, then killed him.
Why *those* cups, though, and why leave the body in *that* room?'

'I know it doesn't seem to make much sense.' Simon corrected
himself after a moment's thought. 'Any sense. For the moment,
about the only thing we can say with certainty is that it seems
to revolve around Mangey. But don't ask me how. I can't make
head nor tail of it.'

Jane watched Sally; the girl was listening with a hard intensity,
jaw set firm as she stared ahead, body tense. Suddenly she raised
her head and spoke.

'Mangey's been dead for a long time. How can he be involved?'

Simon smiled. 'I'm going to talk to Jane about that. Right
now, we need to discover where Kendall had been staying after
he ran off from Foley's house.' He paused. 'We want that, but
we'll take whatever we can scrape up.'

While Sally and Rosie made their plans, he came to sit beside
her.

'How does it feel to be back?' he asked, gesturing at the room.

'Different,' she told him warily. 'The same.'

'When I invited you to see if there was a secret room, I never
expected any of this.' He hesitated before he continued. 'I know
I asked you to help, but what I'd like you to do is something
very different from anything you've done before.'

What? She felt a stab of panic. In the past she'd always followed
people for Simon, hunted them, stopped them. That was what a
thief-taker did, and she knew she'd done it well. But they'd
become Sally's tasks now. What else could he want from her?

'I talked to Mr Armistead,' Simon said. 'He showed me the
material he has on Mangey. There's plenty of it. He's collected
everything he could find and put together books of papers. You've
met him; you can probably imagine.' He gave a quick grin that
disappeared in a second. 'Mangey is an obsession of his. I'm
certain there has to be some sort of connection between what
happened today and what took place back then.'

'Yes.'

'I'd like you to go through whatever Armistead has on the

man. Let him take you through it all and see if you can find the
link between what happened to him and what's going on now.
The killer won't be expecting anything like that.'

'Me?' The idea stunned her. She wondered if she'd just
imagined it.

'You can make sense of it. You like to read.'

'But . . .'

Her thoughts were churning; the worries rushed in to taunt
her. It wasn't much more than a year ago that Mrs Shields taught
her to read. She loved it, but there was still so much she didn't
understand. Those papers would be full of old words and strange
writing. Law. How could she hope to understand any of that?
Did he realize what he was asking?

'I don't know if I can.' It terrified her. Her work in the past
had felt like second nature. The same things she'd done to stay
alive when she lived on the street. Every single moment of this
would be a struggle. She could fail.

'Try,' he said. 'Please. I wouldn't ask if I didn't think you
weren't capable.'

Jane drew in a long breath. Did he really believe she could
do this? 'I can't promise anything.'

'That's fine,' Simon told her. 'I don't expect any guarantees.
Look, I don't even know if there *are* any answers in there. There
might be; it's something we can try. Rosie doesn't have the time,
Sally can't read. You're the only one who can do it. Go and see
Mr Armistead. In the morning; he's busy today. He has the house
with the bright blue door on Kirkgate, just a few yards down
from Briggate.'

She stood, mind still reeling.

'All right,' she agreed, feeling as if she was standing at the
edge of a cliff. A single wrong step and she'd fall.

Her mind was still a jumble as she began to walk along
Swinegate. She heard the rush of footsteps coming behind her and
turned. No surprise; she'd wondered whether the girl would follow.

'I'm glad you're back.' Sally's voice was tentative.

'It's only for this.'

'I didn't know if you ever wanted to see any of us after
everything that happened.' Her eyes moved to Jane's missing
finger. 'That's why I stayed away.'

'I had to stop,' Jane told her. No regrets about that, and now she was filled with uncertainty about what she was going to be doing. 'Are you still happy working with Simon?'

'Oh, yes.' The grin of pleasure spread across her face. She still carried an innocence about her. It was deceptive, Jane knew that; Sally's eyes had seen too much for her years. 'I'm learning all the time and . . .' She groped to find the words. 'I feel like I have a family now. I never had chance to thank you for bringing me into it all.'

The girl she'd known had constantly bristled with fury. This Sally was happier. 'Have you had to use your knife much?'

'Not too often.' Sally shrugged, as if it was nothing. Her face broke into another broad smile. 'You were right about the fees, too. He pays me half of everything we make. I have more money than I can count.'

'Have you been saving it?' That was what she'd advised. What she'd done herself. It had given her freedom.

'Some of it.'

She knew full well what Sally did with the rest. When she'd been out walking at night she'd seen the girl around the homeless children, doling out coins. Sally was small and thin, still starting on the long path to becoming an adult, not ready to leave her own past behind her. Sometimes a deadly history. Jane understood that all too well. In so many ways, Sally's life was a reminder of her own.

'Maybe we'll be able to work together.'

Jane shook her head. 'Simon wants me to go over all the old documents about Mangey with Mr Armistead. I'll be spending my time with him.'

'Oh.' She tried to mask her disappointment. 'Would you mind if I visited you?' There was a plea in the question. She might have a new family, but she needed someone who *knew*.

Jane squeezed her hand for a moment. 'Of course not. You'll always be welcome.'

Simon passed the word in the dramshops and inns: good money for information about Kendall. Small stirrings but so far no takers. *Somebody* had to know. The man had spent a pair of nights somewhere between leaving Foley's and meeting his death. He'd made the offer. In the end, greed would always win.

Finding Kendall's body in that room had jarred him. It turned a case that had seemed quite ordinary upside down and left him looking for somewhere to begin. So far, no luck.

The night tasted of smoke and warmth as he ambled home along Duncan Street. He felt a presence behind him and slipped a knife from its sheath up his sleeve. He carried three, another on his belt and the third in his boot. The twinge of fear grew sharper and colder in his chest.

Close now. He turned, the blade in his hand.

Sally stepped out of the shadows, raising her hands.

'I saw you and thought I'd make sure no one was following.'

'Any joy tonight?'

She shook her head.

'Who do you think is doing all this?' she asked as they turned on to Swinegate. Suddenly, her body stiffened. A moment later, he sensed it, too. A figure ahead of them, waiting in the night. He tried to pick out a shape, but the darkness was too full.

Simon's heart was racing and his palm was damp on the knife hilt as his eyes searched the blackness. Sally had faded off into the shadows, but he knew she'd be there.

The quick rasp of a boot on flagstone. Simon jerked his head at the sound.

Five yards away. Not near enough for a knife. He stood, waiting. Two seconds. Three, four, five.

Another shift of the feet.

'What do you want?'

'You said you'd pay to know where Kendall had been staying.' The man's voice wavered. Thin and scared.

'I will.'

'How much?'

'Sixpence.' Simon was aware of someone else, behind him now, creeping closer. He took a breath, skin prickling, but tried to show nothing.

'Let me see your money first.'

Too easy. He hadn't tried to haggle for more. Simon started to reach for his purse and braced himself for the attack. This was when it would happen. Instead, a quick screech of pain, loud enough to wake the street.

Simon was slow; he felt as if he was forcing himself out of a stupor, watching himself move. But the man in front of him hesitated even longer before deciding to run. Enough time for Simon to be on him, the knife at his throat, smelling the stink of helplessness as the thief pissed himself with fear.

'Well? Where was he?'

'I don't know.' The words rushed from his mouth, tripping over each other to arrive. 'We heard you talking and we thought we could take your purse.'

Two young men who thought they'd found an easy mark. They'd almost been right. He'd let them come too close to success. If Sally hadn't been here . . .

'It sounds like your friend has paid a price.' The noise had softened to whimpers of pain. 'That's what happens when you make a mistake.' The man in front of him was shaking with fear. 'Give me a reason why you shouldn't hurt, too.'

He watched as the mouth opened and closed, but this time nothing came out. Finally, a shake of the head. 'I'm sorry.'

Simon took the man's knife away. 'Go and see to your friend. The next time—'

'No more. Honest. I promise.' He stumbled away.

A few paces and Sally was beside him again, her knife already in her pocket.

'What did you do?'

'Just sliced off the top of his ear, that's all. He'll heal. He was going to stab you.' She said it without concern, a simple fact; he had to remind himself that she'd already seen so much in her life.

Inside, after he locked and barred the front door, she wished him goodnight and ran lightly up the stairs. So often she seemed as if nothing worried her, but he knew it caught up with her sometimes; there'd been a few nights he'd heard quiet crying from the attic in the small hours as bad dreams plagued her.

Simon stood, hands still on the wood, trying to make sense of the encounter. It was the type of thing that had happened half a hundred times over the years. So familiar, almost like watching a play. He should have been in control; there shouldn't have been any kind of problem. This time, though, he hadn't been able to play his part properly. Something had held him back a moment too long. Was it the fear that had been creeping up on him lately?

It could have killed him.

He pressed harder against the door, trying to still the trembling that had begun in his fingers and moved into his hands. He stood, heart still pounding too fast as he tried to understand what had happened. Was it a moment that would pass? Christ Almighty, he needed to believe it was.

Simon took a deep breath. Whatever it was, he had to put it aside. He had no time for this. There was work to do. Tomorrow they'd go hunting again.

FIVE

Jane looked at her good dress again before deciding to wear the muslin she'd bought a few days before. It fitted her well enough, and she looked perfectly presentable. Nerves fluttered in her belly at the thought of going to see Mr Armistead. Was she good enough to do what Simon wanted?

'It's a good choice for the weather,' Mrs Shields agreed. 'All those yellows and greens in the print look like summer.'

She stood by the looking glass, brushing the morning tangles out of her hair, then laid the shawl the woman had given her over her shoulders.

'You're a proper picture, child.' The old woman gave a beam of delight. 'I don't expect he'll remember me, but please give Mr Armistead my regards. He knew my husband long ago. You should have seen the time someone brought him to a ball at the Assembly Rooms. He looked aghast at having to talk to strangers and dance with women.' She laughed at the faded memory. 'I think he fled after ten minutes.'

'Simon said he'll be expecting me.'

'He's a gentleman,' Mrs Shields told her. 'You'll have nothing to worry about with him.'

If only that was true, she thought as she hurried down Briggate, hardly noticing the crowds and the Saturday warmth. Her mind was overflowing with worries. How could she do all this, these old words and lives? Not a novel to sit and enjoy, but a real life to study. Simon had more faith in her skills than she did.

At the corner of Kirkgate, she hesitated. Just a few weeks ago she had her own, calm existence. Then the nightmares began. Now she was being drawn back towards her past. She was becoming a thief-taker again. Did she want that? It wasn't too late to turn and go home. To wrap herself in the safety of four walls. Then someone barged against her and she stumbled forward. Maybe it was an omen. Keep going.

The house had been grand once. Over the years that had faded to a kind of careless poverty, Jane thought, as if the owner had never noticed that the place had grown weary. The furniture was heavy, dark wood, the rugs old and worn threadbare in places. But Armistead paid no attention. He bowed and welcomed her, guided her through to the library.

For a moment, Jane could scarcely breathe. She was overwhelmed. Bookcases on every wall, their shelves bowed under the contents, far more books than she believed could fit in an entire home. Almost as many as the circulating library. She wanted to trace her fingers along the spines, to feel the leather of the bindings.

He pointed to a table.

'I took the liberty of making sure that everything to do with Mangey was ready. All my research.' He managed a bashful smile and she realized he was as nervous as her. 'Do you know, you'll be the first to see it.'

Five thick volumes, each stuffed with documents and papers. How could she ever begin to make sense of all that?

Not long after noon and Jane stood by the corner of Briggate and Boar Lane, buying food from Kate the pie-seller. Her head was ready to explode, crammed to bursting with everything she'd heard and read in the last few hours. She was drowning from hearing fact upon fact about Mangey, his family, and George Norcross, the shoemaker who'd accused him of coin clipping.

Kate eyed her up and down, the muslin she was wearing and the embroidered shawl. 'You're all dressed up today.' She gave a sly grin. 'Meeting a lad?'

Jane blushed, feeling the heat in her cheeks. 'No, of course not. It's work. I needed some air.'

Anything to stop feeling as if she was being swept along in the torrent of language and dates and names. The doubts that had gathered as she walked to Armistead's house loomed stronger than ever.

'You look dazed,' Kate told her.

Jane smiled. 'Trying to take in too much.'

He'd gone through fact after fact, point by point, from Mangey's birth in York to living in Leeds and being commissioned to create the Leeds Mace.

'What's a mace?' she asked him.

'It's a little like a stick,' Armistead replied after long consideration. 'An ornamental one. It's made of precious metal and decorated. Just for show, for ceremony, they use it on civic occasions. Mangey made the one we have in Leeds from silver and gold. It's an elaborate piece, very beautiful.' His eyes shone as he spoke. 'He was able to show just how gifted he was as a silversmith. He was well paid for it, too.'

Yet only two years later, he said, Mangey was hanged on the Knavesmire in York, convicted of treason by a jury.

'Norcross, the man who accused him, he was the one who mentioned the hidden workshop. But he never produced any evidence of it, and nobody ever saw it.'

'Then why was Mangey convicted?' Jane asked.

'That's a very good question. From the trial transcript, I wouldn't have predicted the guilty verdict,' Armistead admitted. 'But it happened. You have to understand that coin clipping was treason, as serious a crime as we can imagine. Cutting little pieces of silver off a penny or a sixpence debases the coinage. It hurts the country. Still, there were a few who believed Arthur Mangey was the victim of some sort of vengeance by the corporation. I've never been able to find out why they thought that, or if it's true,' he said with frustration.

From there, he'd begun with details. Names. Events. Dates. Now they cluttered her head as she sat and ate the pie. The air was warm, heavy and grey with soot, but simply being outside calmed her, with the hustle and bustle of people moving around her like water.

Soon enough it was time to return, her belly fluttering as she walked. Tonight she'd put it all down on paper so everything made some sense.

Saturday morning and Simon was early to the coffee cart, hearing more of the gossip and wild ideas about the hidden room and the body. One or two knew Kendall's name.

No hints, though, no possibilities to investigate. They were starting from nothing. But that wasn't the only thing troubling him.

At least nobody was talking about what had happened the

night before. That was something to keep quiet. Sally had saved him. Without her, he might not have been breathing now. The thought had prodded him awake too many times during the night, anxious and drenched in sweat.

He'd been lucky to come up against amateurs. Any professional would have left him dead on the ground. He'd been indecisive. Impossibly slow. That moment of questioning and doubting himself, of second-guessing a move before he'd even made it: those were death sentences in this trade.

He'd said nothing to Rosie. What could he tell her, that he was losing his nerve? That he might be growing too old for this business? What else could he do in life? This was the only real work he'd known. He had money, but nowhere near enough to last a lifetime and provide for his sons.

No choice but to overcome this. To conquer the fears that snapped at his heels and stay alert.

'Where are we going today?' Sally asked.

'Let's start with Josiah Green,' he told her. 'You thought he was lying about someone trying to sell him the cups. We'll see what he has to say for himself.'

The man started blinking as soon as they entered the shop, glancing away in that curious manner he had instead of looking them in the eye. Definitely hiding something, Simon thought, and making a poor job of it.

'Silver cups.'

'I don't have any,' Green shook his head and spread his arms, then nodded at Sally. 'I told her. Search if you like. Nobody's tried to sell me any.'

'No? Are you sure?'

'Of course I am. I'd remember something like that.'

Simon drew himself up to his full height, broad and commanding enough to look menacing.

'For some reason I don't believe you, Mr Green.'

He glanced away and tried to sound firm. 'It's the truth.'

'I'm quite sure you don't have silver right *here*.'

Piled around, under their claim tickets, were the items that filled most pawn shops. Old clothes, even ancient bedsheets. Anything the poor could sell to buy their food until the wage arrived on a Saturday night. Nothing expensive. With his tattered clothes and unshaven face, Green looked like his customers, a man who was barely sliding through life. It was a sham. He owned a good house across the river in Hunslet.

'I told you, take a look.'

Simon nodded at Sally. She vanished into the back room.

'You'd keep that silver somewhere safer than down in the shop, wouldn't you, Josiah? A strong gust of wind and that front door would fall down in fear.'

'I don't deal in silver.' His fingers began to fidget, rubbing against the counter.

'Really? I thought a man in your trade dealt in everything.' No threat. No need; a sense of intimidation should be enough to scrape through to the truth.

'Who'd bring silver here?' A half-hearted attempt at a smile. 'You can see for yourself.'

'Someone who'd stolen it and needed to sell it. A little quick money in the pocket. You know, I've heard you have a special place where you keep valuable items.'

'Me?' Green's face lost all its colour.

The rumour had floated on the air a few months earlier. It seemed that it was true.

'Up in the attic, wasn't it?' He had a faint memory of somebody telling him that; he'd mentioned it to Sally before they arrived. She was young and agile enough to climb up there.

'I don't know what you mean.'

The girl chose a good moment to return, as if she'd simply been waiting for her cue. She had cobwebs caught in her hair, dust and dirt on her dress. Green's expression fell as he saw her.

'No silver,' she said. 'Some gold rings, a few other things.'

'I told you.'

'You did, Mr Green. Now you can tell me who tried to sell you some silver.'

'No one. Not in months.'

His words had the hard ring of truth. Simon thought and the answer came in a flash: if it wasn't one thing, it had to be the other. 'Who wants you to buy silver for them?'

'Why would anyone want that?' Green's manner was furtive again.

Simon placed his palms on the counter. 'You tell me.'

A quick, frightened shake of the head. Interesting.

'Well, Mr Green?'

Another shake of the head.

Press it or leave him? He studied the man's face. Push him now and Green would lie. Simon would return, take him by surprise and brace him. He was leaving with some useful knowledge. That was a start.

At the door, Simon turned back.

'Does this man want any silver or only pieces made by Arthur Mangey?'

'I'm not saying.'

His answer spoke volumes.

'What did he mean?' Sally asked.

'You heard him.'

She looked at him, confused. 'But he didn't say anything.'

Simon smiled. 'He did, just without coming out and confirming it. Someone's looking for pieces Mangey made.' He frowned. 'It still doesn't explain why the killer left Kendall in that room, though.'

'He wanted to tell us that he knew about it. To boast.'

The girl sounded so certain. Maybe it really was that simple: flaunting that he was far ahead of them.

'Then our murderer knows a great deal, it seems. I wonder how long all this has been going on.'

The auction houses weren't open on Saturday. He'd talk to them on Monday and see if they'd sold any silver made by Arthur Mangey. Five days ago he'd never heard of the man. Now his mind was brimming over with him.

The house was empty. No Rosie or the boys. No note on the kitchen table to say where they'd gone. Richard and Amos didn't have lessons on a Saturday; she'd obviously taken them out.

Sally disappeared up to her room. He sat and read the *Mercury*, but his mind couldn't concentrate on the page. He was trying to hammer the facts he'd learned into a shape that made sense.

Why would anyone want silver made by Mangey? A collector? That was possible, but murder hardly seemed like a collector's tool.

And beneath it all, the undercurrent of worry at what was happening to him. Why had fear come to find him?

The front door opened and a rush of noise from the twins whipped the thoughts away. Just as well; they were carrying him nowhere.

Rosie appeared wearing her finery, a dark blue gown she'd had made at the beginning of spring and a hat with an elaborate feather.

'You're all dressed up to take them out to play,' he said with amusement.

'Mrs Fenton looked after them for a couple of hours. I went to see Sarah Richmond. She and her husband came back from Durham last night.'

Of course. Richmond the banker; Kendall's previous employer. 'What did she have to say?'

'Nothing but praise.' She unpinned the hat and set it carefully on the table. 'She said Thomas Kendall was an excellent employee.'

It wasn't what he'd expected to hear. 'If he was so good, why did they let him go?'

'They didn't; he left them. Claimed his sister was ill and he needed to go and look after her. They gave him a good reference. An honest one.'

'I don't suppose they have an address for her?'

Rosie shook her head. 'It's a curious thing, though. A couple of months later, he turned up again, working for Foley. She asked a few questions. He was paying Kendall more than they had.'

'Hardly the first time something like that has happened.' People often poached good servants.

'The Richmonds weren't happy about it, but they filled his position straight after he left. Sarah could hardly believe it when I gave her the news about the cups and the murder.'

He told her about the visit to Green, and someone seeking silver made by Mangey.

'Why?' she asked.

'That's the question. But a pound to a penny whoever's looking for silver by Mangey is the one behind this.'

'Maybe Jane can discover something in all those documents.' She stretched. 'I'm going to change.'

SIX

'I don't understand.' Jane looked up from the paper and stared at Armistead. Late into Saturday afternoon and Armistead passed her an old copy of the *Leeds Intelligencer* from 1755, the print so cramped and faded that it took time for her to puzzle out the words.

Last Friday as some workmen were pulling down the false roof of an old house belonging to Mr Smith in Kirkgate, they found several instruments for coining, supposed to belong to Mr Mangey, who was executed at York many years before.

'Unfortunately, that's all I know,' he told her with a sigh. 'I've searched everywhere but I've never been able to find any other reference to it. No mention of what tools they might have been or what happened to them. But in his trial there was talk of Mangey hiding tools there.'

'If he had somewhere like that, why would he need a hidden workshop and those tools you found?'

His eyes twinkled. 'An excellent question, isn't it? You've seen the transcription of the trial. So much of the evidence seems to have been pulled from thin air. It's perfectly possible that Mangey used the secret room for storing some of his silver and not clipping coins. We simply don't know. Obviously Norcross, the man who accused him, knew about the place. I've wondered if he placed the coin and shears we found there, to implicate Mangey. But as nobody searched . . .'

'We'll never have the truth,' Jane completed the sentence.

'Exactly.' Armistead nodded. 'Norcross sounds like a very unsavoury character. He'd been a prisoner in Rothwell goal, you know. I'm not sure that signifies anything, but . . .' His face settled into a frown. 'Immediately after the guilty verdict, one of the jurors said he gave no credit to his evidence, and he'd voted to acquit Mangey. After the trial finished, Norcross accused several other eminent men in town of crimes. One of them ended up as the mayor.'

'But it was too late for Mangey?'

'Yes. After those accusations, Norcross vanished.'

'Vanished?' She echoed the word, seeing him nod again.

'The next trace of him in any records in Leeds comes seventeen years later, when he appears to be living here, married and with a child. I have no idea where he went in the meantime. Now, what would that suggest to you?'

'That he'd run off and there hadn't been a word of truth in anything he said.' It seemed plain as day to her.

Mangey hadn't been caught with any counterfeit coins, there was no definite evidence that he'd done anything wrong. Testimony against him had come from a few men, but it seemed to have little solid behind it. There hadn't even been a search for the hidden room in the man's workshop. The accusations had come from Norcross, who insisted that Mangey had asked him to help with the coin clipping, promising him money in exchange.

None of it fitted, Jane thought. Mangey was respected, quite wealthy. He didn't need the money, although she knew that meant little; she'd seen how powerful greed could be. But there was nothing to indicate Mangey and Norcross had ever been close friends. Why would someone in Mangey's position trust a shoemaker he didn't know particularly well when he was doing something as dangerous as committing treason?

Yet even without hard evidence or damning testimony, he'd been found guilty. Nothing about it felt right to her.

'You said that you wondered if it was a plot against Mangey,' Jane said.

'I did,' he agreed, then gave a bitter smile and shook his head in disbelief. 'I still do, but I'm never going to find out. Others seemed to feel that way at the time. I told you, though, I've never come across anything in writing to indicate it might have been true, and everyone involved is long since dead. It didn't affect his son, though.'

'What do you mean?' Jane sensed the start of a tale. She wanted to know more.

'His name was Thomas. Educated at the grammar school here, then went to university in Cambridge. He took holy orders and made quite a career for himself. Ended up marrying the Archbishop of York's daughter. It's quite remarkable when you consider it. It certainly took me by surprise when I found out. We have his father hanged as a traitor, yet those sins were never laid on the son's shoulders. Not the smallest taint of it on him. Thomas is buried in the cathedral in Durham. It's not much more than forty years ago since his wife and son both died.' Armistead gave a wistful sigh. 'Almost close enough in time to touch.'

'Is there anything to connect what happened back then with the body we saw in the workshop and those cups being stolen?' That was what Simon had wanted to know. The reason she was here.

'Mr Westow asked me, but I haven't managed to think of anything,' he replied after a long, considered silence. Armistead took out his watch. 'I'll look again tomorrow and we can see on Monday.' He looked at her and began to smile. 'Do you know, I'm honestly grateful for your interest. I've never been able to share any of this before. Nobody ever wanted to know, and you've shown great intellect.'

Jane felt the blush rise from her throat. It was still there as she walked home in the warm sun. Intellect. She rolled the word around her mouth, relishing the pleasure of the compliment.

Monday morning. After the silence of Sunday, the new week arrived warm and loud as factory boilers heated and their chimneys began to throw out their smoke again.

Simon was at the coffee cart, listening as the talk still churned around the discovery of Kendall's body. Every day the ideas grew wilder and wilder, stretching out to the impossible.

Farther up Briggate, the workmen had made an early start loading the last of the rubble from what had once been Middle Row on to a procession of carts. Now they only had to set cobbles in place and traffic could use the whole width of the street. Leeds would seem like a new, bigger place.

He turned away, starting the stroll home to Swinegate. Jane should arrive soon with all she'd learned from Armistead. Kendall's body had been placed in that secret room for a reason. There had to be some kind of link. He felt it in his bones.

He turned at the sound of boots running along the road and his hand moved towards his knife. Sally was already there, poised with a blade in her fist. But it was a member of the watch, gulping to catch his breath.

'The constable says can you meet him at Mr Armistead's house?'

Simon stared at him. 'Why? What's happened there?'

'He gave me the message, that's all.'

There could only be one reason Porter wanted Simon.

'Find Jane,' he told Sally. 'Bring her.'

A nod and the girl had gone, disappearing in a heartbeat. Simon hurried to Kirkgate.

The inspector, the constable's deputy, stood guard in the doorway, glowering at any curious passers-by who paused.

'Go in,' he told Simon. 'He's waiting.'

Jane blinked against the light as she rushed through the streets, Sally keeping pace at her side. Not quite a run, nothing that would leave people staring, but weaving and sliding between people, wanting to reach Kirkgate as soon as she could.

Her heart was pounding and she tried to push down the thoughts and fears that whirled through her mind. She needed to see what had happened, to arrive before her imagination ran riot.

Simon was waiting with Constable Porter. He placed his hand on her arm.

'In the library,' he said quietly, and moved aside. She stood in the doorway. The air was thick and warm, loud with the buzzing of thousands of flies and sticky with the perfume of death. Books had been tumbled off the shelves to form small mountains on the floor. Pages torn out and tossed around; She wouldn't be able to move in the room without treading on them.

She saw it all, but barely noticed. Her gaze was fixed on the desk. Armistead was sprawled, face down, covered in crawling insects, a pool of blood dried on the wood and soaked into the scattered documents.

Jane felt as if the breath had been torn out of her body. She knew death and murder very well, but this cut to the quick. She felt as if she was trapped in one of the nightmares that had tormented her. This was no dream, though. Her eyes were open and there was a haze of sun outside. She couldn't escape by waking.

She'd liked Armistead. He was a gentle soul, without an ounce of malice, just his quiet passion for history. He'd made her feel comfortable in this place. Accepted her as his equal. He'd been generous with his books, his words. She felt the grip of grief tightening around her heart. Hastily, she rubbed her eyes with the back of her hand, then looked at the faces of the living.

'Who found him?' Her voice shook.

'The housekeeper. She arrived not long after six. He was fine when she was here yesterday morning.'

'I . . .' she began, suddenly terrified that Porter might think she'd done this.

'Don't worry,' Simon told her. She was safe; it was there in his eyes.

'You've been working with him,' the constable began. 'He knew all about Mangey.'

'He tried . . .' She hunted through her brain, trying to find the words that suited. 'He *wanted* to know all about Mangey. What really happened.' Her eyes moved back to the body. 'That was his life. Mr Armistead knew as much as anyone could. He'd put together those books about the case with papers and what he'd been able to find out.'

Her heart sank as she glanced down at the pages and volumes scattered across the floor. All Armistead's work strewn like rubbish.

'First of all, we need you to see if everything's still here,' Simon told her.

'Yes. I'll do that.' She owed it to the poor man. And much more. As she stared at the body, Jane felt the raw, rough knot of anger in her belly, hard, certain and solid. The first time in months. She knew she was going to find the man who'd killed Armistead and make him pay for the murder. She was swept up in this life again.

When the corpse had gone, the sense of him still filled the library as she began to work, trying to ignore the stench of decay all around her. The room had been his joy, filled with the things he treasured in the world. Why would anyone do that? Had he found an answer to the last question? Someone had murdered him and tried to destroy all his work, as if he'd never existed at all. On her knees, she picked up one page, then another, trying to make some order out of the debris. It seemed like a hopeless task.

'Those books were everything to him.' Jane looked up and saw the housekeeper in the doorway. She was a large woman with greying hair, a soft, pained look to her face. Her eyes were rimmed red where she'd been crying. Blue veins stood out clear on the back of her hand. 'I came in and saw him here and I started screaming.'

'He seemed like a gentleman,' Jane said.

'Aye, he was that, pet. He was that. Always good to me. Why would anyone do him that way?'

'I don't know,' she answered bleakly. 'I really don't. But I'm going to find out.'

Simon stood on Kirkgate with Porter. The constable's hands were pushed down into his trouser pockets, his face dark and angry.

'A man like Kendall ends up dead, people aren't going to fuss,' he said. 'He was a thief; they'll say good riddance. But Armistead . . .'

'An upright citizen,' Simon said.

A nod. 'He was. That's when they start squawking and pushing me to solve it. We know damned well the two deaths are connected.'

'Mangey,' Simon agreed. 'He's the link. But we need to find out how.'

'Maybe Armistead discovered it. That would be a good reason to kill him.'

'Let's see what Jane can find.'

'I'll have a man keep watch on the place.' He cocked his head. 'Does Foley still want you to find the cups?'

'He does. It looks as if we're going to be working together again.'

Porter strode away, the inspector at his side. Simon turned to Sally; she'd been standing, listening in silence.

'You saw the body. What did you make of it?'

'It didn't look as if there had been a fight,' she answered. 'All that with the books thrown all over the place, it was done later. Armistead was sitting at his desk when he was killed.'

Sally had a quick, sharp eye. Sometimes she noticed a fine detail that he'd missed. This time she'd seen the same as him. No sign that the door had been forced. The man had let his murderer in, and later not put up any resistance. He'd fallen face down, as if he was searching for something among the papers. He might well have known his killer. If he didn't, then Armistead hadn't believed he was a threat.

'What do you want me to do?' she asked.

He didn't know. The only thread to twitch was Green, the pawnbroker, and that was one for the pair of them.

'Ask questions. See if you can hear of anyone who might have gone to see Armistead. We'll meet at noon.'

She looked up at him doubtfully before nodding and moving off. He knew he was wasting her skills, but she couldn't come with him to the auction houses.

Jordan, Taylor and Sons had premises on Boar Lane, close to Holy Trinity church and just as hushed and reverential inside. The clerks talked in quiet voices as Simon waited to see Mr Taylor.

His son, at least. It was an old firm, and the father had died ten years before. Edmund Taylor sat behind a large desk, looking harried by the piles of paper in front of him.

'Forgive me, Mr Westow. We have a sale coming up at the end of this week and things are hectic. Do you have something you want to auction?'

'No.'

The reply took Taylor by surprise. 'Then—'

'A question, that's all.' He smiled. 'Very simple and straightforward: has anyone asked you to keep an eye out for any silver made by Arthur Mangey?'

Taylor narrowed his eyes and licked his lips.

'That's certainly a curious thing to ask,' he said slowly. 'Would it be connected to the hidden room and the body that everybody's been talking about?'

Simon smiled. 'It would.'

'I'd heard of Mangey before that, but only as a silversmith. Nothing about coin clipping.'

'It seems that not many had. Do his pieces often come up for auction?'

'No.' He pursed his lips. 'At most there have been two or three in the last five years. They always spark a little interest. I assumed it was because he was from Leeds, but maybe it's his notoriety.'

'That's possible,' Simon agreed. 'Has anyone been asking for silver he's made?'

'No. Nobody with a special interest, no requests to seek out pieces by Mangey.'

'I see.' He stood and extended his hand. 'Thank you for your time.'

It was the same story at Walker's on the corner of Swinegate and Briggate, close to Leeds Bridge. No matter; it had been worth the try.

Sally was eating when he arrived home. She still possessed the insatiable appetite of a street girl, wolfing down the bread and cold meat on her plate and shaking her head when he asked if she'd discovered anything.

Rosie listened as he recounted his visit to the auction houses.

'I was thinking about Kendall's body,' she said. 'The message of where it was left.'

'Go on,' he said.

'It's a challenge. He's telling us he's out there, taunting us to catch him.'

'That's exactly what Sally said,' he answered, with a glance at the girl. 'Why, though?'

Sally raised her head. 'What if we hadn't known the room was there?'

'The workmen would still have found the body,' Rosie told her.

'Would it have meant anything? The shears and coins would have been destroyed or stolen. It would just have been a body in an empty building. There wouldn't have been any . . .' She cast around for the word. 'Any *story* with it. The killer must have heard we were going to look, that Armistead knew all about Mangey and would be there,' Sally continued. 'The story has to be important.'

Rosie nodded. 'It makes sense that way,'

Sally's mind was racing now. 'He must have believed that Armistead would be able to identify him. That's why he killed him.'

'If they knew each other,' Rosie said, 'it would certainly explain why Armistead let him in and there wasn't a fight. It was probably a man from the same class as him.' Her eyes narrowed. 'He might have believed he could trust someone like that.'

Simon picked up the idea. 'The killer must have imagined there could be something in those books and papers that could link him to what had happened. That's why he went through them that way,' Simon continued the thought. 'He was trying to destroy any evidence. Jane's examining it all, but I don't know if she'll be able to tell much. He could have taken it and we'll be none the wiser.'

Rosie nodded. 'That's just how he wants it. Leaving us behind him.'

Jane worked all morning, starting to put Armistead's library into some sort of order. First she returned the fallen books to the shelves, placing them back in alphabetical order, exactly the way he'd had them. She put all the Mangey papers to one side. Some had his blood on them. Dried, dark stains in the warm May weather, still with their harsh iron tang.

It was impossible to judge whether every scrap of paper was there. She'd been able to put some together, places she remembered where one item followed from the other. But there were still too many gaps.

At noon she went out to see Kate the pie-seller, grateful for a change of scene, the chance to sit and eat and try to ease everything out of her head, at least for a while. Then a short walk, stopping to listen to Davy Cassidy's fiddle and letting it clear her head.

The air was gritty and hazy, but anything was a relief from the cloying sweetness that clung in her throat as she worked in the library. There, she could feel Armistead watching over her shoulder.

Less than five minutes after her return, she heard the tap on the door. Simon entered, Sally on his heels, staring around at all the books back in their proper places.

'You've done well,' Simon said.

'I've made a start,' Jane told him. She gestured at the small mountain of papers needing attention. 'Most of those have to do with Mangey. Still a long way to go.'

'Any sense that things have been taken?'

'I don't know. Mr Armistead hadn't shown me everything he had.' She frowned. 'I'm trying to put the pieces together, but it's hard when you don't know if they're all there.'

'What about anything to connect the Mangey case to these killings?'

'No,' she replied firmly. 'Not yet.'

Jane heard herself and realized she sounded as if she knew exactly what she was doing. Armistead's murder had torn away the last shreds of worry she'd had about this work. Now there was just determination.

'How long do you think it will take you?'

She bit her lip as she tried to calculate. 'I'm not sure. The books were the easy part. The papers are going to take time.'

'Porter will want to know what you find,' he warned. The constable had arrested her once and put her in a cell. She had no love for him or his men. 'Come to the house once you've finished. We'll leave you to work.'

Simon was turning the door handle when she spoke again. Her voice was quiet and even but determined.

'I want to be part of this. Finding the one who killed him.'

The decision felt natural. Someone had to give Armistead justice. Jane could feel the anger coursing through her, a fury for the man who'd taken the life from him. This was a promise she could make to the dead. Now she was beginning to understand what the dreams had meant, the reason she'd been drawn back into all this.

Simon stared at her, then nodded.

SEVEN

'Do you think Armistead read all those books?' Sally asked as they strode up Briggate.

'Very likely,' Simon said.

'Why?' she asked, curious. 'Why do people like it?'

'There's plenty of knowledge in them.'

'I suppose so, but . . .' She let her words drift away and shook her head.

Mudie was totting up his accounts, scowling at the figures as he sat with a bottle of brandy and a glass.

'Hard to make an honest living these days,' he said. 'I might have to turn to crime.'

'Don't do it, George,' Simon laughed. 'I'd only have to come looking for you. You must have heard about Armistead.'

'Poor devil.' He took a sip. 'Is it connected with Foley's case?'

'Beyond a doubt. Have you ever heard of anything present day involving Mangey the silversmith?'

'I'd barely heard Mangey's name until last week. Someone told me once about the treason and the mace, but that was ancient history; I can't say I paid it much attention. Then Sir Robert mentioned him when he wanted someone to find the stolen cups.' He shrugged. 'That's all. Didn't Armistead collect everything he could find on Mangey?'

'He did. Jane's going through it.' He saw Mudie raise his eyebrows in surprise. 'Can you think of anyone who might know more?'

'Not—' he began, then cocked his head. 'Wait, have you met Henry Fowler?'

Simon stopped to think, running through names in his mind. 'Is he the clerk at the Parish Church?'

'That's him.'

He didn't understand. 'What would he have to do with this?'

'Probably nothing, but he enjoys researching people's ancestors and descendants. Could be worth talking to him.'

The thread sounded so slim it was invisible, but he was ready to explore any possibility. Simon stood and thanked Mudie.

'If you're really grateful, you'll do these for me.' He gestured at the columns of numbers.

'I said I'm grateful, not forever in your debt.'

'Mangey. Mangey.' Fowler had a habit of tapping a finger against his chin as he spoke. He was a man with a jowly face, eyes blinking behind heavy spectacles, much of the hair gone from his head. He kept glancing towards Sally, as if her presence left him uneasy. 'The only Mangey I know about is buried in Durham Cathedral. He married the Archbishop of York's daughter.' His expression brightened. 'He was from Leeds.'

'He's the son of the man who was hanged as a traitor. Do you know anything about his children?'

'A traitor?' The man's eyes widened. 'No, I don't know anything about them. Why?'

Simon explained about Arthur Mangey and a possible link to a murderer, seeing Fowler turn pale. But the interest glowed in his eyes.

'I don't expect I'll be able to find much,' the man said slowly. 'We only have our own parish records here, all the baptisms and marriages and burials. If there was anything somewhere else, I wouldn't be able to tell.'

'I'm willing to pay,' Simon said. Foley would foot the bill for that.

Fowler raised his head and tapped his chin again. The temptation was there in his eyes, but he had disappointment in his voice. 'It's a kind offer, but I can still only look at what we have, Mr Westow.'

'Could you find out what you have in a day?'

'I have my duties here.' He waved his hand around the church. 'The best I can say is that I'll try.'

'I'll come back tomorrow afternoon.' He was certain it would be another avenue that led nowhere, but for the moment it felt like progress. Just not the kind he'd ever experienced. History, papers, family connections that stretched through generations, it was unlike anything he'd come across before. It left him unsure, treading carefully, casting around for the right direction.

'There was someone in the burying ground,' Sally said as they began to march up Kirkgate. 'It might be nothing, but he began to walk as soon as he saw you.'

Simon felt the twinge of fear return. 'Is he following us?'

'I didn't look, didn't want to make him suspicious.'

'See if you can find him again.'

Simon checked his knives, the old habit; one, two three, all there. He felt his heart thumping, the prickle up his spine. This time he'd be ready. No wavering. Decisive. At least he felt no worry for his life with Sally here. But he couldn't have her at his side all the time.

He kept walking, cutting along High Court and down to the Calls, their warehouses lined up against the river. He could hear the barges creaking and grinding against each other as they were loaded and unloaded. The laughter and shouts of the workmen.

No hurry, ambling along as if he didn't have a concern in the world. Luring the man. Then it was time to see who was behind him. He turned down Pitfall, the short street by Leeds Bridge that ran to the water's edge. Only one way in or out.

He took ten paces, most of the way to the river, then Simon turned, arm by his side, knife flashing in the light. A man had followed, young, slender, his eyes hidden in the long shadow of a building. No weapon in his hand. Panicked, he looked around, ready to bolt, but Sally was waiting, armed and wearing her hunter's face.

'What do you want?' Simon called. The young man didn't look like a threat, but his chest still felt tight.

'To talk.' He had a weak, worried voice, glancing over his shoulder again at Sally.

'Talk?' He echoed the word. 'What do you want to talk about?'

'A man called Kendall.'

Simon nodded for him to come closer. The man took halting, nervous steps until he stood three yards away.

'That's enough. Stand there.' He could feel the sweat on his palms, the beat of his heart, the sharp fear in his gut. 'What do you know about him?'

'I can tell you where he spent his last two nights.' The trepidation was still there in his voice. Sally hovered close by, ready to strike.

'If that's true, it's worth a little money.'

'It's good, I promise.' He sound so earnest, so real. 'I can take—'

'Just tell me.'

'He was staying with a woman.'

'How do you know her?'

'She's my aunt.' He swallowed, gazing at Simon's knife. 'I can take you to see her.'

It had the ring of truth. Simon drew in a breath. 'All right. Sally will search you, then the three of us can go together.'

A small house in Holbeck, close enough to the Round Foundry for all the banging and clattering to resound along the street. The man took a key from his pocket, turned it in the lock and opened the door.

Sally ducked ahead of Simon, right behind the man, too quick to notice the way he held back for a moment before he forced himself to plunge in. The door opened straight into the kitchen with a sink, small range, table and chair.

A woman was sitting, pushing scraps of old fabric through hessian to make a rag rug. There were others all around, brief splashes of bright colour across the flagstone floor. She looked up, terror across her face as soon as she saw the weapons.

The man hurried to squat by the chair. 'Don't worry, Aunt Katy. This is Mr Westow. He's looking into Thomas's death. I told him that Thomas spent two nights here after he ran off from his job.'

She let out a long sigh and gazed up at Simon with eyes that overflowed with grief.

'You didn't know him, did you?' she asked.

'No,' he answered.

'He was a good man. Used to give me money from his wages, Thomas did. Yes, I know he stole that set of silver cups.' He could hear the faint lilt of Ireland in her voice.

'Why did he do it?' Simon asked.

'So he'd have enough for us to go somewhere once he was paid for them.'

'What happened?'

'They were lovely things, so delicate. Thomas wrapped them very carefully when he left. He went to meet the man who was supposed to pay him for them.' Her words turned bleak. 'That was last Wednesday evening. He never came home again.'

Simon felt his heartbeat quicken. The day before they'd found his body in the hidden room. 'What was the man's name?' If she knew that . . .

'Just that he was called Mark. He told Thomas an ancestor of his had made the cups.'

Simon stiffened. Now he had a name, and the connection to Mangey was real. The pulse began to twitch in his neck. And for a moment all the fear fell away from him. 'Did he say anything else about him?' he asked urgently. 'What about the rest of the name?'

The woman shook her head. 'No. Just Mark. Thomas promised he'd tell me everything when he came back with the money.'

She'd known Kendall for almost eighteen months; he'd visit every time he had a day off. He made promises, hopes of some future together, and they seemed as if they might happen after a man approached him about the cups. He'd grown more excited, more nervous as the time to steal them drew close. From Sunday night until Wednesday morning he'd stayed with her, keeping out of sight. Full of anticipation, making eager plans for where they might go, what kind of life they could enjoy. Then . . .

'I want to find the man who killed him,' Simon said. 'Did he tell you anything else at all that might help?'

'No.' She shook her head, hopeless. 'Don't you think I haven't gone over everything? Every sentence. Every little word he spoke about it. He believed, so I believed. There's just the name, Mark. From the way Thomas talked, he must have had money. He promised to pay handsomely. I don't know. I'm sorry.'

Her anguish filled the room. He thought about asking why she hadn't come forward, but what difference would it have made? Simon counted out coins, some for the young man, more for the woman left bereft, and walked out into the warmth.

Fowler was in the vestry of the Parish Church, the record books spread across the desk, astonished to see Simon so soon.

'Mr Westow. I've barely had time to start yet . . .'

'I'd like you to keep an eye out for someone called Mark in your search,' Simon said.

'I will. But I told you before, I don't have anything for births or marriages outside the parish of Leeds . . .' He spread his arms in a helpless gesture.

Jane hadn't expected to see Simon again today. The afternoon was moving along, and she was comfortably lost in the papers, reading and thinking about them, when he bustled into the room.

'Don't worry, I'm only here to ask one question. Have you come across anyone named Mark in Mangey's family?'

She closed her eyes, concentrating, trying to recall everything she'd read.

'He had a nephew named Mark, his sister's son. Mark Michael Williams. Why?'

Very quickly, Simon ran through what he'd discovered. 'Did they live in Leeds?' he asked.

'I think so.' A few seconds as she began to scrabble through sheets of paper, then she said: 'Yes. But he died more than fifty years ago.'

'Was he the only one?'

'All I've found so far. I'll keep looking,' Jane said.

'Please.' Finally, he had a name. A good lead. Simon felt the surge of hope roaring through him; now he had to hold his breath so that it didn't crumble to nothing between his fingers.

Alone, Jane raced through the documents until she found the record of Mark Williams's baptism and felt grateful for Armistead's thoroughness. He'd been born ten years before his uncle was hanged.

She dug into the documents, hoping for any trace of more descendants, but Armistead hadn't gone further down that family line. She could feel Simon's urgency pressing on her. But she wanted the answer, too; she needed to know who'd murdered Armistead. Jane turned her head, and for a fragment of a second she saw him sitting at his desk. Alive, whole again, smiling at her with approval.

She letting her mind settle again, then kept going through the papers, looking for something that Armistead had mentioned in passing. Nothing more than a rumour he'd come across somewhere, gossip drifting down through the years, that the silversmith had a child with a woman who was not his wife.

But wherever he'd come across it, she couldn't find any trace now. Mangey's son Thomas had a son of his own, but Armistead's notes said the man had died leaving only a widow, no children. Maybe the rumour had never been written down. Or perhaps the murderer had taken them. That would make sense, yet so far she didn't have any feeling that any pages were missing. But how could she distinguish the absence of something she didn't know existed? Jane felt her frustration building. So close, but still so very far from anything that would help.

She worked until the light outside began to fade and the words were swimming in front of her eyes. Time to go home before her head began to ache. She checked the catches on the windows and made sure the back door was locked, before turning the key at the front and handing it to the guard from the watch. His name was Edward Lister, too old to do much more than this. A portly, kindly man, with a gentle smile and pleasant manner.

'Goodnight, miss. Going to stay warm all night, I reckon.'

Jane looked up at the sky with its pall of cloud. Somewhere beyond that, the last of the evening sun.

'At least that will be good for you out here, Mr Lister.'

She spotted Sally as soon as she turned on to Briggate. The girl was tucked away in the shadows by the entrance to Turk's Head Yard, but Jane felt her presence; a long, pointed glance before she set off up the street ensured Sally would follow. She heard the lulling sound of Davy Cassidy's fiddle from somewhere down by the bridge.

'Have you managed to find anyone named Mark in those papers?' the girl asked.

'No.' Jane looked at the ground and kicked a pebble over the cobbles, watching it bounce until it landed in a pile of rubbish. 'Nothing.'

All the rubble from the Moot Hall and Middle Row had been carted away. Only ghosts would roam through their old haunts in the middle of the street now. A coach took advantage of the space, roaring up from the Albion hotel, the driver shouting and cracking his whip to scatter people out of the road.

They walked in silence until they reached the Head Row. Warm enough for the men to be sweating in their dark wool coats and the women to fan themselves as they strolled. She sensed Sally's frustration. She need to be doing something, but there was little to test her skills.

And here *she* was, Jane realized. Back in the life. Whether she liked it or not, it had opened its arms and drawn her back in.

As they parted in Green Dragon Yard, Jane said, 'Tell Simon I'll come and see him, but I haven't found what he wanted.'

Simon finished reading to the boys and blew out the candle. The curtains were drawn, the room was dark, the warmth of the day still clinging inside. A few minutes and they'd be fast asleep. Young, with no worries to drive rest away. Never having to wonder about themselves.

In the kitchen, he looked at Sally.

'Josiah Green,' he said. It was time. Every pawnbroker stayed open late; most of their business came after dark. He'd given the man long enough to believe he was safe. Now, Simon knew more about what had happened. He had some pointed questions. This time he'd make sure he left with the answers.

But the shop was locked and bolted, the shutters up in the window.

'Go around to the back,' he told Sally. 'See if you can find a way in.'

She returned shaking her head; Green had been careful there. Window blocked, door barred. No small space even she could squeeze through.

The grocer next door said Green had never opened up that morning. He wondered if the man was ill; last year he'd been closed for a week with a chest problem. Maybe he'd be back tomorrow.

He might, Simon thought as they marched over Leeds Bridge and into Hunslet. But he could feel the tingle of fear. Far stronger, though, a creeping sense that something was very wrong.

Green was a widower. He recalled that much. Children? He didn't know.

The house was in darkness. Simon tried the door. Locked. A nod and Sally scurried off, moving quietly.

'No way in,' she said when she returned.

He knocked, but all he heard was a dully, empty sound. A glance around to be certain no one was watching, then he selected the right lock pick from his case.

It took time; Green had spent money to make sure his house was secure. Finally, he felt the lock give and he turned the handle, holding his breath. No bolt. They were inside.

Simon had his knife in his hand; he couldn't even remember drawing it from his sleeve. His mouth was dry, goose pimples up his arms. Sally moved quietly through the rooms. Heart pounding fast, keeping his breathing soft and trying to force down his fears, he went upstairs, alert for anything.

Two rooms. The first held an empty bed and a wooden chest. As he opened the door of the second, he heard thousands of flies buzzing and he knew.

Jane had the book open on her lap, but she wasn't reading. All those words she'd gone through about Mangey kept fluttering and floating through her mind.

'You're distracted, child,' Mrs Shields said.

'I've been thinking.' She managed a smile, but it was a weak, wan offering.

'Have you finished at Mr Armistead's house?'

'Not yet. Probably tomorrow or the day after.'

'Have you found what you needed?'

She shook her head. 'I'm not even sure if it exists. That's the problem.'

'Maybe it will all look better after a good night's rest. Most things do.'

Perhaps she was right. Jane was weary. For the last few days she'd done things she could never have imagined just a week or two before. Reading old papers, making sense of all the words in them, and everything under the eye of a dead man. Each time she looked around in Armistead's library, she saw his body. It was strangely reassuring.

'I hope it will,' she said as Catherine Shields returned from the kitchen with a cup.

'Drink this.' A soft taste, some herbs and a sense of fruit. Pleasant on her tongue. She needed to ask the woman to teach her how to make all her tinctures. Someday she might need to know. Perhaps after this was done.

* * *

She woke early. A restful, dreamless sleep, all the nightmares banished. Jane moved softly through the house, buttering bread and pouring a drink. Mrs Shields was still asleep, nightcap tied in a bow under her chin.

In the small yard, flowers were blooming in all their bright colours. She breathed in the scents as she sat and ate, relishing the soft chill of the dawn. Jane lightly stroked one of the blooms, surprised as ever by her missing little finger. History. The price she'd paid for not being sharp.

For ten minutes she ran her knife over the small whetstone until she was satisfied with the edge. So long since she'd needed to use it. But it was still a comforting weight in the pocket of her dress.

She saw Dodson the beggar sitting on the pavement along Albion Street. The day had quickly turned close and sultry, but he was still wearing his old greatcoat. The man had lost a leg during the wars against Napoleon; there was no pension for wounded soldiers, so he was forced to ask for charity to buy his food and a room. To live on kindness.

He'd always been alone; Jane had never imagined him any other way. Today, though, he had a figure at his side, a man curled up against him, as if the beggar might keep him safe from the world. Sleeping, his face and hands covered in cuts and bruises, he looked like he'd been given a hard beating.

'I found him last night,' Dodson told her. 'He was on Kirkgate, just by the Crown and Fleece.'

'What happened to him? Do you know?' She knelt, peering at the man. He was thin, little more than a skeleton of bone and rags, wrists as spindly as twigs.

A small shake of the head. 'He hasn't said anything yet. I took him home and washed the wounds on his face. I couldn't just leave him there. I thought I could help him. It's something I can do.'

A kind, trusting man. Too few like him in this town, she thought. 'He needs to eat.'

'Yes,' Dodson agreed. One word, but she understood. It was difficult enough for him to keep his own body and soul together, let alone taking responsibility for someone else. He was a good man, observant, too – an excellent source of information over the years. She fumbled in her pocket, drawing out coins and dropping them in his cup.

'Thank you,' Dodson said. The other man hadn't stirred; the only sign he was alive was his chest rising and falling as he breathed.

He'd been wounded, hard used, but there was something about the figure that disturbed her. He was like a wraith, someone not fully alive, as if he was trailing darkness behind him. Stupid, she thought, a ridiculous notion on a bright morning. But as she glanced back over her shoulder, the sense of it remained. From nowhere, a chill ran through her body.

EIGHT

'The door wasn't locked,' Simon lied. Constable Porter stared, the disbelief clear on his face, but said nothing. Josiah Green's body had been taken to the infirmary for Dr Hey to examine, but his bedroom was still thick with the buzz of flies.

As soon as he discovered the corpse, Simon sent Sally to find someone from the watch. One look and the man scurried off, needing to bring someone more important. Almost an hour passed before Porter arrived, with the inspector and two other men.

It gave Simon ample time to search the house. The place appeared undisturbed; if the killer had looked, he'd been careful and neat. No cups, nothing related to Mangey.

'Is this connected to the others?' the constable asked.

'I'm certain of it,' Simon replied.

'This makes three of them.' Porter sighed. 'Kendall, then Armistead, now here. Do you understand what's going on?'

'Only fragments of it.' He explained what they'd learned about a man called Mark, where Kendall had spent his last two nights, how he'd believed Green was lying. 'I should have asked him more right then and there,' he said with regret. 'But I didn't know enough.'

The constable gave a slow nod. 'We're never going to now. The girl who's going through Armistead's papers, has she managed to turn anything up yet? Nothing on this Mark?'

'Not when I last saw her.'

'Then we're almost stuck in the same place as last Thursday.' He slapped his fist into his open palm. 'Nothing more to do here tonight. I'll go through it in the morning.' Simon felt his stare. 'Unless you've already done it.'

'Just waited for you.' He gave a small bow. 'Goodnight.'

Late out, a little cooler with the night wrapped around them as they started back towards the house on Swinegate. Sally kept silent. Simon tried to think and found himself scrambling.

* * *

'Green's death changes things,' he said. Morning, and they were seated around the table in the kitchen. The tutor's voice drifted in from the parlour, and the high piping of the boys as they repeated what they'd just learned. He turned to Jane. 'I don't suppose you've managed to discover anything about Mark.'

'Nothing more than I told you yesterday,' she answered, 'and he's dead. But whoever killed Armistead probably took any papers that could lead to him. I might never be able to tell.'

'We'll have to hope he didn't,' Rosie said and turned to her husband. 'This man. Mark.'

A shake of his head. 'We're groping in the dark.'

'We're assuming he gave Kendall his real name.' She hesitated for a heartbeat. 'But what if he didn't?'

He let out a long, aching sigh. 'Then we're absolutely nowhere.'

'He could have lied about everything,' Sally said. 'Having money to pay for the cups, too.'

Impossible to tell. He glanced up and saw an empty space where Jane had been, then heard the soft click of the front door as she left. 'I can try Barnabas Wade. He knows about most of the people with money.'

'I'll come with you,' Sally said. That made sense; she wasn't likely to know anyone who could help find Mark.

'I'll go shopping.' Rosie offered a bright smile. 'Maybe one of the women will remember a man called Mark. If he exists.'

Hoping they'd find another scrap of luck. The first one had given them a push, but it hadn't carried them too far.

Later in the morning and the coffee cart had gone from outside the Bull and Mouth. It would be back tomorrow, setting up before it was light. Simon began to check the inns. Wade spent his days moving between them, waiting for the coaches, ready to prey on their exhausted passengers. He was a disbarred lawyer who made a precarious living hawking worthless stocks. By the time the customers realized, they were miles away from Leeds. Wade knew enough about the law to make sure his contracts were tight; no comeback in the courts.

Simon found him in the Rose and Crown, sitting quietly in a corner reading the *Intelligencer*, and settled across from him. Sally stayed outside on Briggate; no girls would be welcome in here.

Each year the man looked a little less prosperous. His jacket grew more threadbare, his collars dirtier and more frayed.

'You picked a good time, Simon. A little break before the next coach arrives.'

'How's business?'

'Good.' He smiled. 'Booming.'

His voice was bright, but fragile, and his appearance gave the lie to the words. No sense in challenging him on it, not when he wanted to employ the man. Simon took coins from his pocket and slid them across the table.

'Tell me, Barnabas, do you know of any men named Mark who might have money?'

Worth a little money and time to see if the man existed. It was Wade's business to know the wealth of any men of consequence in Leeds.

Simon brought him a glass of rum and Wade sipped it as he went through his memory.

'There's Mark Rose, but he must be eighty now. I doubt he's been out of his house in two years.'

'Someone younger than that.'

'Do you know Tobias Hart?' He waited until Simon shook his head. 'I believe he named one of his sons Mark, but the lad's not even ten.'

'Any others?'

Wade shook his head. 'That's all. Why do you want a Mark, anyway?'

Simon stood. 'I'm not sure I do,' he replied. 'I can't even be sure he exists. There's another tot of rum waiting when you've finished that.'

He left before the man could ask any more questions.

Jane had always worked best on her own. Keeping her own pace, able to disappear into her own thoughts. Here, in this house, there was nobody around. If she stopped and listened closely, she could make out the low rattle of voices outside on Kirkgate, but they rarely intruded. Her mind had space. She could still feel Armistead's presence in the room.

She'd worked steadily but found nothing that mentioned anyone named Mark. Only a small pile of documents remained, the last of everything the killer had strewn around the library. By now she felt as if she knew as much about Mangey as Armistead had. His work, the crime he was supposed to have committed, and those who claimed to have seen the coin clippings. If they were all speaking the truth, the man had been reckless. No, far more than that: he'd been stupid. He might as well have begged to be caught. That was hard to believe when the crime was treason and the penalty was death.

Jane believed he was innocent, that there had been a plot of some kind against him. The same as Armistead; like him, though, she hadn't been able to discover a reason for it. It wasn't lurking in anything she'd read. And she still hadn't managed to unearth any kind of link between what happened over a hundred and twenty years before and the murders of the last week.

She pulled another of the papers close and began to read. It was one she hadn't seen before, and Jane pored over the words. Her frown deepened, and near the bottom of the page she drew in her breath quickly. Her chest suddenly felt tight and her heart started to thud.

Jane rushed through the rest, hoping for another reference to what she'd just seen. Nothing at all. Quickly, heart still drumming a rapid tattoo in her chest, she went back over the morning's work in case she'd missed something or pages has stuck together. No.

On her hands and knees, Jane scrambled under the furniture in case she'd overlooked something when she searched before. But there was nothing to find.

Only this.

The killer must have believed he'd taken everything that could point to his guilt. He'd almost succeeded. This single page remained. She folded it, once, twice, kept going until it was small enough to fit in her pocket. Carefully, she placed the other pages in the final volume and returned it to the shelf.

One last walk around the room, the luxury of tracing the leather binding on all the books. By the desk she made her farewell to Armistead. He'd made her feel welcome. He'd accepted her. No questions or demands. Never looked at her as if she was too young or too uneducated. Now she was all done here, and there was no reason to return.

Jane gave the key to the watchman. He looked content, lounging against the wall in the warmth.

'That's it, Mr Lister,' she said. 'I've finished.'

'Pity in a way, miss,' he said. 'I've enjoyed this.'

'So have I,' she said wistfully. 'Do you know what will happen to everything inside?'

'I'm not sure. I suppose it depends what's in his will, miss. I don't think he had any relatives.'

Who would care for all those books? Jane wondered as she hurried down Briggate, aware of what she was carrying. Her senses stayed alert for anyone following her.

She stopped by Kate the pie-seller.

'You have a strange look on your face,' she said.

No surprise. Her heart was thumping, pulse twitching in her neck. What she had was important. Other pages had been stolen; she'd be willing to swear on that.

'I'm fine,' she answered. 'Honestly.'

Jane glanced back up the street. She'd miss working in Armistead's library. Hard to believe that a few days ago it left her terrified. She'd quickly come to feel at home there. Even the murder, and Armistead's ghost lingering in the room, hadn't changed that feeling.

She moved on, wiping her hands together as she finished eating. Davy Cassidy was playing nearby, a rapid flurry of notes that were full of fire and sparks. A little further down Briggate, close to the entrance of Queen's Court, Dodson stood, resting heavily on his crutch, the wooden leg. The man he'd helped sat next to him, head slumped.

She needed to show what she had to Simon. But a quick moment wouldn't alter things. 'How is he?'

'Not well,' he answered. Dodson had a cut on his cheek, another on the back of his hand. 'It's nothing.'

'What happened to you?'

'An accident.' No expression on his face. 'It's nothing.'

Jane bent and put three coins in the old cup.

Something was very wrong. That was obvious. The man on the ground raised his head and leered at her. His teeth were rotted to an ugly shade of brown. He pursed his lips and spat, watching the phlegm land next to the toe of her boot.

Her fingers started to inch towards the hilt of her knife. The man stared at her with contempt in his eyes. Did he imagine that she was so delicate that a look would scare her? She turned and marched off down the street. The feeling she'd had before was right; he made her skin crawl. He had evil in his soul.

'Look,' Jane said as she unfolded the paper and placed it on the table. She pointed. 'There, in the very bottom corner.'

Simon watched her face. Her expression was mix of trepidation and triumph. He picked up the sheet, straightening the corner where it had been folded over, and read it quickly. He turned it over, searching for more, then handed it to Rosie.

'Is that all?' he asked.

Jane nodded. 'Yes. Just one sheet. He must have taken the rest.'

'What does it say?' Sally asked, anxious to know.

'It's a name,' he told her, and ran his finger over the word. 'Mark.'

The final sentence on the page. Very smudged and smeared, but he could make out the words. The beginning of a sentence. Simon felt the surge of relief inside. *Mark came to see me again* – Mark existed. No doubt about that, at least. But what did it mean?

'That's Armistead's writing,' Jane explained. 'He made those notes. He probably never needed to write them up properly. They're definitely not referring to Mangey's time. It's something more recent. There's no date, so I can't tell when he did it, but the man must have visited him before. Armistead didn't remember the name when I asked him last Saturday. He probably never imagined it was important. You saw the way the corner was folded over. That must be why the killer missed it.'

'There's only the name,' Rosie said as she read the page again. 'Nothing else to give it any meaning.'

'I know,' Jane replied. 'But it's important, isn't it?' She looked hopefully from face to face. 'It has to mean something if he took whatever came after.'

'Very important.' Simon studied it again. Mark. For someone to want to steal every mention of it, the name had to be important. But on its own like this it was little more than a tease.

'What does it mean, though?' Sally asked.

'We don't know,' he answered quietly. 'Not yet, at least.' Simon turned to Jane. 'Have you gone through everything now?'

'Yes. If I hadn't seen the name, I'm not sure I'd have realized anything had been taken,' Jane replied. 'The papers were quite muddled.'

'It explains why he murdered Armistead. His guilt must have been right there on another page.' A pause as he tried to picture the scene. 'It looks as if he took whatever he could find that mentioned him, then tossed the other papers and books around to cover it.'

Sally's finger traced the word, over and over. 'What can we do with this?' she asked.

'We keep going,' Simon said. 'The murderer told Kendall his name was Mark. It seems that's the truth, at least.'

Mark was real. One big step forward.

'Come with me.' Jane took Sally by the arm. The girl glanced over her shoulder at Simon before following.

'Where are we going?' the girl asked. 'Do you know who Mark is?'

She ignored the question. 'I want you to see someone.'

Standing in the shadows at the entrance to Byrd's Yard they could watch Lower Briggate without being seen. A clear view over to Queen's Court.

'It's that soldier. The one you know.'

Jane nodded. 'Dodson.'

'What about him?'

'Do you see the man with him?'

'I can't make out his face. He has his head down. Why?'

She explained the little she knew. Dodson hadn't had an accident; the longer she stared, the more certain she became. The man had injured him.

'Can you ask the children and see if anyone knows him?' They lived from day to day and slept where they could. But they saw and heard things most people missed. They were Sally's people, they trusted her. Some of them must have come across the man.

Sally stood, mouth turning down as she gazed at the figure. 'There's something about him. Something bad.'

'Something dangerous,' Jane agreed.

The girl stared for another few seconds. 'One of the children is certain to know who he is. I'll find out tonight.' She turned to Jane. 'What about Mark?'

'You saw what I found. It's not much.'

Jane gazed up and down Briggate. She saw the folk moving along the pavements, all the carts and coaches crowding the road. How many lived here now? It had to be many thousands. Figures beyond counting. She felt as if she rarely saw the same face twice and new people were arriving every day. It wouldn't be difficult for a killer to hide himself in all that.

Mark was a man who knew the town. Who understood its history and its secrets, the entrance to that hidden workshop. He knew people of a certain class. Armistead, for one, but he'd only realized the danger once the man was in his house. By then it was too late.

'What are you thinking?' Sally's voice roused her.

'I . . .' she began, then shook her head.

Where had Sally gone? Simon called out her name, but there was no response. He knew what he needed to do, but for a second he hesitated, wary of going anywhere without the girl behind him. Stupid, he thought. It was daylight. He was safe. He needed to beat this fear.

But he still checked his knives as he left the house and felt a tightness in his chest.

Over in Holbeck, he knocked on a door. Maybe the woman who'd first told him about Mark had remembered a little more. But nobody answered, there was only the hollow sound of emptiness. As he peered through the window, a voice said: 'You're too late. They went last night. Her and that nephew of hers.'

'Do you know where they've gone?'

The woman stood on her front step, arms crossed, a shawl over her hair.

'They never said. Put what they owned on a handcart and left. Wasn't much for her round here, not after that man she liked was killed.'

He hoped she'd find happiness somewhere. If only she could have waited a day longer . . .

'What's wrong, child?' Mrs Shields asked. 'You've been up and down from that chair all evening.'

They hadn't needed a fire in the hearth for weeks; today, the warmth and closeness of the day had lasted long into the evening and under the skirt and petticoat Jane's legs were prickly from the heat. But the old women kept a rug over her knees; she grew chilled so easily these days.'

'I'm sorry.' She hadn't realized she was doing it.

'You haven't settled to that book. Don't you like it?'

'It's not that.' Jane set *The Scottish Chiefs* on the small table. 'I have too many things cluttering up my head.'

'When I was a little girl, my governess always told me that a trouble shared was a trouble halved.' Her lips curled into a smile. 'Do you know, I never believed her. I think she just wanted to know what I'd done wrong.'

A minute and Jane began talking about Armistead and the way he'd encouraged her. Her sorrow for him. Discovering Mark and what it might mean. The man Dodson had taken under his wing. Everything that seemed to be weighing her down.

'I wish I had some advice I could offer you,' Catherine Shields said when she'd finished. 'But you live in a very different world, child. I don't understand it.'

'No need.' She reached across and gently squeezed the woman's hand. All bone, barely an ounce of meat on it. 'I think I can sleep now.'

NINE

'I heard you come back last night,' Simon said as he and Sally crossed Leeds Bridge. No problems yesterday, but he felt easier having her by his side. He glanced across at the warehouses lining the Calls, all full of activity. The river was busy as ever, barges tied up two and three abreast alongside the wharves. She'd arrived home late. The sound of her footsteps as she climbed to the attic woke him.

For a second, she looked embarrassed at being discovered. 'I went to talk to the children.'

Simon knew she enjoyed living in the house; she'd quickly become a complete member of the family. But he'd also learned she had other ties, other demands on her heart. She gave the children money for food, for shelter if they were desperate. Things to keep them alive. She seemed to see it as her duty, as if she owed them a debt for the time she'd spent living out there. He never asked how much she gave; that was her business.

Simon was shown through to Foley as soon as he gave the servant his name. He kept Sally at his side. She gazed around with wide eyes, studying the house as they passed through the hall and into a parlour.

The tall window looked over the neat garden that ran down to the river, the flowers in full, colourful bloom. Sir Robert was at his desk, a nib in his hand.

'Westow. Young lady.' From the corner of his eye, Simon saw Sally bob a small curtsey. 'Any good news for me?'

'I'm afraid I don't. The only thing I have is a question: do you know anyone named Mark with an interest in silver, especially anything made by Mangey?'

'Mark,' Foley replied after long consideration. 'I know two men with that name, but I can't say either of them has ever shown any interest in silver. They've both been here and never said anything about the cups. I don't believe Mark Preston even bothered to look at them.'

'What about the other man?'

'That's Mark Walker. He admired them, but no more than a passing comment. Politeness. I always pay attention to how people react to them—' He stopped himself. 'Reacted. Tell me, do you honestly believe you'll be able to find them?'

'I'm doing all I can.' Three murders complicated everything.

'Of course. I'm curious: why the interest in Mark?'

He frowned as Simon explained, his fingertip tracing circles on the paper in front of him.

'No, I don't know of anyone with an interest in Mangey. Besides poor Mr Armistead, of course, God rest his soul. Mind you, he seemed more interested in the man and his history than anything he made. But I don't see either of the Marks I know as murderers, Mr Westow. They're gentlemen.'

One hardly precluded the other, and Foley was deluding himself if he believed it did.

'Do you know those men he mentioned?' Sally asked as they strolled back towards the bridge. Nowhere near noon and already he could see men sweating as they hurried along.

'I've never heard of them before.'

'You didn't ask him about them.'

'We can find out. If they're friends of his, they probably have money.'

'No,' Rosie said. 'I believe I was introduced to a woman named Preston once, but I don't remember her face.'

'Walker?' Simon asked.

A shake of her head. 'It's hardly a rare name, is it?'

So much for that. If the men were anything of consequence in Leeds, George Mudie would know them.

The print shop was busy when Simon walked in, Sally a step behind him. Three men were crowded around the desk. One of them was burly, dressed in a shabby coat that had been crudely mended a few times. Unshaved, with ideas of destruction in his eyes. His gaze passed over them, just a man with a young girl. But Simon read trouble in his eyes and felt a tingle on his skin. He drew in a breath and glanced at Sally; she'd seen it, too.

One of the men speaking to Mudie turned his head.

'Please excuse us, sir,' he said. 'We're talking business. It might take a while. You might do better to come back later.'

The thick-set man reached out to push Simon. He found himself facing a knife. No thinking. He'd just acted.

'Thank you, but I believe we'll stay.'

Sally had moved, positioning herself off to the side. Her blade was out, eyes watching the men who'd been busy with Mudie. But the conversation had ground to a brooding silence.

The air crackled with the threat of violence. The man facing Simon burned with anger, tensing his shoulders under the old coat and clenching his fists.

'You won't have a chance to land a blow,' Simon warned him and raised his voice a little. 'Is there a problem, George?'

'These gentlemen have come to collect on a bill. Let me introduce Mr Westow,' he said to the pair in front of him. 'He's a thief-taker.'

One of them gave a dismissive glance and returned his attention to Mudie.

'You owe us money.'

'I owed Mr Gill money. As I told you, I had an agreement with him. I'd pay him an amount each month until the debt was cleared.'

'Any agreement you had ended when we bought out his debts. You need to pay in full.'

Mudie shrugged. 'I can't. That's why I had the arrangement with Gill.'

'If you can't pay, we'll have to take over this place.' The man's voice was iron.

'How much does he owe?' Simon asked.

The men turned his head again. 'A little over ten pounds. Why, what business is it of yours?'

A good deal of money, but hardly a fortune.

'I'll see you have it in full.' Simon offered the man a smile. With Sally here, his fear was under control. 'Will that satisfy?'

'There's the interest.'

'Waive it. Let's call it goodwill for a quick payment.' He stared at the enforcer in front of him. 'What kind of honest businessmen need a bully boy with them?'

'Too many don't want to pay.'

'Come back without him tomorrow and it'll be waiting. I'll expect a receipt marked paid in full.'

For a second they didn't stir and Simon braced for a fight. A bad place for it, with all the trays of type around.

'Tomorrow morning,' the man said finally.

'No trouble. Agreed?'

Another long hesitation, then a nod. Simon watched the men as they left, squeezing past him. Then a sudden movement and a cry of pain. Metal clattered to the floor and the bodyguard was clutching his right hand.

Shielded by his body, he'd drawn a knife. Sally had speared the back of his hand and now she stood, glaring, ready to hurt him again.

'Try that once more and she'll kill you,' Simon warned him. The man stooped to pick up the weapon, but Simon rested his boot on it. 'Leave it. Call it the price of foolishness.'

He glared as he went, still cradling the wounded hand, blood seeping through his fingers.

'Thank you,' Simon said to Sally, and the blush rose from her throat at the gratitude. For a moment he felt cold, as if someone had plunged him into ice. That made twice in just a few days she'd saved him. He'd believed everything was fine, allowed his attention to slip and it had almost been deadly. Christ, how stupid. He needed to change that.

'Who were they?' he asked Mudie.

'You know as much as I do. Never seen them before. They turned up here saying they'd taken over Gill's debts and they'd come to collect in full.' He tried to sound as if it was nothing, but his face was pale and his hand trembled as he poured himself a tot of brandy. 'Did you mean it, Simon? Going to give him the money?'

'Of course I did. How much exactly?'

'Ten pounds, two shillings and threepence three farthings. That's what they claimed.'

'I'll see you have it first thing in the morning. Pay me when you can. The same arrangement you had with Gill.'

'I . . .' he began, then words seemed to fail him.

'What happened to him, anyway?' He'd met the old man a few times, always pleasant and cheerful, happy to oblige friends with a loan.

'He had a palsy, poor devil,' Mudie said. 'I went to see him last month. His left side was useless, he could hardly speak. I think it was probably a blessing for him when he died. His sons must have sold off his list of debts.' Another sip. 'I can't tell you how—'

'No need. I came here to ask you a question.'

Mudie snorted. 'Got more than you bargained for. What is it?'

'A man called Mark.' He explained what they knew and gave the names of the two that Foley knew.

Mudie shook his head. 'Let me think when I'm calmer. I'm sorry, that shook me, Simon. I'm too old for threats and beatings.'

'I'd like to find out about the men who were just here. They didn't sound local; I've never come across them before. Do you know anyone else who owed Gill money?'

'I've never heard any names.'

'Can you ask?'

'They'll be scared.'

'I daresay.' Fear was the friend of men like that. A powerful one. 'I'll bring you the money tomorrow.'

'We're going to have trouble with them,' Sally said as they left.

'We are,' Simon agreed, swallowing hard as his eyes moved around, searching for any sign of the men. 'That one you stabbed . . .' Bested by a girl; his reputation would be shredded. He'd want his revenge for that.

'I'll keep watch for him.' She'd pocketed the man's knife.

'Thank you,' he said again, but she shrugged; it was nothing. Damnation. He should have anticipated the attack. He'd made another error. It might have been a fatal one, if it hadn't been for Sally. His mouth was dry and he felt fear starting to creep up his body again. What would happen to Rosie and the boys if he died?

'I've heard nothing about them,' Porter said when Simon told him about the men at the print shop. 'They must be new. Gill hasn't been in the ground a month, not enough time for the will to go through probate. Those sons of his were always greedy devils, just waiting for the old man to breathe his last.'

He'd spotted the constable on Boar Lane and hailed him, wondering if there had been any more word on the murders. Not a thing on anybody named Mark and no hints on the killing of Green the pawnbroker. The watch's investigations were hitting a wall whichever way they turned. This new problem left him looking more haggard than before.

'Is there a way to stop them?' Simon asked.

'I don't see how. Collecting a proper debt is legal enough,' the man answered slowly.

'Not with threats, though.'

'No,' he agreed. 'But taking over a business if someone can't pay sounds above board to me. Did you *hear* any threats?'

'No, but why would they need a bodyguard if they were businessmen?'

'Could be any number of reasons.' He held up his hand as Simon began to bristle. 'I'm not trying to start an argument, Westow. I'm simply pointing out what a magistrate would say if someone tried to swear a complaint.'

He was right, of course, and Simon knew it. Unless these men slipped up, there was going to be no legal way to stop them.

A nod of acceptance and Simon was striding away to Beckett's Bank to withdraw the money he'd promised Mudie.

Bank notes in his pocket, he turned up Albion Street, and round to the small cottage behind Green Dragon Yard.

She was surprised to see Simon appearing out of the blue, more so when he suggested an hour sparring with knives. His eyes were bright, he looked on edge. Haunted.

'How long since you used your knife?' he asked.

'Months,' she admitted.

'Then we both need some practice.'

'All right,' Jane hadn't missed this side of the work, but if she was hunting Armistead's killer, she'd need to be sharp, quick with her knife. Together, they walked up towards the quiet place on Woodhouse Moor they'd used in the past.

Another sultry day; two minutes and they were sweating. He was a little rusty, but she was slow. In a fight with someone good, they'd both have been beaten in seconds.

Half an hour and they'd both improved a little. Her old skills started to come out of hibernation: reactions quickened, acting faster. Simon still seemed hesitant, a heartbeat behind. The instincts he'd once possessed seemed to have deserted him. He had no flow to his movements. Jane knew she was still too slow, nowhere near as good as she'd once been. But the memory was beginning to return to her muscles. She gulped in air and wiped the sweat off her palm, drying the hilt of her knife on her dress.

'You'd be better doing this with Sally,' Jane told him.

He chuckled. 'She's far too quick for me. This way we can push each other.'

It was more than that, she thought. He trusted her, but she wasn't a part of the family, not likely to say anything to Rosie. Any secret he was hiding would stay with her.

Like it or not, she was fully part of all this life again. Hunting Armistead's killer, looking out for Dodson and trying to keep him safe from his new friend, she needed to have her skills honed. To be ready. To be completely ruthless.

Finally, Simon slid his knife back into its sheath. His face was streaming with sweat, shirt sodden. But he looked a little happier than when they'd arrived, Jane decided. Whatever he needed, he'd found some small part of it.

The exercise had been good for her, too. She felt more alive. Skin tingling, heart beating faster, face flushed. Maybe she'd test herself against Sally next time; someone truly dangerous. Yet under the exhilaration she felt a tug of sorrow; there was no escape from the past.

As they walked, Simon talked about the men at Mudie's print shop. Her ears pricked up as she heard what Sally had done. Now she understood why he'd needed this. No matter; whatever the reason, it had been a good idea. She'd enjoyed it, she realized as they parted by Green Dragon Yard.

A wash, a drink of cordial, and she felt refreshed.

'Your eyes are shining,' Mrs Shields said happily.

Jane smiled. 'It was good.'

As the light began to fade, Jane laced up her old work boots and wrapped a thin shawl around her shoulders. The knife sat in her pocket; she'd spent a quarter of an hour sharpening it over the whetstone, losing herself in the rhythm of the strokes. She couldn't do much more to help identify Armistead's killer, but she could try to keep Dodson safe.

'I'll be back in an hour,' she said as she leaned over to kiss Mrs Shields's cheek. 'Maybe a little longer.'

The old woman stared at her with concern. For the last several months, Jane had spent her evenings at home. She knew things had shifted.

'There's no need to worry.' A squeeze of the thin hand. 'Honestly.'

The homeless made their camps where they could. They chose empty buildings that would soon be demolished before factories started to rise from their ashes. But there was nobody in the spots she used to know. Jane wandered along the river. Ten minutes passed before she felt someone watching her. She drew out of sight into the entrance of a court, pulling out the knife and holding it down by her side. She was surprised: no worry, only the sense of anticipation.

A small figure stood in the gloom. 'Sally says you're to come along with me.'

She put the weapon back in her pocket and followed. The girl skipped along, as if she was playing a game. They passed Cavalier Hill, then took a track that led towards the river. Jane smelled the smoke of a bonfire and started to pick out the silhouettes.

She'd entered Sally's kingdom, a shifting place the girl visited as often as she could.

'They saw you right away,' she said. 'They haven't used those old places in months.'

'I wanted them to find me.' She turned her head towards the group gathered by the fire; even on a warm night, the blaze felt like comfort and safety. Boys, girls, men, women, from four years old to twenty. Some sleeping, others talking softly. Nothing had really changed from the years she'd lived this way, Jane thought; it simply felt like another age now. Maybe it would stay this way until the end of time. She was aware that many of them were observing her. 'Have they come up with anything on the man with Dodson?'

'His name's John,' Sally told her. 'None of them have heard him called more than that. No surname. He arrived in Leeds a few days ago. They're scared of him.'

That was easy to believe. He carried darkness and decay within himself.

'Do they know if he's hurt anyone? Threatened them?'

Sally shook her head. 'A group of men beat him bloody one night when he tried to beg money from them.'

'Dodson must have found him right after that.'

'One of the girls said it feels like he has a shadow all around him.'

She nodded; that was the truth. 'Simon told me you saved him today.'

'He did?' she asked in astonishment. 'It wasn't that much. I saw something, that's all.'

'He came and asked me to practise with him. We're both too slow. I need someone to make me work harder.'

'Who? Me?' Sally asked.

'You'll be better than me these days.'

The girl cocked her head. 'When?'

'Tomorrow morning. Eight, up on the moor.'

'Unless Simon needs me.'

TEN

He'd barely arrived at the coffee cart when someone started to talk about damage done overnight, a brick heaved through the window of a business.

'Where was it?' Simon asked.

'Mudie the printer, up on—'

He put down the mug and hurried away. Up Briggate, past the place where Middle Row had stood. It was difficult to believe that only a week had passed since they discovered the secret workshop and Kendall's body.

George Mudie was sweeping up the glass from the floor. Tiny shards and specks glittered in the light.

'I heard.'

He snorted. 'No doubt it's all over Leeds by now. Gives everyone a chance to gloat.'

'Nobody's doing that.' He took the money from his jacket and placed it on the desk. 'Now you can pay them, George.'

'You know who did this.'

Of course he did. The bully boy. A small, spiteful piece of revenge. But he'd have been careful not to be seen. There would be no way to prove anything unless he grew boastful in drink. Until then, though, they were helpless.

'Sometimes I wonder if it's worth it, Simon. Now I have to pay for the bloody glazier, on top of everything else.'

He added two more shillings to the pile. 'That should see you right.'

Mudie's voice was glum. 'All it means is I owe you more.'

'I told you, pay me what you can, when you have it.'

'You're a friend. I appreciate that.'

Simon saw two figures standing by the door. 'Looks like you have company.' He raised his voice. 'No bodyguard today, gentlemen?'

'We're only here for a moment,' one of them answered, the undertone of menace in his voice as he gazed at the shattered window. 'As long as you have the money, of course.'

Mudie counted it out. 'We're clear now. All that's missing is the receipt.'

The other man passed it over, and they touched their hats as they turned to leave.

'If only it was this easy to do business with everyone. Good day, sirs.'

Mudie exhaled slowly. 'God knows what they'd have done if you hadn't helped.'

'You don't need to think about that. It's over now.'

'For me.'

There would be others. Leeches like that would feast wherever they could.

Simon strolled to the Parish Church, and through to the vestry to find Fowler.

'Mark . . .' Simon began.

The clerk shook his head. 'I'm sorry, Mr Westow. I haven't been able to find anything.'

It had gone nowhere, but he hadn't expected much else; if the man had discovered any information, he'd have sent word. He stood in the church porch, surveying the town. A heavy pall of smoke from the factory chimneys, so thick in places that it dimmed the light. It grew worse with each year; God only knew what it would be like by the time Richard and Amos were grown.

But Leeds was his home. It always had been. He couldn't imagine living anywhere else.

He walked along the Calls, thoughts flickering through his mind. Working with the knives yesterday had helped, but it only made him realize just how slow he'd become. He'd questioned each move before he made it, wondering, second-guessing himself instead of trusting his instincts. He'd allowed caution to rule.

'Do you need me?' Sally asked. 'Jane wanted me to help her for an hour.'

'You go,' he told her, hiding his sudden worry. 'I'll be fine.'

A small test of his mettle for the few hundred yards to his house. Still, he kept alert, gaze sweeping around, hand resting on the knife in his belt.

*   *   *

Sally could have killed her twenty times over. She was a far deadlier opponent than Simon, fast and cunning; she'd learned so much in the last few months. Jane felt clumsy as she tried to parry the attacks and find an opening for her own. Old and awkward. It wasn't that long since she'd been the speedier one. Now she was struggling, while the girl hardly needed to try.

Jane was a little faster by the time they finished, starting to anticipate moves. But she knew the truth: she'd just received a lesson in how far she had to go to recover her ability. It would take work. Time. Did she have that? Did she want it?

They walked through town together. Down Briggate, watching the faces. The handsomely dressed and the poor, jostling side by side. The children who swooped, trying to pick a pocket or snatch a purse, vanishing again as if they'd never been there.

Jane spotted Dodson on Commercial Street, the wooden leg stretched out in front of him, the man called John by his side. She nudged Sally and they strolled towards the pair. No new injuries on the crippled soldier, and for a second she wondered if he really had had an accident. But the merest glance at the hatred on John's face and she knew he'd been responsible.

Coins in the cup, a few words and they moved on. She sensed John's gaze burning into her as she walked away.

'You've had a proper look at him now.'

'There's . . . .' Sally began. 'I . . .' She shuddered in the heat. 'I felt cold when I was close to him.'

'Those coins I put in the cup were the only ones there. People are usually charitable to Dodson. They're avoiding him.'

No surprise; John would repel any honest soul.

The pavement was dry and dusty, the cobbles of the road littered with mounds of horse dung. A boy with a shovel dodged between carts and carriages to scoop it up and tip it into a handcart. The market gardens that fed Leeds would buy all he took them to fertilize their crops. He looked up, spotted Sally and waved.

'Do you know him?' Jane asked.

'He used to live on the streets. Picked pockets until he managed to put enough aside for that cart. He does well these days.'

Like Sally, like her, he was proof that there was always hope, even if you had nothing.

'John,' she said, with a glance over her shoulder.

'He's going to have to go, or that soldier friend of yours won't last.'

Jane took a deep breath. The thing she hadn't dared say. She'd hoped she was wrong. But no.

Suddenly she raised her head.

'Do you feel that?'

A nod. Sally had a hand in the pocket of her dress, gripping her knife.

'Why don't you go around and then come up behind,' the girl said.

Jane slipped away, pulling the shawl closer over her hair. A minute and she returned, trailing fifty yards behind, touching her gold ring for luck. Following was one skill that hadn't withered. The man was easy to spot. She knew who he was from the way Sally had described him yesterday. Big, with his right hand poorly wrapped in a bandage. He was walking with fast, measured strides, anger rippling off him as he moved. He wouldn't be stupid enough to try for revenge in daylight on a busy street, would he?

She edged closer. Just in case.

Abruptly, the man turned away. Had he realized she was there? No. He was nothing more than brute strength, not the type to be aware of anything like that. She'd seen too many like him.

Warily, she followed. Invisible in the shawl, just another woman hidden by the crowd. Sally would realize he'd gone and guess what she was doing. Her nerves were taut, her missing finger throbbed, back to haunt her. If he turned on her . . .

This wasn't her battle. But somehow it had come to her and she couldn't stand aside.

Jane kept her distance, moving cautiously. Glancing around, hand tight around the hilt of her knife.

He went back through town, crossing Briggate, along Cheapside, where the butchers cut up carcasses, over Vicar Lane and down, all the way to the far side of High Street and into a rooming house. Cheap, shabby, probably no more than a penny or two a night. She waited until the door closed behind him, then hurried away.

Kate the pie-seller was doing brisk business with people hungry for their dinner. Jane bought two pies and gave one to Sally.

They ate as they walked to the middle of the bridge and gazed down over the parapet.

'I wonder why he left like that?' Sally said. 'I thought he was going to follow me all the way home.'

'Maybe he already knows where Simon lives.' Or it could have been any one of too many things. 'He's the type who'll burn for revenge. You bested him in front of the men who hired him.'

Sally nodded. 'Humiliated by a girl.'

'He won't be able to do much while his hand is bandaged.'

She smiled. 'If he's angry enough, I don't think that will stop him.'

'He's big,' Jane said.

'Then I'll need to be fast.'

'Just be careful.'

'I will,' Sally told her. 'I'm going to stay alive. We need to practise again soon.'

Sir Robert Foley had mentioned two men named Mark: Mark Preston and Mark Walker. Time to go back and see if Mudie knew either one; he'd had time to think about them.

He was turning the handle of the printing press, casting an eye over each sheet as it came out before feeding in a new one. A pistol sat close to his hand. His eyes darted up as Simon opened the door.

'No more problems?'

'No.' He saw Simon eyeing the gun. 'Just in case. Before you ask, it's loaded. Not much point otherwise, is there?'

'None,' he agreed. 'When I interrupted things the other day, I wanted to ask you about a pair of men . . .'

'Mark Preston's very upright,' Mudie replied once he heard the names. 'Involved with the Methodists, a lay preacher or something like that. Never heard a bad word about him. Mark Walker . . .' He pressed his lips together for a minute. 'He's completely different. Sly as the devil, and you wouldn't trust him as far as you could throw him. I'm surprised you've never come across his name before. What's he done?'

'It might be nothing. He came up, along with Preston.'

'Is this related to Mangey and those cups that were stolen?'

No point in lying; Mudie was the one who'd introduced him to Foley. 'Yes.'

'For what it's worth, Walker's the type who'd pay someone to steal them, but I can't see him killing anyone himself.'

'Where can I find him?'

'The last I heard, he owned one of those big houses on Hanover Place. Right there off Park Lane. That was three or four years ago, mind; he could have moved since then.'

That was a start. Simon walked out along the Head Row, past the dignified elegance of Bedford Place and Hanover Street, and followed the curve of Park Lane. Hanover Place stood back, just beyond the grandeur of Vauxhall House and its grounds.

The houses were a fair size, with long, immaculately tended gardens that ran down to the road. The people who lived there weren't short of a penny. Metal railings with tips pointed like spears kept everything private.

He'd need a way in. But first he needed to discover which of the eight houses belonged to Walker – if he still lived there.

'He still lives in the same place,' Porter said. He was sitting at his desk in the courthouse, smoking a pipe. 'I was out to his house just a few months ago.' He squinted as he tried to recall it. 'Third one along from the left, I think. Dark green door.'

'What took you there?'

'He'd reported a burglary. Small items, a waste of my time. More a job for you. What do you want with him, anyway?'

'His name is *Mark* Walker.'

'Ah.' The realization spread across his face. 'I know he has a shady character, but do you see him as a suspect?'

'He knows Foley, he's seen the cups.' Simon gave a shrug. 'I need to find out.'

'I don't see him as a murderer.' Porter gave a shake of his head. 'It would mean dirtying his hands.'

'Men like that can kill if they're desperate.'

'Or they're certain they'll never be discovered.'

'Would he be the type to leave Kendall's body where we'd be certain to find it?' Simon asked.

The constable shook his head again. 'Never. He's too clever by half.'

'Living where he does, he must be a gentleman of sorts. Armistead would have let him in.'

Porter shook his head. 'Unless Walker's lost his mind, he wouldn't have done it. I don't buy it, Westow. From the look on your face, you're not certain, either.'

'I've never met the man.'

'Find a way to talk to him. You'll see.'

He returned to Hanover Place armed with a short note from Foley. *This gentleman might be able to help with the problem you had some months ago.* Not much, but enough to get him through the door and into Mark Walker's presence.

The man was smooth. Impeccably dressed and groomed, but his clothes hadn't come from any local tailor. The coat fitted too snugly to his form, the trousers tight against his thighs, neckcloth tied with some elaborate knot, and a brilliant sheen to his boots. All very exact and dazzling, Simon thought. Very likely the height of fashion. Clothes designed to awe the provincials. He had London style in his appearance and the arrogance to match.

The items in the room were carefully selected, delicate porcelains, all artfully arranged to catch the light and the gaze. No silver at all.

'I'm sure it's a kind gesture from Sir Robert to recommend you,' Mark Walker said after he'd glanced at the piece of paper and handed it back. 'But the incident happened too long ago. Having your name then would have been more useful to me.'

He had a severe face, the type to repel, with heavy, dark brows and hooded eyes, his hair thinning. Not forty yet, but already looking older and careworn.

'You had items stolen. It might not be too late to recover them.'

The man spoke slowly and clearly, as if he was addressing a child. 'As I said, Mr Westow, all of that is history. Forgotten.'

'Very good.'

'I'll wish you good day.'

Curt, Simon thought as he strode down the path back to the street. Cold. But a murderer? Unless the man was an excellent play-actor, he couldn't see it. Porter was right. Could it have been one of his servants? He'd only seen the man who let him in and out, and he wore the same condescending air as his master.

It seemed unlikely. The man obviously had plenty of money;

why would he need to steal and murder? Yet something niggled inside, and he wasn't willing to write him off completely. Maybe it was simply his manner that rubbed Simon the wrong way. A very slight possibility, nothing more than that. He needed a better suspect.

'Walker looks out of place up here,' Simon said, spreading butter across a hunk of bread. 'He ought to be strutting around in London.'

'You didn't like him,' Rosie said.

'Is it that obvious?' He laughed. 'He was very . . . dismissive.'

'Of you?'

'He seemed willing to forget that he was robbed a few months ago. I can't understand that.'

She gave him a weighted look. 'He did? Most people would be desperate to have it solved. Any sign of a woman around?'

'Not that I saw.' He thought about the house with its clean angles and bare space and shook his head. 'No sense of one, either.'

'A pity,' Rosie said thoughtfully. 'I could have made her acquaintance. We need something with more substance.'

'We've had no luck with Mark so far.'

'We will.'

He valued her confidence; he just wished he could share it. His seemed to be in short supply these days.

As he left the house, Sally was coming down Swinegate. Every few yards she glanced over her shoulder. Twice she crossed the street.

'Has someone been following you?' Simon asked.

'That man from the print shop. He was around this morning.' She shrugged. 'Where are you going?'

'To ask more questions about a man called Mark.'

The coffee shops, the better quality of inns. For three hours he went from place to place. Vague answers at best until a man placed his pipe on the table, raised his eyes said: 'Mark? What is that? His surname?'

The breath caught in his chest. Surname? For the love of God, he'd assumed . . . he was stupid.

ELEVEN

'D o you still have the page from Armistead's house?' He'd hurried up the Head Row, Sally scurrying to keep pace. His heart was beating fast, thoughts cascading through his mind. Down Green Dragon Yard, then through the gap in the wall to the garden of the small cottage. Jane had opened the door, astonished to see the pair of them. 'The one with Mark in the bottom corner?'

'Yes.' She looked confounded by his question as she brought it from her pocket. 'Right here.'

Outside, in the light, he peered, bringing his face close to the paper. The ink was blurred and smudged. Could it really be a surname?

'What do you think?' he asked Jane after he'd explained.

She studied it carefully, eyes moving over the words on the page. Simon was holding his breath, waiting for the answer.

'It could be,' she said eventually.

'How likely do you think that is?' He needed to hear something. Words that might help him believe.

He watched her study the paper, scowling, wondering, biting her lower lip.

'I don't know,' she replied. 'I'm sorry.'

'Mark can definitely be a surname, too,' Mrs Shields said. She'd followed them outside. 'I knew a Mr Mark once.'

'In Leeds?' Simon asked. His throat was dry, every muscle in his body tight and on edge. Maybe . . .

'He lived next door to us when my husband and I had a house on Park Square.'

Simon looked into her face and pictured her there, back when the square was new, the fashionable address in town.

'What was his full name? Do you remember?' He tried to keep the urgency out of his voice.

'William,' she told him. 'Mind you, he must have been close to sixty when I knew him. That was over thirty years ago now.'

No help at all. He felt urgency clawing at him. 'Did he have any children?'

'A son and two daughters.' She smiled. 'The son was married, and he had a boy of his own, before you ask. The son was called George, I do remember that. But for the life of me, I couldn't tell you the boy's name.' She thought for a moment. 'I suppose George would be about sixty himself these days, and his son is probably in his thirties. Does that help at all?'

'Very much,' he told her gratefully. The woman might look so frail that a slight breeze could carry her away, but her mind was still clear. She'd given him a line to follow.

'What do we do now?' Sally asked.

'I want you to find out if there's still anyone with the surname of Mark in Park Square.' He glanced at Jane. 'The pair of you. I'll see what I can find elsewhere.'

'Keep your shawl over your hair when we get to the houses,' Jane said. 'Yes, like that. Nobody will notice us.' She smiled. 'They certainly won't remember we were there.'

At the back door of one of the grand places on Park Square, Jane drew in a deep breath, then brought her hand down on the metal knocker. Sally stood behind her, head bowed.

With her long apron, and the cap covering her hair, the hard-eyed woman had to be the cook. She stood, hands resting on her hips.

'Yes?' She sounded harried and ill-tempered, her face was sweaty from the damp heat escaping from the kitchen. 'What do you want?'

'I'm sorry, ma'am. Our mistress sent us with a message for Mrs Mark,' Jane said.

'Mark?' The woman glared. 'Nobody called that here. Not anywhere on this side of the square, neither. You've got the wrong place, stupid girl.'

Before Jane could reply, the cook shut the door on her.

Houses ran along three sides of the square. On the corner, Jane paused. The place must have changed since Mrs Shields lived here. She liked to think of her as a young woman, pretty, charming, holding her husband's arm as they strolled around and stopped to talk to other couples.

A second side, but the answer was the same. One throw of the dice left.

It was a maid who opened the door, an older woman with a sunken face where her teeth had been drawn, but kindly blue eyes.

'Mrs Mark? You have the wrong house, pet. It's next door but one.'

'An hour and she'll have forgotten we ever existed,' Jane promised as they hurried away.

'Mark,' Mudie nodded his head in approval. 'Mark. I must be getting old, I never thought about it as a surname.'

'George Mark?'

He began to laugh. 'My God, I'd completely forgotten him. You'd do best to talk to Barnabas Wade. No love lost between those two.'

'Why?'

'You really never heard that tale, Simon? He's the lawyer who started the action that ended up with Wade disbarred. The fool gulled some relative of Mark's, and he brought an action against him. Won, of course. Died soon after.'

'Does he have a son?'

'I've no idea. Barnabas probably has chapter and verse on the whole family.' He bent over the type he was setting. 'I've spent enough time running my mouth. I need to work if I'm going to make money to pay you back.'

But no sign of Wade in any of his usual places.

It didn't matter. Simon began to feel hopeful, as if the stones were starting to shift. Maybe Jane and Sally had found something . . .

'We know where they live,' Rosie said after she'd heard Jane. The boys were out in the yard, kicking a ball against the wall, enjoying the freedom after a day of lessons with their tutor. Simon had seen the reports on the twins. They were clever, their teacher said; soon they'd need more than he could give them. He and Rosie had decisions ahead. Not only about that; maybe other things, too, he thought, unless he conquered this draining fear.

'Now we need to find out about Mr Mark,' he said and looked at his wife. 'Do you know anyone on that side of the square?' She pursed her lips. 'I'll pay a call tomorrow. Mrs Bartholomew would be perfect. She's the nosiest woman you can imagine. I'll probably have their whole history by the time I come home.'

'We could definitely use something like that.'

'I don't think it's him,' Jane said quietly.

'Why not?' Simon asked.

'Park Square is still a very good address,' she began. 'He must have money or a respectable job.'

'Go on.' What she was saying made sense, but he wanted to hear it all.

'He probably has a family, too. That's a great deal to lose. Why would he risk it?'

'Maybe he has, maybe not. He could be clinging on to what's left. Until we know about him, we can't be sure. Plenty of people we've taken in the past have risked everything. Some of them have been of good standing, too.'

She nodded, pulled the shawl closer and left quietly. He heard the click of the door as she went. She was still so good at this work, but he'd never understand her.

Jane had been walking for an hour; without thinking, she'd counted the chimes of the church clock. Over to Cavalier Hill and back, sorting through the jumble in her head. The work this afternoon had seemed completely natural and easy. Too much so. Following the man that Sally had stabbed, pretending to be a servant to find out about people . . . she'd slipped back so easily into the old ways, as if she'd never stopped. It was all simple, but she'd walked away from it before. *Chosen* to walk away.

She wanted the man who killed Armistead. The cold fire of her anger burned in her belly, but this wasn't why she'd come back. Jane had agreed to return to go through the papers. She needed to understand what she truly desired and what she was willing to do for it.

But as twilight edged into darkness, she felt no clearer. Slowly, she drifted back towards home. She'd barely turned from Vicar Lane on to the Head Row when she felt something. Dangerous, threatening. A tremor that ran through her entire body.

She drew her knife, grip tight on the handle. Someone was close. Waiting there, down in Rockley Hall Yard. The light had dwindled, the buildings cast thick, black shadows. All she could see was a faint, shifting form against the night. Something bad lay down there. Something evil.

Jane hesitated. Her heart was hammering. There was no real noise from the yard. Nothing human, just the rustle and scratching of rats. Maybe her senses were playing tricks. Her mind was jumpy; she knew she was too ready to imagine things. A moment, then she turned and hurried on towards home, boots tapping briskly on the flagstones.

The beershops were doing brisk business. Clouds of smoke hovered below the ceiling and talk was loud. Even in the corners, Simon had to raise his voice to be heard as he found the men he needed and asked about the family called Mark on Park Square.

One or two had come across them. Done small jobs for them – carting this or that, mending something in the house. Nobody who *knew* them; not even any pointers in the direction of someone who might.

By the end of the evening, he was frustrated. He knew a little more, but it was all dribs and drabs; he was still nowhere close. No sense of whether anyone in the family could be involved in theft and murder. Probably Jane was right: it was unlikely that any man with some wealth and standing would risk everything by leaving a corpse where it would be found.

Yet people did strange things; in his years as a thief-taker he'd learned that many times over. It might seem improbable, but it certainly wasn't impossible.

No Sally with him tonight; he told her he was going out alone. Time to cut those leading strings and look out for himself. The way he'd been before she arrived. He'd forced himself, but every minute he'd been outside, Simon had felt fearful. Skin prickling, heart beating too fast. He had to do this. It was the only way.

His mind eased as he unlocked the front door. Then he was aware of voices in the kitchen. Porter was sitting at the table, talking to Rosie. No sign of Sally.

'Westow.' The constable rose and gathered up his hat. 'There's something I want you to see.'

'Is it related to . . .'

The man shook his head. 'No. But you need to look at this.'

They marched through the streets. Even in the night, smoke and soot from the factories gritted the air. Still a lingering, teasing warmth. Porter's face was set hard, in no mood to talk. Men saw them and slunk out of sight.

Up Briggate, all the way to the market cross, then down the Head Row. He stopped at Rockley Hall Yard.

'In here. Not a handsome sight.'

The inspector and two members of the watch were there, holding lanterns on poles to light the scene.

'Christ.'

'I told you,' Porter said.

Simon wanted to turn away. But all he could do was stare, the horror rising through his chest.

Not just cut. The body had been mauled. Mutilated and slashed everywhere, curls of flesh hanging from the cheeks and throat. Clothing ripped away, skin torn to shreds. Hair ripped from his scalp, leaving bare, bloody patches. An ear almost ripped off.

'It's . . .' he began, but the words failed him. He shook his head, not wanting to believe. 'God Almighty. How..?'

'I know. It's like an animal's been at him,' Porter said bleakly. 'Do you know him, Westow?'

There was enough to identify the man. The bulk, the eyes, the bandage still wrapped around his right hand. The man who'd been the bodyguard for the men in Mudie's shop.

'You told me about them.' The constable nodded. 'That little girl who's working for you did him some damage.'

'He pulled his knife first. But she couldn't have done this—'

'I know. I talked to her. She was at home with your wife and your boys.'

Simon tried to pull his gaze away, but he couldn't. He kept staring, fixed by the sight.

'We don't have animals capable of doing that,' he said finally. 'Not in Leeds.'

'No,' Porter agreed. 'But it seems we have a man who can. That's worse.'

TWELVE

She tried to find a place to sleep. Somewhere safe. Exhaustion made her bones heavy, dragging her feet down the ginnels and courts. People everywhere, glaring, telling her to leave. She tried to run, but all she could manage was a shuffle. Finally, down at the back of a yard, she found somewhere up against the side of a wall, close to a midden.

All she owned was in a small bag, clutched tight against her belly as she lay down. The night was frigid, her teeth were chattering. A sudden tug, someone trying to rip her belongings away from her. Low, dark laughter. Rank breath on her face. She held tight, desperate. She couldn't lose it all.

Jane's eyes snapped open in the darkness. Another nightmare. She sat up, breathing slowly as the wisps of the dream vanished. She was crying and she didn't know why.

The night seemed to stretch out ahead of him. Simon began to doze, then the image of the man's torn face slipped into his head and his eyes opened again. His mind whirled, plagued by all the dead. After them came the man named Mark, lurking deep in the shadows. Then the doubts about himself arrived, fresh and ready to taunt him. Just as he was drifting away once more, the face returned.

He was grateful for the first streaks of dawn, sliding out of the covers, leaving Rosie to sleep. Once he was dressed and washed in cold water, he felt awake. As long as he lived he'd never be able to forget what he'd seen, but the morning would banish it to the back of his mind. That killing was not his concern. There were too many other things he needed to think about.

Swinegate was quiet, not a soul around as he strode along the street. The usual early crowd had gathered around the coffee cart outside the Bull and Mouth. The conversation swirled around the discovery of the corpse; what other topic could there be?

Simon listened to all manner of theories; none of them sounded likely. Nobody knew the name of the dead man. After a few minutes he drifted away and returned to the house.

Jane was sitting with Rosie and Sally.

'I walked past there last night,' she said. 'I heard something inside—' She paused for a moment. 'I felt something. I thought it must be rats.'

'No,' Simon told her. 'It was very human.'

'Porter was shaken,' Rosie said.

'It was the worst I've ever seen.' No need for details. Bad enough that he'd relived it all through the night; he didn't need to see it in the morning, too. 'Someone's out there. We all need to be very careful at night. *Very*.' He turned to look at Sally. 'Especially those children.'

'I'll make sure they know,' she said. 'Are we going to look for the killer?'

'No.' He was grateful it wasn't their business. 'We need to decide what to do about Mark.'

Jane passed on the other side of the Head Row. A few people had gathered around the opening to Rockley Hall Yard. The curious, the ghouls with nothing better to fill their time. If she'd gone in to look last night, she might have become another corpse.

Luck, she told herself, and twisted the ring on her finger.

Up on Woodhouse Moor, she sparred with Sally, knives flashing in the light. At the end of an hour she felt quicker and slyer, the old skills emerging from their long sleep. But still a long way to go.

'What does Simon want you to do?' Jane asked as they strolled back into town.

'I don't think he knows,' Sally replied. 'We're not even sure who we're looking for, are we?'

'No.' That was the problem.

'What about you?'

Jane shrugged. She'd offered what she could. First with the books and then impersonating a servant. There was nobody Simon wanted her to follow.

'That body they found,' Sally began. She looked up at Jane. 'Do you think John could have done it?'

She'd wondered that as soon as she heard about the damage

to the corpse. She'd had no sense of him as she passed last night, but everything seemed to fit. The darkness, the raw violence. Jane had watched Simon's face as he talked about it; the slaughter must have been brutal. She'd ask Dodson if she managed to see him on his own.

'If it's him—'

'Let's find out first,' Jane said. There would be time to decide once they knew.

From the grim look on his face, Porter only wanted to discuss one thing.

'His name was Walter Smith. That's what he told people, anyway. We took a look at his room. Nothing to show who he really was. You said he was working for the men who bought up the debts old man Gill was holding.'

'That's right.'

'It's funny. We've been searching for them this morning. Can't find hide nor hair. Discovered where they'd been staying. Paid their bill and left first thing. They took the early coach to London.' He cocked his head. 'Strange, that, isn't it?'

Very, he thought. Very. But he didn't know what it meant.

'I spent an hour with Mrs Bartholomew.' Rosie tucked her gown around her legs as she settled at the table. Light wool, a good weight for the warm June weather, a rich burgundy colour that suited her well.

'Was she able to tell you anything about Mr Mark?' Simon asked.

'Everything you'd want. He's called George, just like his father. The rumour is that the family has some very vague blood connection to Arthur Mangey. No one seems certain on the details. *She* thinks it might be a by-blow.' Her bright expression faded. 'He doesn't sound like our man, though. A clever enough mind, she claims, but a cart overturned on him when he was a child. His body's not very strong; needs a cane to walk and his right arm is nigh on useless.'

Maybe it was still possible, he thought, then stopped himself. Rosie was right. It couldn't be him.

'But he does have a cousin. Two or three times removed, something like that.' The faint glimmer on Rosie's face became a proud grin. 'Or so Mrs Bartholomew's heard, which means it's definitely true. He's called William Mark. She doesn't know much about him, other than he spends most of his time in Leeds and he's supposed to be an outcast in the family.'

'What did he do?' Sally asked.

Rosie leaned forward, elbows on the table. She lowered her voice, as if she was passing on a secret. 'All the usual things you'd expect of a man with some family money and nobody keeping him in check. Made a servant girl pregnant, in debt to everyone. A short temper.'

'He can't be from here or plenty of people would know his name.'

'Collingham,' she said with a triumphant smile.

Simon had heard of the place, nothing more than that; a village a dozen miles away, he thought. No great distance on a horse.

'How old is William Mark?'

'Somewhere in his middle twenties, she believes. His father grew tired of paying his debts and cut him off.'

That made him even more interesting. 'How long ago did he do that?'

'Mrs Bartholomew isn't sure. She thinks it was a few months.'

Mark would be desperate for money. If he knew about the cups . . . but how could he have learned about the secret room in Middle Row? Even Armistead had no idea how to get in and out. Simon's thoughts fell over each other. If Mark murdered Kendall, leaving the body there could have been the arrogance of someone who realized he wasn't known in Leeds. Stop, he told himself. Things were growing too tangled.

'We don't have anything better, do we?' Rosie said.

'Not at the moment,' Simon agreed. He was a likelier suspect than Mark Walker. Still, it was thin. Not much better than water. He sighed.

Sally raised her head. 'There's a boy and a girl who mentioned that place once. They came from there.'

'Collingham?'

'Yes.'

'How old are they?'

She blinked. 'I don't know. I never ask. A little older than me, I think. I can tell them his name.'

He nodded. It wasn't likely that anyone homeless would know the man, but a question cost nothing.

No evidence at all, but he had a feeling in his belly about William Mark. Or was he simply hoping he was right?

The streets were dirty. Carts and carriages threw dirt and dust into the air. Somewhere up above the smoke, the sun was shining. Even in a thin cotton dress with just a light shawl on her shoulders, Jane was hot as she walked through the press of people on Briggate. A few stopped to gaze at the place where the Moot Hall and Middle Row had stood in the middle of the road for over two centuries. She couldn't begin to picture that amount of time. Now traffic moved easily up and down, no longer squeezed on either side of an old building.

No sign of Dodson.

She handed over her money to Kate and chewed the pie the woman gave her.

'You look like you're not quite here today.'

Jane gave her a worried smile. 'I suppose so. Have you seen the soldier?'

'The beggar?' She thought for a moment. 'No, I don't think so. I never notice him. He's always around.'

'I haven't seen any sign of him.' She felt a chill starting to creep up her spine.

'He's been looking after that man.' Kate gave a dark look. 'You know the one I mean.'

'I do.'

'I used to give him food, but I've kept my distance since that one appeared. There's something about him.'

'He's dangerous.'

'Between him and the madman killing people, Leeds is becoming a terrible place.' She spotted a group of men and began to call out her wares as Jane wandered away.

Dodson had told her once that he had a room in one of the old folds on the far side of Timble Bridge that long ago had been pens for animals. Now they were built up, home to workshops and cheap, battered houses.

A few questions and she discovered his address; people knew the gentle old soldier with a wooden leg. They liked him.

She stood by the door, one arm raised, the other in the pocket of the dress, clasping the hilt of her knife. A deep breath and she brought her fist down on the wood.

No sound from inside.

She tried again. Nothing.

The lock was cheap and old, but she had no tools to pick it; she wasn't even sure if she still had the ability.

She'd return later. Maybe Dodson would be back. But as she trudged away it felt like a vain hope.

'William Mark?' Foley echoed the name. The doors to his garden were open to the warm, thick air, the water in the distance. 'My God, I'd forgotten about him. We've met a few times. I used to know his father a little.'

Simon's pulse quickened. 'Has he ever been here?'

The man frowned as he tried to remember. 'He might have. I have a vague image in my head of him attending a party. Why, do you think he . . .?'

'I don't know,' he replied quickly. 'His name came up. He appears to have a reputation.'

Foley's mouth twitched into a smile. 'I recall hearing rumours.'

'Do you remember if he admired the silver cups?'

'Honestly, no. I can't even be certain he was here. I'd know if he asked me about them, though.'

'It seems that William has been cut off by his father, he's heavily in debt, and I'm told he likes to fight. The family's supposed to be distantly related to Mangey.'

The man's eyes opened wide. 'Is that right? He might believe he had a good reason for taking the cups, then.' Foley nodded thoughtfully. 'If he knows about Mangey, he'd understand their worth.'

'It could explain how he knew about the secret room, too. It appears that the pieces are all on the board.'

Another nod. 'I see that, Mr Westow.'

'You said you know his family.'

'A little. I've hunted with his father a few times. That was long ago, now. We both rode out with the pack in Harewood.'

'Could you write me a letter of introduction to him?' It would be the best way to discover everything about William Mark.

'How much do you want me to say about the reason?'

'All of it.' The man had pushed his son away. He might be willing to give Simon the truth.

'I'll have it for you this afternoon.'

On the way back to Swinegate, Simon hired a horse for the next morning. Twenty miles in the saddle; his thighs would be agony by the time the day was over. He was staking his hopes on the family being willing to see him.

'Did you talk to those two from Collingham?' he asked Sally as they sat around the kitchen table.

'They'd heard his name. That was all.'

Of course. There had never been much chance of more. Different classes, different lives.

He was up before dawn on the Saturday morning and out to the coffee cart to catch any new rumours. Sally was already there, quiet in the shadows on the other side of Briggate as Simon drank and listened. As he walked away, she fell in beside him.

'I could go with you,' she said.

'Not today,' he told her. 'I'll be on horseback.'

Sally jutted her chin. 'I know how to ride.'

He remembered last year, just after the girl had begun helping Jane, the way she'd soothed a nervous horse. Completely natural and unafraid around it. He'd thought then that she seemed to be familiar with the animals. It wasn't a skill he'd ever expected in a girl who slept on the streets.

'How long since you were last in the saddle?'

'I don't know,' she said after a long hesitation. It was there behind her eyes: she knew exactly, right to the month. 'But I remember,' Sally said defiantly.

'All right. Let's see if the ostler has anything that would suit and a saddle for a girl.'

Her eyes shone.

She was awkward at first, but no worse in the saddle than him. By the time they passed through the tiny village of Harehills she had the feel of the animal, more at home off the ground than he'd ever feel.

'How did you learn to ride?'

It was conversation for the journey, but she stayed silent for
so long that he believed she wasn't going to give him an answer.
They'd gone another half mile along the Wetherby road before
she began to speak. Even then the words arrived hesitantly, as if
she wasn't certain she should allow them out.

'We had a farm. Only a very small one,' she added quickly.
'Enough for us. My parents and my brother. He was older than
me. I was up on a horse by the time I could walk, I think.'

Sally kept her eyes ahead, scanning the ground, never turning
to look at him. Simon kept quiet; he'd let her tell the story at
her own pace. He suspected she'd kept it locked inside for years;
bringing it into the open was desperately hard for her.

'My father wasn't strong. I could see that even when I was
little. My mother used to do most of the work. We helped her,
me and David. He's my brother.' Another long gap. 'When my
father died, my aunt and uncle came and took over the farm.
They had children of their own. Four of them. The place couldn't
feed everyone. Not if they were going to have anything left to
sell, too. David was big enough to earn his keep. They decided
I wasn't.' Finally Sally looked into his eyes. 'They turned me
away.'

'You came to Leeds.'

'Not straight away. I knew the countryside. I was sure I could
survive there, that they'd change their minds, or some other
family would take me in. I'd learned things. When you live in
the country, you become used to seeing things killed. Pigs,
chickens, foxes. I had a knife. I was going to show my aunt.'

'You have,' he said.

Everybody carried their wounds. Simon knew that; his parents
had died and he went into the workhouse, sent to labour in a
factory when he was six. Jane's father had raped her when she
was eight; her mother had thrown her out rather than lose a
husband's wage.

They were still here. So was Sally. So many hadn't lasted.

He waited, but she'd said her piece. Instead, she pointed out
the types of birds, the kites and the falcons that glided in the air,
the different crops growing in the fields. When she did that, he
could see the pleasure on her face. She lived in town, she'd grown
the armour to last there, the hardness that being on the streets

in Leeds demanded to stay alive. But here, this was where she seemed properly alive. He understood why she'd wanted to come with him today. Her chance to be in the open spaces, even for just a few hours.

They followed the signpost from the main road. Collingham was a hamlet. A straggle of houses and an inn. Simon's thighs ached as he dismounted and asked for directions to the Mark house.

It stood half a mile away. Large and old, built of warm, rosy brick. An inviting building, Simon decided, with the grounds carefully tended; nothing was falling to ruin here. In the courtyard behind the building, he watched Sally slide gracefully from her pony and lead the animals toward the stable to talk to the grooms and the farm hands.

The introduction from Sir Robert Foley did everything that Simon had hoped. Five minutes and he was shown through to a parlour where a stocky, florid man was sitting at a desk.

Charles Mark stood, extending a thick, strong hand. A proper countryman, his skin had the worn texture of old leather, burned dark by years out in all weathers, his eyes clear and a deep, startling blue.

'I remember Foley, he stayed in his saddle in the field,' he said. 'What can I do for you, Mr Westow?'

Mark's voice boomed, as though he was outdoors and used to making his words carry across the fields.

'Your son—'

An abrupt storm of anger boiled up on the man's face.

'Don't have one. Threw him out and cut him off.'

The violence in the man's tone took him by surprise.

'I see.'

'Does he owe you money?' Mark asked.

'Nothing like that,' Simon replied, and realized he suddenly had the man's attention.

'You're lucky, then. What's he done?'

'I believe your family is related to Arthur Mangey, the silversmith—'

'—and traitor.' Mark snorted. 'We are. My great-grandfather was one of his distant relations. Too damned convoluted for me to worry about. Why does it matter?'

'Was there something passed down in the family? Some knowledge about a secret room?'

Mark was silent, gazing at Simon. Finally he asked, 'How do you know about that?'

No choice but to tell him the tale and watch his expression darken.

Mark shook his head. 'I never hear the news out here. Not that interested, either. Enough to keep me busy, especially this time of year.'

'Could your son have known about the workshop?'

'His grandmother,' the man said. 'Damned woman. It was bad enough she passed it on to her own brood. We had no choice but to put up with that nonsense, but I asked her not to fill the children's heads with it. She didn't listen. She was the one who kept hold of all that family ridiculousness. She was proud of the Mangey heritage, God knows why. It's not as if he was any manner of close ancestor. Claimed he wasn't a traitor, although how the devil she worked that out, I don't know. She must have told William everything when he was a boy and it stuck with him.' He snorted with anger and disgust. 'Probably the only damned thing he learned that did.'

William Mark had known about the room. That was what Simon had hoped to learn when he came out here. Now he knew who'd killed Kendall, the reason for his knowledge and why he'd wanted the cups. Well worth the aching muscles of the ride.

'Did you ever know a man called Armistead in Leeds?'

'No,' Charles Mark replied with a firm shake of his head. 'Never heard the name.'

Perhaps it didn't matter. William Mark could have shown up on Armistead's doorstep and claimed he had information on Mangey. The young man had been raised in this house; he'd at least have the veneer of a gentleman; Armistead would have happily invited him in.

'Do you believe my son is a murderer, Mr Westow?' He asked the question with a dark finality.

'I think it's possible.' Simon made sure his voice was wary. Even if Mark had disowned his son, something like that would still be terrible to hear. 'I'm sorry.'

A slow intake of breath, a nod of acceptance and sorrow.

'If he is, then he must face the law. Hang if he's guilty. I knew there was never much good in him, but I'd never suspected that.' He shrugged, as if that might dislodge the feelings in his heart. 'I hoped he might learn something if he had to fend for himself. I never imagined it would be that.'

He'd turned his son off at the beginning of January. No more allowance, changed the will so he'd receive nothing, and seen him go with his tailored clothes, shiny boots, and all his debts. A new year, a fresh start for them both. The young man had been a wastrel. He had plenty of charm, a persuasive tone, but something rotten at his core. Not like his sisters; both of them were settled in good, steady marriages, never a sense of wildness in either one of them.

He looked drained. Bereft. 'You've told me something I didn't want to hear, Mr Westow. But in a curious way, I'm glad you did. I can wash my hands of William with a clear conscience now.'

'One last question – what made you choose the name William?'

He snorted. 'My mother again. She said it was a family name and we ought to keep it. More fool me. Should have got rid of every damned thing to do with the past. I don't know Leeds, maybe seen the place five times in my life. Too big for my tastes, too many people to feel comfortable. If I need something, I go to Wetherby or Harrogate; they're quite large enough for me. But *he* liked the place. Town, he called it. Always gadding off there, every chance he had. Nothing to entertain him out here, he claimed. Will you be able to catch him?'

'We will. I'm working with the constable and the watch.'

'Then I hope it's before he does anything more.' Another sad shake of his head. 'I'd never expected to say this about my own son, but I wish you well.'

THIRTEEN

S imon had his answer. It had taken time and a fair sprinkling of luck, but he was finally there. Once he'd found the right person things had quickly snapped into place.

Very little conversation on the ride back to Leeds. Sally was content simply to be in the saddle; her face showed how much she was relishing the peace and pleasure of the countryside.

Simon had ample to fill his mind as he swayed on top of the horse. William Mark must have felt certain he'd never be identified. That was why he'd been arrogant enough to show off his family knowledge, to kill Kendall in the hidden workshop and leave the body to be found.

He had the cups. Maybe those ideas his grandmother had put in his mind made him believe they were his birthright. That somehow they belonged with him. But by now he had to be desperate for money, and they would fetch a handsome price. Probably the only thing of real value that he still possessed. He was trapped.

They'd passed the turnpike toll house at Sheepscar, on the final stretch back into Leeds, when Sally broke the silence: 'Up there.'

She pointed up the hill, to something moving on the horizon. Simon looked. He had to squint into the glare before he could make out two figures in the distance.

'What—' he began, but she was already urging her pony up the slope. All he could do was follow, digging his heels into the horse's sides.

It was a steep, sharp climb, following a winding track through the long grass. By the time they reached the top, his old animal was winded. Sally had her knife in her hand as she slid from the saddle and began to prowl through the undergrowth. Simon took out his own blade.

There were woods around, with plenty of young trees and thick bushes. A fine place for someone to hide.

'Here,' Sally called and he walked over. His legs were slow and stiff from the time in the saddle. She was squatting, staring at a place where the grass had been trampled. 'See there?' She rubbed her fingers on the dirt. 'It's blood. Everything's been tramped down going that way, you see?'

It looked as if it had all happened in a frenzy, Simon thought as he watched from the corner of his eye for the smallest movement. Had the bodyguard's killer found another victim? But nobody dead, and everything was still now. A few birds were calling. Breathing in, he could just taste the scent of Leeds. Looking around, a chill of fear touched his heart. This was something for Porter and the watch.

'No sign of anything now,' he told Sally. Whatever had happened here, it was over and done. A final gaze around. 'Come on. Whatever was going on, it has nothing to do with us. Not unless it's Will Mark. We have plenty of work of our own.'

Jane stood in front of Dodson's door with Simon's lock picks, hoping she remembered how to use them. Another knock first, in case he'd come home, but all she heard was a hollow silence.

It took five attempts, and with each one, her fear grew. Someone could come and see her. Her hands were slick; she had to keep wiping the sweat from them.

As the pick slipped yet again, she wondered why she was doing this. What did she hope to find? To be sure that Dodson was still alive—

Finally it held and she turned it, holding her breath as the lock clicked open. Jane took hold of her knife and turned the doorknob.

A table, a chair, a chest of drawers, a bed with an old mattress and a sheet stretched tight over it. The shutters were open; the window faced a brick wall, and there was little light.

No sign of any fight or struggle.

Jane looked around, running her hand over the surfaces. A layer of dust and a stale smell were the only things to show the room had been empty for a few days; Dodson kept everything clean and in perfect order; years after having to leave the army, he was still a good soldier.

A spare shirt and trousers neatly folded in one drawer. A single old, thick sock. The other drawer was empty. If he'd ever owned a purse of money, he kept it well hidden.

No indication that the man called John had been here. Whatever he possessed, he had to be wearing it on his back. She had no sense of him in the room. He might never have set foot in here. But he had. Deep inside, she knew he had.

Jane turned a circle. Staring, thinking. Feeling. A part of her wanted to believe that everything was fine. That she was worrying too much about the soldier with one leg. But something was wrong. She knew it, the sense of it filled her.

It took time to lock the door again. Her grip seemed awkward, wrong. She kept staring at her missing little finger. Done, finally; Jane allowed herself a tiny sigh of relief before she hurried away.

Another check of the places where she usually found Dodson. Kate the pie-seller still hadn't seen him. The thoughts were chasing each other round her head, but with each minute her certainty grew: the old soldier was dead or close to it.

She kept searching for an hour, dashing from place to place as she thought of them, panic rising in her body. There were so many spots he could be, on either side of the river. Or in the water itself. She couldn't look everywhere on her own.

Sally. She could ask the children to watch for Dodson. A reward for the one who found him.

But the girl had gone with Simon to talk to William Mark's father, Rosie told her.

For now she had no choice but keep up the hunt alone.

The church bells had rung seven in the evening before Sally found her. The girl looked calm, nodding as she listened.

'Come with me,' she said, darting through the courts and alleys between Briggate and Lands Lane. Jane knew each single inch of Leeds. It was imprinted on her mind; she followed without thinking, always certain where they were.

Past Lands Lane, beyond Red Hall, where the smoke and soot had turned all the ruddy bricks deep black. Not far from Green Dragon Yard and home. To a small clearing. She remembered an orchard here. That had only been a few years ago; now only three trees were left to offer some shade. Seven children sat under them, one barely out of leading strings.

They gathered round Sally. She handed out halfpennies and farthings and told them to pay attention.

'This is Jane. She wants you to find someone. I need you to pass the word. Everybody looking.'

They eyed her warily, but listened as she described Dodson. Most nodded; they were used to seeing him.

'Five shillings for whoever finds him,' she finished. Enough to keep them alive for weeks. But worth every penny.

'Someone will spot him,' Sally said after the children had dispersed.

They were sharp, and went everywhere. But would he be alive or dead when they found him?

'Now there's something I want you to see,' the girl continued.

The blood had drained into the ground, a darker stain on the earth. Jane tried to make some sense of the way the long grass on the ridge had been trampled. A fight, someone wounded, that much was certain. But with no weapon and no bodies it was impossible to say.

'I saw it when we were riding back,' Sally said. 'There were two of them up here.' She shaded her eyes and look down toward Sheepscar and the toll house.

'There's nothing now,' Jane said. Her mind was filled with Dodson. Could it have been him up here? Where was he? Still alive? Injured? 'Do you think it was John?'

'I was too far away to see. It could have been.' A final look and they started to walk away. 'A man called William Mark killed Kendall and Armistead and the pawnbroker. Simon talked to his father.'

'How did he know about the secret room?'

'They're related to the Mangeys. Simon can tell you, but that's the reason.'

William Mark. Now she knew who they were pursuing. The man who'd murdered Mr Armistead. From up here, she could gaze down on Leeds. Was he still here or had he run somewhere, trying to find some safety? A new start with his precious silver cups.

She was a hunter again.

'William Mark.' Constable Porter repeated the name. 'Are you absolutely sure?'

'Everything fits,' Simon told him. 'How many would be likely to know how to get in and out of the hidden workshop?'

'Do you know the names of any of his friends?'

'Nothing at all, really. But he likes rich living.'

The constable snorted. 'All he needs is the money for that.'

'There's his problem. He has nothing.'

'He should be easy enough to find, then.'

'Anything on that other killing?'

'Not yet.'

'You ought to know about something we saw coming back to town . . .'

By evening, Simon hadn't managed to find a sniff of William Mark in any of the inns and beershops. Nobody recognized his name. Or maybe it was the wrong class of company for the man.

His thighs burned and ached from the ride, but it sharpened his mind and kept the fears at bay. On the street he rested a hand on his knife. Ready, alert and tense. He had to beat this.

Simon walked into the Yorkshire Grey, down near the bottom of Kirkgate. Matthew Hutton commanded a corner of the place. Light from a hanging lantern fell on his face as he sat at a large, scarred table. Hutton claimed he'd been a master's mate on naval vessels during the wars against Napoleon. Someone had once called him Captain and the name had stuck.

Simon placed a glass of rum in front of him. Hutton glanced at it, then raised his eyes.

'You must want something.'

The man had arrived in Leeds six years before, a shovel over his shoulder, whistling as he led a horse and cart up Briggate. Within three days he had contracts to remove the night soil from four of the grandest houses in town. At first he worked alone, labouring every hour of daylight. Two months later he employed four men and he'd won more business, still doing a full share himself. These days Hutton had eight different crews working for him, charging householders for the removal of their waste, then selling everything he collected to the market gardeners who planted the fields outside Leeds. Earning on both ends.

He'd become a wealthy man, dressing in cambric shirts and tailored clothes these days, always with a naval cut to remind people of his past. Part successful businessman, part pirate. Still hungry, going out six days a week to sell his services.

Hutton shook his head at the name William Mark. 'Don't know him, matey.' He sipped the rum. 'What's he done?'

'It could be nothing.'

'No, it's not. A thief-taker don't go round asking about someone for no reason.'

'I'd like to find him, that's all. You have crews that visit plenty of houses. People with some money.' Hutton nodded to acknowledge the fact. 'Mark knows people like that. He might be a guest in one of those places. Your men could ask around.'

'They could. But what's in it for me?' He rubbed his thumb over the fingertips of his right hand.

'A little money.'

Hutton was a man who kept his eye on the main chance 'Maybe he'd want to give me more if I tipped him the wink.'

'Maybe.'

The captain was a distrustful man. But he had a secret, one Simon had chanced to learn. He'd never told a soul about it, not even Rosie. The man had come to Leeds from Hull, discarding the name Thomas Tyler along the way. Never more than an able seaman, he deserted the navy to become part of a smuggling gang until he peached on them, exchanging their lives for his horse and cart.

'He could be gone and you'd never know, would you, matey?'

'I'd find out,' Simon told him. 'But you wouldn't do that.'

'Wouldn't I?' He smirked. 'Don't put money on it. Why do you want him? What's he taken?'

'Some silver cups. He might be responsible for the body in Middle Row and a couple of others.'

'Is that right?' Hutton stroked his chin. 'Then happen he'd pay handsomely to avoid the law.'

'If he had a penny to his name.' He waited until the Captain was staring at him. 'Still, if I heard that something like that had gone on, I'd send word to some people in Hull that a man named Thomas Tyler had done well for himself here. You think that might interest a few folk there, Captain? I don't know if you've ever heard of Mr Tyler.'

Hutton glared daggers. If the men from Hull came looking,

he'd have to flee his good life here. 'You're a right bastard, Westow, you know that?'

'We have an agreement, then?'

'Do I have a choice?'

'No.'

No reason to trust Hutton, Simon thought as he hurried home. But he was willing to try every avenue; one of them might come lucky. He kept his right hand tight on the hilt of his dagger, listening for any unusual sound in the darkness. His body was taut, mouth dry. Fear: by now he knew it all too well.

Sally was waiting by the front door on Swinegate.

'You're as loud as an army when you walk,' she told him. 'It doesn't look as if anybody followed you.'

'Good.' The muscles in his legs ached, the inside of his thighs were chafed and tender from the ride. He was ready for a night's deep rest.

But he was satisfied. Things were moving.

FOURTEEN

Sunday morning and the bells were pealing. The Parish Church, St John's, Holy Trinity all set up a ringing that resounded around the town as they called for their worshippers.

No noise of machines; the only day of rest in the week for the workers. The pall over Leeds thinned with no new smoke or soot to claw at the throat.

Simon had been up since first light, waiting by the coffee cart as it set up outside the Bull and Mouth, listening to the latest gossip in Leeds. Nothing new, only more strange ideas on the old topics. Walking over from Swinegate, his legs still ached from being on horseback and last night's fear was still alive in his mind. Just a few years ago he'd have been fine after a night's rest. One more reminder than he was growing older.

He wandered up Briggate, feeling safer in the daytime. The morning was still quiet. Out beyond the Head Row, light reflected from the clear new glass in the window of Mudie's print shop. Nobody inside; George must have allowed himself a day off. He thought about the men who'd come demanding money. They'd left Leeds, the constable said. Why had they vanished so suddenly? They must still have had business here, collecting on the debts they claimed to have bought. Where had they gone? And at the same time that their bodyguard was murdered? The most brutal killing Simon had ever seen, and he'd known his share. The debt-collectors had run off with his money in their pockets; that gave him an interest.

At least the bodyguard's death wasn't his problem. He had enough on his plate trying to find William Mark. Maybe Hutton and his men would help; maybe they'd do nothing. At the least, it was one road to try.

He needed more. Much more. To spread a net that would snare the man. Simon had no doubt that Mark was still in Leeds. He knew people, he'd spent most of his time in town, his father said.

He might still have credit with some of the tradesmen here. Then there was Mangey, the connection that had started all of this.

Mrs Shields was still sleeping as Jane laced up her work boots. Only a few days since she'd started wearing them again and they already felt normal, comfortable, as if she'd never taken them off. A final check on the old woman, listening to her steady breathing, then she slipped out into Sunday morning.

The beggars would all be out early, hoping for charity as people passed on their way to the churches. They'd remain, waiting for the penitent to leave with their souls freshly scrubbed. The sabbath was always a hopeful day for generosity.

Jane had seen Dodson on Sunday mornings many times before. But not today None of the others holding out their cups knew where to find him, either.

'He's not been around for a day or two,' Manchester Minnie said, then turned her head and began to cough until she was shaking. A ha'penny for her, then on and on.

Nobody knew. The old soldier had vanished. Most blamed John.

'Should have left 'un to fend for himself,' one man told her. 'Got a heart that's too big, has Charlie Dodson.'

Davy Cassidy put up his fiddle for a moment. He shook his head and said: 'I know his walk with that wooden leg, but I haven't heard it, miss. I'm sorry.'

She scoured the town, heart sinking deeper with each step.

Jane found Simon ambling around the streets. Ideas sometimes came to him as he walked, he told her once. He remembered the one-legged soldier, promised to keep watch for the man. But he wasn't listening closely, distracted and tangled too far in his own thoughts.

She prowled along the riverbank, wishing to find nothing, but half-expecting she might.

Jane had been criss-crossing Leeds for three hours by the time Sally found her. The morning church services were done. Most families had gone home for their dinners; others promenaded up and down Briggate, stopping to look in the shop windows.

She came out of Pack Horse Yard to see the girl waiting.

'Come on,' she said, and turned.

'Have they found him?'

'You'll see.'

Her heart was thumping in her chest. Was he dead? Alive? But she kept her mouth closed, following along Commercial Street, past the soft gentility of Park Square. Another mile, until they'd gone far beyond the factories and the houses, off into the countryside.

'Over there.' Sally pointed towards a copse and Jane found herself running, desperate to see. To know.

Two girls sat with him. Dodson was breathing. He'd wake, they said, then slide away into sleep again. He had wounds on his face, blood dried to a crust. Some of his bones might be broken. His wooden leg was missing, the old greatcoat he treasured slashed into shreds.

'Who found him?' Jane asked. One of the girls keeping watch over him raised her hand; Jane handed over the two half-crowns she'd promised.

'What are you going to do?'

'Find someone to move him.' Her mind was clear, making plans. He needed care, and plenty of it.

Jane was waiting anxiously when the carter stopped in Green Dragon Yard with Dodson in the back, resting on straw.

As soon as the soldier had been put in the cart, she'd hurried on ahead to speak to Mrs Shields. Hoping the old woman wouldn't turn him away.

As soon as he was settled, Catherine Shields examined him.

'He has a fever,' she said with a deep frown. 'Two of his ribs have been broken. I think everything else is intact. Plenty of cuts. He'll need to be cleaned. He's probably been lying there for hours. Overnight, maybe even longer.' She added after a moment, 'There are bound to be wounds we can't see when he's clothed. That one on his neck looks infected.' She stood, pressing her thin fingertips against the small of her back. 'It's his head that worries me. Someone hit it hard. Looks like it must have happened a few times.'

'Can you help him?' Jane asked.

'I can try, child.' The woman gave a comforting smile.

Dodson slept. The woman was right; there were wounds all

over his body. Clean now, ribs strapped tight, and Mrs Shields
had tilted his head to drink something she'd prepared.

'He should sleep for a long time. I doubt he'll wake before
the morning. If he rests, his body can start to heal.'

Jane glanced out of the window, surprised to see the slant of
late afternoon light. Where had the day vanished? She looked
down at the man, the strange imbalance of his body with half a
leg missing. She held up her left hand and spread the fingers,
the little one gone. She barely noticed the loss now. Was he the
same with his missing limb?

'You know who did this, don't you?'

She nodded. John.

Mrs Shields wiped Dodson's face with a damp cloth that
smelled of lavender.

'Tomorrow should tell us if he'll recover properly,' she said.
'He might not, child. You need to be prepared for that. I can't
tell what will happen.'

'Yes,' was the only word Jane could manage. Fury flared inside.
A few minutes later, content that the man wouldn't wake for
hours yet, she slipped away. Coming on dusk. Night was a perfect
time for hunting.

The quiet of Sunday darkness, Simon thought as he walked down
Kirkgate. A few hours and the machines would start up again.
Noise would fill the air and smoke would rise from the chimneys
as people returned to work in the factories and the mills.

He turned his head. For a second he thought he'd heard footsteps, moving at the same pace as his own. His heart started to
race. He'd dreaded this. Simon speeded up, breathing faster and
listening closely. No mistake. It was there. Someone was
following him. He eased the knife from his sleeve, keeping it
out of sight against his side.

Fear spread through his body. Cold sweat in the hollow at the
base of his spine. No Sally to guard him tonight; he told her he
didn't need her and she'd hurried off to her homeless children
as soon as she'd eaten. His choice, and now he was going to
have to face this on his own. A pointless thought flickered like
lightning in his head: he needed to practise again, to sharpen
every skill. If he stayed alive tonight, he'd do that.

The man came just as Simon turned down High Court. He was in the shadow of the buildings. A shape that moved like quicksilver.

Simon took the second knife from his belt, standing, waiting as his eyes became used to the gloom around him. He knew the short street well, the two missing cobbles halfway down, the opening to the Calls at the far end.

The flash of a blade and he just had time to draw back, then a lunge. But he was only cutting the air; his opponent was already moving away. Who was it? he wondered. Why? But only the winner ever had chance to ask those questions.

Don't think. That was the secret. Let the body take over and do what it knew. Push. Parry. He had to use those years of experience, not weigh and calculate each move. Act and react. The tip of a knife ripped through his coat. For the smallest moment, it snagged on a knotted seam and he could push his own blade home into the man's shoulder. No yell of pain. Nothing more than a grunt, but it drove him back.

A little further. Simon kept pushing forward. He'd hurt his attacker. The man's movements had become slower, heavier, as if his boots had filled with lead.

Simon slid to the side as the man lunged, then brought the knife hilt down on his skull. It was enough to make him stagger off balance for a step or two as Simon's body slammed into him and sent him sprawling backwards on to the road. The ring of metal as the blade was jarred from his grasp and landed on the cobbles.

His fingers started to grope for it, but Simon brought his boot heel down hard on the man's hand.

'Who are you?'

No answer. He pushed down harder, feeling a bone snap under the flesh. It would be a few weeks before the man wielded a knife again. Simon was breathing hard. A tiny difference in luck and the fight would have gone the other way.

'Who hired you?'

The man turned his head and spat. Two seconds before he spoke. A grimace of pain and his voice was tight as he struggled to control the pain.

'Someone who reckons you deserve to be hurt.'

'What's his name?' Across the years he'd made too many

enemies. There were plenty in Leeds who'd love to see him wounded or dead. He dangled the point of his knife near the man's face. 'Last chance.'

The man hissed out the words: 'Everyone calls him the captain.'

For a moment, Simon didn't know what to think. One answer he hadn't expected. Matthew Hutton, the man grown plump on night soil, trying to make sure his past stayed hidden. But for a clumsy piece of tailoring, he might have succeeded.

Simon stepped back, kicked the man's knife so it went skittering into the darkness, and looked down at him.

'Go back and tell him you failed.' That message would be enough. Hutton was clever enough to know that Simon would follow through on his threat. The captain would run if he wanted to stay alive.

He walked away. By the time he reached Swinegate, he could feel the tremors starting to rack his body as everything caught up to him. He tried to control his breathing, to calm his body as his heartbeat danced all around.

The skirmish had taken seconds. The kind of fight he'd experienced so many times. He'd won, but he was beginning to feel the cost. The shock that arrived once it was over. It had never been like this in the past. He was starting to wonder just how far he could trust himself.

His hands were shaking hard as he tried to push the key in the lock. It took three attempts before he was able to jab it home. All safe now. In the kitchen, a tot of brandy. Down in one, letting it burn in his chest and his belly.

The feelings gradually ebbed as he sat, keeping quiet and still, with everything safe and familiar around him. But it was the perfect time for all his ghosts to rear up. The face of the bodyguard that he'd seen in Rockley Hall Yard, everything human stripped away from its bones. The skeletons of the dead children they'd found last year, dug up from the ground. Corpses crowding in on him. He wanted to fling them away. To have a full night's rest with the world leaving him some peace.

Simon poured a second drink and swallowed it in a single gulp, gasping as he felt it bite. Enough. If he decided to walk down that road, he'd end up a drunkard. It would be so easy.

He put the glass aside went up the stairs to bed.

FIFTEEN

If she walked in the darkness, Jane knew that word would reach Sally. She'd been out since the church bell rang the hour, ranging around Leeds with a heart full of hate. For William Mark. For the man called John.

The girl came out of the night near the market cross at the top of Briggate and they fell in step, following the road out towards Sheepscar.

'None of the children have seen John today,' she said. 'They've been keeping watch.' A fragment of hesitation. 'How's the soldier?'

'Alive. Sleeping.'

'John's probably gone,' Sally said. 'There's nothing to keep him here.'

She nodded. The man had appeared from nowhere, easy for him to vanish the same way.

'I looked at Dodson's room again, in case he'd gone back,' Jane said. It had been exactly the way she'd seen it before. 'I haven't had a sense of him anywhere.'

'If he's gone . . .'

If he had, Jane knew there was little she could do. How could she follow? She didn't know which direction to take. But if he was still here, she'd find him. He was the one who'd attacked Dodson. Who else could it be? The bodyguard, too, the killing that had horrified Simon. She felt certain he'd done that. Maybe it was in his blood. Maybe his soul was tainted.

It had only taken a few days for her heart to start brimming over with hate. She couldn't stop the feelings. The fire was raging inside.

'The children will find him if he's still here,' Sally said.

'They need to keep their distance.'

'I've warned them.' Her face softened. 'You're never going to find him by walking around. Why don't you go home? We can meet on the moor tomorrow morning. I'll find you when they tell me anything.'

Jane sighed and nodded. Sometimes the girl was wise for her age. A few paces and she turned her head. Sally had already gone.

Early Monday morning and stokers were feeding the boilers in the factories. The machines were running and smoke plumed thick into the skies. The day was already warm, closer still with soot filling the air.

Simon stood at the coffee cart. People were talking nineteen to the dozen all around, but he barely paid attention as he thought about last night. He knew how fortunate he'd been, but Lady Luck was capricious. At least this time he hadn't hesitated when opportunity came.

He'd always shrugged things off, let them float along behind him. Lately, something had changed. Fear had clung to him. It had found its way into his head and it was playing wild and free.

He needed to shut it away again. To press on and find William Mark.

Before that, there was the matter of Matthew Hutton.

Simon wrote the letter. Just a few lines, but enough to sign the captain's death warrant. He addressed it to a man he knew in Hull and slipped it into his pocket. Two stops before he went to the post office.

Hutton's house lay south of the River Aire, out along Meadow Lane, two hundred yards from Sir Robert Foley's. A spacious home, showing how well he'd done for himself in such a short time. He'd worked hard for it. Would the captain really be willing to abandon all this?

'The master left this morning,' a grave-faced servant told him. 'Had his chaise brought around and loaded three chests on to it.'

'What about you? Everyone working here?'

'He's paid us for this week,' the man replied with a scowl. 'That's it. He's written to his man of business to sell the house.'

No point in asking if the servant knew where he'd gone; Hutton wasn't a fool. The man would find a new home far enough away, change his name and his past and start over.

Was it fear or anger that had made him send the man to hurt

Simon? He worried at the question as he walked to Foley's house. In the end, perhaps there was precious little difference between the two emotions.

'I have no idea where Mark might be, Mr Westow,' Foley said. 'If I did, I'd have told you.'

'He knows people in society. Mark is used to them. He's staying *somewhere*.'

Foley nodded. 'I can ask.'

'Please. You know these people. But if you do come across anything . . .'

'Don't worry, I'm not fool enough to go after him myself, Mr Westow. If I hear the smallest word, you'll have ample chance to earn your fee.'

As long as he caught Mark and returned the cups.

After the post office, the courthouse. Constable Porter had no new information, sweating over papers in his office and dictating letters to his clerk.

'Do you know what the council wants now? I have to document every damned thing my men do. For the love of God, most of them can't even write. Half of them try anything they can to avoid any real work whenever they have the chance.'

No surprise on the wages they were paid. Criminals could offer them more to look the other way.

'Come and be a thief-taker.'

Porter snorted. 'It's not a bad idea. You've done handsomely for yourself. Do you have anything new on Mark? I've not managed to come up with a sniff.'

'Not on him, but did you know Hutton's run off from town?'

The constable sat back and lit his pipe. 'For some reason, I imagine you know what's behind it.'

None of it brought him any closer to William Mark. Sally was off somewhere; she hadn't been with him at the coffee cart. But the people she knew wouldn't be familiar with Mark. If he ever grew desperate enough to try and hide among the homeless, she'd quickly hear.

The image of Dodson shone clear in her mind. Something to hold on to there; behind him, gentle Mr Armistead. She needed them, needed the anger they gave her. They stoked the fire that was bright and hot as she sparred with Sally.

Months before, Jane had been glad to put all that aside; fighting to survive had been part of her life since she was eight. Every day had been a battle, and she'd felt lighter once she left that behind. Different, calmer. Now she needed it again. As she practised with Sally in the morning light, Jane knew she was growing quicker. Nowhere near good enough yet but edging closer as the sharpness returned. Anyone going against her would need to battle hard.

'How's the soldier?' Sally asked as they walked back from the moor.

'The same.' Mrs Shields was dosing him with her medicines and potions when she left. Caring for a patient had brought her alive again; it gave her a purpose. She bustled around the house, quick and anxious. At least the old woman seemed hopeful that Dodson would recover.

'I can't tell if his mind will be the way it was before he was attacked,' she'd said cautiously. 'But I believe his body will be whole.'

He'd need a new wooden leg. But she'd have time to consider that after he was well enough to walk. She was aware of Sally's voice.

'—Simon was going to see Hutton this morning.'

'Didn't he want you there?' Jane asked.

'No.' Her eyes flashed. 'He warned me not to try and follow him, either.' She began to smile. 'It doesn't matter.'

'Why?'

'Three of the children found me first thing and said they'd seen the captain leaving in that fancy carriage he has. Going west just before dawn like the devil was breathing down his neck.'

The past caught them all, Jane thought. As soon as you believed you'd put it away, it returned to put its claws in you. Those nightmares had foretold it. They'd warned her and kept her close. She glanced at the girl.

They found Simon on Park Row, just coming out of the courthouse.

'We're no closer to Mark,' he said. The only description they had was vague: not especially tall, with carefully arranged fair hair, expensive tailoring and a charming, empty smile. None of it meant much; too easy to change.

'Who knows him in Leeds?' Jane asked.

'Foley's going to ask. Mark has always been around people with money.'

'Young men?' she asked.

'Yes, but they all have mothers and sisters,' Simon continued after a moment. 'Rosie knows one or two of those. She'll start talking to them. We're wasting our time searching out here.'

'What do you want me to do?' Sally asked.

'Young men like whores,' he said. 'Talk to them. They might know him.'

By the time he looked again, Jane had drifted away, shawl over her hair, already swallowed up in the crowd of people on the street. He gave Sally a questioning glance.

'Dodson,' she said as explanation.

Evening, and they were gathered around the table in the kitchen. Jane had arrived moments before, a curious look in her eye. She settled quietly while Rosie was speaking.

'I paid a few calls this afternoon. Some of the women I spoke to know William Mark. He's been in their homes, for dinners and dances.' A dark smile crept across her face. 'He won't be welcome back anywhere in society. The word will already have passed.'

'Have any of them seen him lately?' Simon asked.

'Not in the last fortnight; they were definite about that. Wherever he's hiding, it's not with them.'

'What about with their sons?' Sally asked. 'They're grown. Some of them will keep their own rooms around town.'

'They'll be told soon enough. Their mothers and sisters will make sure of that.' She pursed her lips. 'But I did notice one young woman who turned very quiet and worried when I told them what Mark had done. My guess is she's hiding something.'

'Did you try to talk to her?'

Rosie shook her head. 'No chance, and I could hardly press her.'

Simon trusted his wife; if she suspected something, he did, too.

'How can we find out?' he asked.

'You could follow her. She might try to warn him.'

It sounded like a desperate idea, more hope than substance. From her face, Rosie thought that, too.

'I'll do it,' Jane offered before he could say anything more.

One of the old addresses on Kirkgate, not far from where Armistead had lived. As she passed his door, Jane touched the wood lightly and thought of the man. The house she needed to watch had probably been a grand Leeds address once upon a year, but that had been a long time ago. Very likely in the same family for generations, in desperate need of care and money.

She needed a good spot, one that was out of sight. It took five minutes' searching before she found it; a small, dark nook where she could watch both the front door and the entrance to the ginnel that ran behind the street. Jane settled into the small space and studied the building. Curtains were drawn against the night, but lights burned in two of the rooms and she heard the faint sound of a piano.

Charlotte Hawley. That was the young woman's name. The only daughter of the house. Two sons in the family, Rosie had told her, both of them older. One was an attorney in London, the other had rooms on Basinghall Street.

Jane stood, silent, waiting. After telling herself she'd never do this again, here she was, with the old ways as familiar to her as breathing. Before coming out to work, she'd ground up seeds for poultices and mixed liquids at home under Mrs Shields's direction. She'd sat with Dodson, watching the rise and fall of his chest and the flutter of his eyelids. But his mind remained hidden somewhere beneath the surface.

'It can take time, child,' the old woman warned her. She placed a hand on the man's wrist. 'He's improving; his pulse is stronger than it was. We need to have patience.' Her thin, bony fingers squeezed Jane's hand. 'Have faith.'

She wanted to believe. She'd tried to settle, to read her book, but her mind kept shifting, thoughts crowding each other. Out here, even if she was standing in one place, she was doing *something*. Most likely it would be a dead night, a few hours wasted. People passed, but she was so still that nobody noticed her.

The town quieted and the darkness deepened around her. Finally, the last lights were doused in the house, flaring briefly in the bedrooms before turning to blackness again. The night air was still warm, gritty in her throat.

If anything was going to happen, it would come soon. She was attentive for the smallest movement, any sound out of the ordinary. But she only heard the snuffle of rats and the distant, angry screech of a cat.

Then . . . the click of a door gently pulled closed. Barely louder than a breath, but she caught it, suddenly standing straighter, pulling the shawl close around her hair.

A black dress, another shade of night that crept out of the ginnel, pausing to look warily to left and right. As the woman began to move away, Jane was behind her. One hand in her pocket, gripping the handle of her knife.

Following . . . for so long this had been the work she did for Simon. It still felt absolutely natural. She walked quietly, cautiously; the woman ahead was never aware of anyone there.

Up Vicar Lane, down George Street towards Millgarth, then ducking away into a court. Jane paused at the entrance, listening carefully and catching a quick undertone of words. A woman's voice, then a man answered. Guttural, raw. No polish to him; definitely not the way she'd imagined a man like William Mark sounding. Any man from a good family would stand out down here, in the back-to-back houses where people emptied their chamber pots into a drain that ran down the middle of the street.

Jane pulled back. Across the way, into the shadows. It hadn't been Charlotte Hawley who'd come here. Very likely nothing more than a servant girl finding a few secret minutes with her lover. Still, she waited. Ten minutes and the woman hurried past, going back to Kirkgate.

She stayed far enough behind to barely keep her in sight. A silent escort all the way to the ginnel, waiting until she heard the soft hiss of a door closing and the click of a key turning in the lock.

Then home.

Mrs Shields was sleeping, a nightcap tied around her sparse hair. No change that she could see in Dodson. She held a candle near his face; his eyelids began to flutter and his lips parted. For a second, Jane believed he was going to speak, but the moment passed without a word and his mouth closed again. Was he close to returning? If she said something to him, could he hear her? Things to ask the old woman in the morning, she decided as she settled in front of the empty hearth.

SIXTEEN

One more day that brought little. Rumours and hopes that were nothing when Simon examined them closely. Late in the afternoon, he stopped at Mudie's print shop. The man was sitting at his desk, sipping a glass of cheap brandy.

'Keeping an eye on your investment, Simon?'

'Frustration.'

'Not managed to find your man yet?'

He shook his head. 'Looks like he's gone to earth.'

'He might have left Leeds.'

Perhaps he had. Simon hadn't found a sniff of the man in town. Sally was watching the house on Kirkgate, but that was beginning to feel like no more than a faint chance.

'Better hope not, for Sir Robert's sake,' Simon told him. 'If Mark goes, he'll probably never see the cups again.'

He raised his glass in a toast. 'I wish him well for their return.'

'William Mark has murdered three people.'

Mudie's face turned serious. 'Believe me, I haven't forgotten. The pity is that he can only swing from the gallows once.'

'If we find him.' At the door, he turned. 'Sorry, I'm poor company today.'

A bitter laugh. 'Simon, I'm poor company every day. It's never stopped you visiting.'

On the other side of the Head Row, he stood by the market cross, marvelling at how wide Briggate looked without the Moot Hall and Middle Row dividing it. He felt a tug on his sleeve. A child, a boy perhaps a year younger than his sons, a scrawny bag of bones with dark, angry eyes.

'Sally wants you.'

'Where?' Could she have found Mark?

He followed. The boy scurried ahead, stopping every few seconds to look over his shoulder and make certain Simon was still there. By the entrance to the Methodist church on Queen Street the lad halted, pointing towards the shade of a hedge.

Simon blinked twice before he picked out the girl hidden among the leaves. A penny for the boy, then he slipped through the undergrowth.

'She's over there, on Chariot Street,' Sally told him.

'With Mark?'

'I don't know.' Her gaze never moved from the front door of a house. Six of them stood in a row, green, tended gardens, a different, more expensive world. He had no idea who lived here, but they had wealth.

'What happened?'

'I was watching the house on Kirkgate and Miss Hawley came out with her maid. She was looking in the shop windows. After a while, she began to walk faster. The maid could hardly keep pace with her.'

Very curious. 'Where was she going?'

'Nowhere. All over the place.' A frown. 'She'd start off down a road, then turn and come back on the other side. I couldn't make head nor tail of it.'

'Trying to make sure nobody was following her, do you think?'

'It seems that way. I thought she'd seen me, but I must have been quick enough. She ended up coming here down West Street, and Savile Street, then along Wellington Street until she turned at the corner down there.'

Definitely not a normal social call.

'How long has she been inside?'

'About half an hour. I saw one of the children and told them to find you.' She turned her head to look up at him. 'What do you want me to do? Follow her when she leaves?'

'No. Stay here.' Had Rosie's hunch about the young woman been right? It was beginning to look that way. He stared at the house as if he could see through the solid walls. Was William Mark really in there? 'If a young man leaves, follow him. You didn't catch a glimpse of anyone, did you?'

'Nobody.'

His mind was trying to calculate all the possibilities. He couldn't talk to Miss Hawley; there would be nothing proper in that with a girl from a respectable family. But if Rosie should happen to see her, she could begin a conversation. An accidental meeting on the street . . . that would catch Miss Hawley off guard, and Rosie knew very well how to dig for the truth. Gently, never forcing, but learning everything.

'You've done well,' he said before he left, watching her blush. 'Any luck with the whores? Have they seen him?'

She shook her head, still watching the house.

'I didn't see her,' Rosie said. They sat at the table as late afternoon drifted towards early evening. 'She must have come back before I could get to Kirkgate.'

'She came out of the house on Queen Street just after Simon left,' Sally told them.

'I'll try and find her tomorrow,' Rosie promised.

He'd spent the afternoon trying to discover who owned the house Charlotte Hawley had visited. A family called Baker, with a son in his twenties. Nobody knew of any connection between him and William Mark, but that meant little. For the moment, this was all they had. He had no choice but to seize it.

'Sounds to me like you've got nothing more than hot air and suspicion.' Constable Porter puffed on his pipe. 'Or did I miss something?'

The twilight was hurrying into darkness and the man was still in his office at the courthouse. Down below them, the town was still alive, men in the gin shops and alehouses.

'You're right,' Simon sighed. 'I don't have the smallest shred of proof.'

'Then why are you telling me?'

'The way we agreed. I'm passing you infor—'

'But it's not good information.'

'How can you know that?'

'Perhaps I'm wrong,' the constable agreed. 'It's been a long day. One of my men collapsed and died from a heart attack and another said he's too ill to come back to work. He's not likely to survive until the middle of the year.'

Death, sometimes quick, sometimes slow. The only inevitability.

'We both want to catch Mark.'

'Of course we bloody do,' Porter said. 'He's murdered three people.'

'All I want are the cups that belong to my client.'

'That's fine, you can have the damned things. Tell me, Westow, what do you think I should do? March over and accuse Baker of having Mark there? Even if the man's asleep upstairs, Thomas Baker would never tell me. He's a nasty bastard, always has been; he'd throw me straight off his property.'

'Do it quietly. Keep watch.'

The constable snorted and the acid dripped in his voice. 'You mean have men who could be doing better things standing around on the off-chance Mark might be there. Which we can agree is nothing more than a faint possibility,' he added.

'Do you have any better suggestions?'

Porter scratched the back of his scalp and blew out a plume of smoke. 'I have nothing at all.' He stared at Simon. 'Exactly the same as you.'

Five minutes and he was back on Chariot Street, watching the Baker house. A brilliance of candles glowed through the windows downstairs. On the floor above, curtains were drawn tight, only a hint of light through the material. Was William Mark in there? He stared, trying to judge, to feel. But nothing came.

God knew, he wanted the man to be in the house. It would make everything so simple. But the constable was right; all he had was Rosie's hunch, and not a scrap of evidence to back it up. Miss Hawley's route when she visited was suspicious, but it hardly made her guilty of loving a killer.

Another ten minutes, letting thoughts swirl. It wasn't so long since he'd been able to feel certain about everything, when all the pieces of a puzzle lay exactly where he expected.

Now, though, all that had faded. No more black and white, just shades of grey. Caution and fear gnawing at him every day. Questioning himself instead of acting. If his instincts were really failing, that could be a recipe for death to a thief-taker.

Too full of doubts. Too . . . fragile. That seemed like the only word. Scared that his world might snap apart, not quite certain where he fitted in it any more.

He turned and strode out for home, one hand resting on the hilt on his knife.

Dodson had surfaced. Jane was sitting by the bed when he slowly opened his eyes and looked around him. In an urgent voice, she called for Mrs Shields, then leaned forward so the old soldier could see her.

'You're safe,' she told him in a soft voice.

He gave an unsure smile and opened his mouth. Cracked lips, and a feeble croak as he asked for water.

Tenderly, the old woman raised his head enough for him to take a few sips. Cordial, with the taste of fruit and summer. Jane beamed with the joy of having him back.

His gaze settled on her. 'You,' he said.

'Yes.' She placed her hand on his. 'We've been taking care of you.'

'Who . . .?'

'My name is Jane. This is Mrs Shields. You're in her house.'

A moment before Dodson gave her a tiny nod then he closed his eyes again.

'Let him rest, child. He's come a long way.'

'Yes.' He had, but he was so nearly here now.

He woke twice more during the day, for a little longer each time. He remembered her name, but his face clouded when she asked if he knew what had happened to him.

'I can almost . . .' he began, then he shook his head, and a tear fell from one eye before he drifted off.

She stayed with him. Probably Simon had tasks for her, but this was more important.

SEVENTEEN

S
ally had just taken over from him to watch the Baker house. A warm, sticky afternoon and Simon's thoughts wandered as he walked. He recalled what the tutor had said to him that morning about the twins' education. They needed to go to school, the man had insisted, with harder lessons and more discipline than he'd given them. That would set them up for life. Simon knew that Richard and Amos had already learned more than many children. He could end the lessons there and find apprenticeships for them. They could be earning. God knew, the family might need the money if anything happened to him.

Simon held out his hand, studying it carefully. Steady, not a single sign of a tremor. For now. At least there was that. But when the next thing happened to overwhelm him, how would he be?

He pushed the thought away and moved, going from inn to inn until he found Barnabas Wade. A coach was pulling out through the arch of the Rose and Crown, the driver calling to disperse people in the road before flying towards Newcastle and Edinburgh.

'You look pleased with yourself.'

'I've made some money, Simon.' The smile seemed more relief than satisfaction.

'Congratulations to you. Let me stand you a drink.'

'I won't turn you down,' Wade said. 'But you're here for a reason. I can see it in your eyes.'

'You're close.' He laughed. 'It's two reasons. First: what do you know about the two men who bought up old Arthur Gill's debts?'

Wade took a sip of the rum Simon handed him. 'Claim to have bought,' he said. 'That's according to one of Gill's sons, at least. The will's still going through probate.'

'I don't understand.'

'From what I was told, after Gill died, a pair of men stole the book where he kept track of the money he'd lent. They said they'd bought the debts and went round collecting what they could.'

That explained why they employed the bodyguard, Simon thought. It was very likely the reason they'd left Leeds in such a hurry when the man was murdered, too; a few pointed questions would have uncovered the truth. The men had fooled Mudie. They'd been clever enough to gull him, too. Maybe one or two others. A lucrative little line for the time it lasted. If they ever returned, he'd have them.

'I see.'

'You said two things, Simon.'

'William Mark. Does it mean anything?'

The man's eyes narrowed. 'Related to that bastard George Mark?'

'Yes. But not close.'

Wade shook his head. 'Doesn't matter. I'd keep my distance. If you have a grain of sense, you will too, Simon.'

'I'll let you know once I find him.'

The man's expression sharpened. 'What's he done?'

For a moment, Simon weighed whether to tell him; Wade already loathed the family. But he might know something . . .

'It's an interesting tale . . .'

Jane kept vigil by Dodson's bed, always there when he woke for a moment, a minute at most. Each time, he smiled when he opened his eyes and saw her there.

By evening he was able manage a few sentences before drifting away again. But the soldier only seemed to hold a bare memory of John.

'Was he the one who's been hurt?' he asked, voice unsure.

'Yes,' Jane told him. 'Did he hurt you, too?'

'I don't know.' He paused, frowning, as if he was trying to take stock of his body. 'What happened to me?' The beggar tried to turn his head. Eyes wide. 'Where am I?'

'You're safe.'

That seemed to satisfy him. He smiled once more and his eyes closed.

* * *

Dark. Jane closed the shutters against the night. Time to go out and hunt.

'I've given him something to make him sleep,' Mrs Shields said. 'Rest is the best medicine for him now.'

'Will he be the way he used to be?' Jane asked.

Her face grew serious. 'It's still too early to say, child. We can hope and pray.'

She thought about the words as she walked. Sally found her, but the girl looked exhausted, the kind of tiredness that only a fruitless day could bring.

'Any sign of John?'

She shook her head. 'None of them have seen him.'

Easy to believe the man had left Leeds. The children would surely have found him if he was still here; it was difficult to escape them.

Jane felt hollow inside. He was cheating her of justice.

'Any luck with William Mark yet?'

She shook her head. 'I don't think he's in that house we've been watching.'

'You don't have any sense of him?'

'Nothing at all.'

'But why would . . .' Jane had to grope for the young woman's name.

'Miss Hawley?'

'Yes. Why would she go all over town like that to reach there? That doesn't make any sense.'

'No,' Sally agreed. 'It doesn't.' She shrugged.

'Go home and rest your legs,' Jane told her. 'Simon will probably have you back there tomorrow. People don't know how tiring it can be to stand.'

'I will. I just need to . . .'

No need to finish the sentence. Coming out to check on the homeless children, that was the duty Sally took on herself. Something she needed to do, even when she was bone weary.

Jane woke suddenly, not sure what had pulled her from sleep. In a panic, she checked on Dodson and Mrs Shields. Both resting, breathing evenly.

A quiet scrabbling at the window, and she reached for her

knife and slipped on her dress before she turned the key in the lock. She wrenched the front door open. A girl, tracks of tears etched through a grubby face.

'Sally says can you come quick, Miss.' Her eyes begged. 'Please.'

Less than a minute to pull on hose and boots, hurriedly throwing a shawl over her shoulders as they moved along the streets. No faint blur of morning on the horizon yet, night air warm and still against her skin. The girl kept glancing back, anxious, wanting to be certain Jane was still with her.

On the river, barge crews were just beginning to stir. She followed the girl over the bridge, out past the end of Dock Street and Leeds lock, halfway to the ferry that crossed the river. She spotted Sally, standing in some scrubland, apart from a group of children that huddled together as crows circled overhead.

She sensed the death before she could see it, slowing to a walk as she approached.

The body lay on the hard ground, tangled in the dirt. A boy right on the edge of a manhood he'd never have chance to see. Bones broken, flesh pulled away, exactly like the corpse Simon had described in Rockley Hall Yard. A deep slash across his throat. Face staring up at the lightening sky, but no eyes left in his head to see the start of the day.

'His name was Harold,' Sally said. Her voice was dull, empty and dulled. 'Sweet as you like. Swore he was going to marry me as soon as he was rich.'

Jane couldn't pull her eyes from the horror on the ground.

'Someone saw him this afternoon,' the girl continued, 'but that was the last time. He liked to go off on his own. Said he needed it.'

'When did they find him?'

'An hour ago. Some of them were camped close to the river. They heard dogs fighting and came to look. One of them came for me. I was still out.' She raised her head from the corpse. 'Something was nagging at me. I don't know what it was. I just hadn't been able to settle to the idea of going home.' For the first time since Jane had known her, the girl sounded as if she was on the verge of tears, forcing them down. 'Now I know why.'

Neither of them spoke the killer's name.

'You should tell Simon and the constable.'

'I know,' Sally said. 'I'll see to it.' Her face hardened. 'He's still here. You and me?'

Jane nodded. They both had debts to pay.

He lay in bed. Wanting to sleep, hoping to, but scared of it, too. All his fears returned as he closed his eyes. His heartbeat quickened. He kept still, not wanting to wake Rosie. No need for her to be infected by all this. It would pass. It had to pass.

Simon was still awake when he heard the soft click of the key turning in the lock and Sally moving quietly up the stairs. Very late, he knew that, but no idea of the time. Maybe very early. All he knew was that sleep had yet to find him.

At the first glimmer of dawn he slipped out of bed, not sure if he'd managed to rest at all. The day was already sultry. A few minutes and he was standing by the coffee cart outside the Bull and Mouth, feeling the hot liquid revive him.

'Have you heard about the body?' one of the men asked him. Britton, a clerk in a lawyer's office, another one who liked to start his morning here.

'No.' Suddenly every sense was sharp and prickling. 'Who was it?'

'A child, somewhere over the river.' He waved his hand, a vague indication of direction.

'I heard it was a boy,' another voice began, and soon all of them were offering details and opinions. Simon listened, knowing he was hearing nothing worthwhile. He finished his drink and strode along Boar Lane.

'Just like the one in Rockley Hall Yard,' the constable told him. 'The same injuries. Throat cut.'

'A boy?'

Porter nodded. 'Looks like he was one of the homeless.'

'I might be able to find his name.' Sally would know him. One of her flock.

'If you can. I need to find whoever did this, Westow. First that hard man, now one of those feral children. Most people won't care about them, but once word starts to spread, people will be scared. It could be decent people next.' He sighed. 'Truth is, I can't blame them, although I never said that. I know it's nothing to do with you, but . . .'

'I'll see what I can find.'

Sally was walking with Jane. He only needed to look at the girl's face to understand. She looked as though she was barely able to contain the pain and the fury inside her.

'What was his name?' Simon asked quietly.

'Harold.' A breath. 'I want to pay for his funeral. A proper one, in the churchyard. With a curate and a headstone. Everything.'

She was asking for his help. No one at the Parish Church would pay attention to a girl like her.

'I'll arrange it.' He turned to Jane.

'Is your friend beginning to heal?'

'Yes.'

A question for the pair of them. 'Who did all this?'

'A man called John.'

He listened as Jane gave him the few scraps they knew.

'Porter will be grateful for the information.' The look the pair exchanged was enough for him to guess their plan. No need to pass that on to the constable. Whoever caught him, this John would never face a trial. His body would probably never be discovered. 'Now,' he said. 'William Mark.'

EIGHTEEN

'I managed to talk to Miss Hawley.' Rosie's voice was triumphant as she placed her basket of shopping on the table and unpinned her hat. She wasn't dressed in one of her visiting gowns; nothing more than an ordinary day dress.

'Where did you find her?' Simon asked.

'It was sheer accident. I was on my way to the butcher and saw her with her maid staring in the shop windows along Briggate.' Her smile broadened. 'She was grateful to talk to someone who might be able to advise her.'

'About William Mark?'

Rosie shook her head. 'No, although apparently she did have a passion for him once.'

'Once?' he asked, baffled.

'Long ago. Until she discovered what kind of person he was.'

He pursed his lips and frowned. 'Then why would she take such an awkward route to the Baker house?'

'It's not to see Mark. It's a woman, a friend. Her father doesn't approve of her associating with Margaret Baker. She's the daughter, and Mr Hawley seems to believe she's a wayward chit who's leading his little girl astray. He's forbidden her to call. She was making sure he hadn't sent a servant to follow her.'

He laughed. Such a simple, innocent explanation, but one he could never have pictured.

'I don't suppose she has any idea where we might find Mark?'

'Ah.' Her eyes widened. 'She told me he has a friend called Jonas Catesby. Miss Hawley knows him from the assemblies.' Rosie chuckled. 'Evidently he's the type who's always full of himself. He and Mark became so drunk on the punch at one dance that they were told to leave. From the way she spoke, I suspect that's when any feelings she had for Mark withered.'

'Any other little gems?'

Rosie beamed but shook her head. 'The only person she'd been able to speak to about this was her maid. She was so eager to talk that all I had to do was listen.' Another smile. 'It poured out of her. Do you know, she even thanked me when she'd finished.'

All too often his wife surprised him. Before the children were born, they'd worked together. Back then, she'd been very capable, a core of iron under the sweet exterior. She'd started doing more as Richard and Amos grew, eager to be a part of things again. Now, it seemed, she'd turned into the sympathetic matron willing to lend an ear.

'Sometimes you still surprise me,' Simon said, and kissed her.

'Keeps you on your toes.' She winked. 'Now you can go and find out about Jonas Catesby.'

'Catesby? Another young devil with an allowance and a father with too much influence in town,' Porter said. Simon had found the constable hurrying up Park Row; the man told him to come to the office in two hours. 'He's Sir Joseph Catesby's son.'

'I don't know him.'

'No reason you should. The family lives in one of those villages out towards Selby, but the son spends all his time here. Has rooms somewhere in Leeds. Likes gambling, drink, whores . . .' He shrugged. 'The things most young men with money enjoy. Probably running up debts for his father to pay. Never worked a day in his life.'

No need, Simon thought, and images of his years in the mills when he was a workhouse child flickered through his mind. The overseers with their rods and punishments. Trying to do your job when you were asleep on your feet after standing there for twelve hours and the brutal treatment if you made a mistake. Never in his life would he be able to understand men like Jonas Catesby or William Mark.

'Do you know where he lives?'

The constable shook his head. 'Seems to move every few months. I've had a few complaints about him, but nothing serious. I've never needed to act on any of them. Why are you interested in him, Westow?'

'William Mark might be staying with him.'

'Oh?' The constable's eyes narrowed as he weighed the idea. 'Yes, that's possible. They're a bit of a matched pair.'

'I have something else for you.'

'Have you now? You've been a busy man, Westow. What is it?'

'The dead child from last night was called Harold.'

'Was he one of the homeless?'

'Yes.'

'What's his surname? Do you know that, too?'

'No, but I can tell you the man who killed him and the body-guard in Rockley Hall Yard is called John.'

'Are you sure?'

'People are terrified of him.'

'They should be. We've seen what he can do. Do you have any more information?'

'Just that your men should be careful.'

'Did you hear about the boy who was killed last night?' Simon asked the curate.

The man was old for his post, with grey hair and a face that was beginning to show its age in the jowls and weathered, sagging skin.

'Poor child. It was terrible, I'm told.'

'I want him to have a proper funeral. A coffin, burial plot in the churchyard.'

'Really . . .' the man began in astonishment. 'I thought he had no relatives.'

'Maybe not here,' Simon agreed. 'But there are people who are willing to pay.'

The curate chose his words carefully. 'Do they understand it's not cheap?' He gestured towards the far corner of the burial ground. 'There's a place for the indigent.'

'I'll cover the cost.'

'I—'

'Tomorrow morning. Nine o'clock,' Simon continued. 'Just the service at the graveside will be enough.'

A talk with the gravediggers, a few coins passing between them. A visit to the solemn hush of the undertaker. He'd done all that Sally could wish.

Only a question or two before he learned that Jonas Catesby kept rooms on Boar Lane, across from Holy Trinity church. One of the main streets in Leeds, businesses everywhere. Loud night and day. The young man lived above a game butcher who displayed his dead birds outside for customers. Cheek by jowl in the next building, a nest of lawyers.

Simon studied the area; plenty of places to stand and watch where he'd never be noticed. That was helpful. But he had no description of Catesby, no idea which rooms the man rented; he could be gazing down right now. How could he discover if Mark was there?

An hour and he knew it was a hopeless task. He needed to think of something better. Something certain.

Yet another hour, but walking and thinking brought no ideas. Nothing more than tiny slivers of fear when he passed the places where he'd needed to fight in the last two weeks. He had to try and ignore them. Had to.

'Tomorrow morning at nine.'

Jane nodded. She'd never known the boy when he was alive, but she'd be there. The funeral was important to Sally. The last chance to show Harold that someone had cared about him.

The girl wore her grief like a veil over her face. The power of it was carrying her along today. But Jane knew that as soon as the last sod was tamped down on the grave, that sorrow would ignite into a blazing rage. The children would all be searching for John. If he was still in Leeds, he couldn't stay hidden for long once they were all hunting with vengeance in their hearts.

Dodson was improving. Awake a little longer each time, eyes brighter, he was beginning to recall that he'd known her before all this. He could recognize Mrs Shields, he understood where he was and why. But no memory of what had happened to him. When she said John's name, he had no real notion of the man. A description brought nothing, as if almost every trace of him had vanished from his memory. Maybe that was best, she thought as she walked through the evening.

Jane talked to the whores and the drunkards. One or two faces she'd seen from the days she used to come here with her questions, but most were fresh. A few hopeful, many already sunk into a gin haze. They'd seen John, right enough, and were always careful to stay clear of a man who seemed to ooze decay. But no sign of him in recent days.

Finally she gave up, marching home through town. Frustrated, temper beginning to fray, she kept her hand on her knife hilt, ready for anything that might happen. Almost eager.

Simon came with Rosie and the boys. Lessons, work, they could all wait a few hours. Time to pay respect to the boy who'd been murdered. The knowledge that death was waiting for everyone, never knowing when it would call them. Or how. The undertaker had done his job well, a stout coffin made of ash. The gravediggers had gone deep into the earth.

It seemed as if every homeless child in Leeds was standing in the burial ground. Dozens of them, maybe more than a hundred. Even the tiniest stood and listened to the service in complete reverence. A few held small bunches of wildflowers they'd picked.

Once the body was in the ground, Sally stepped forward, picked up a clod of earth and let it fall into the hole. The only one, and soon the dirt was back in place, everything beaten flat. He watched as the children placed their flowers and made their farewells.

After the last of them had gone, Sally came up to him.

'I want a stone flat over him to stop any grave robbers. If I try to buy one, the masons might take my money and do nothing.'

'Do you know how you want it to read?'

No hesitation. 'Harold. Lost but loved.'

'That's it?' he asked. 'Nothing more?'

'What else is there?' She took a breath and he saw something change in her face; all the sentiment disappeared.

She and Sally divided the town. The girl would search north of the river and Jane would take everything on the other side of the bridge. There were two dozen children eager to help them. Every single one of them knew exactly what had happened to Harold, down to the finest detail; they understood John had to be found. The next victim might be another of them, their sister or brother.

'He's dangerous, miss,' a girl explained to Jane as they walked along Hunslet Lane. She stumbled over the long word and glanced up, proud that she said it correctly.

'He is,' Jane agreed. She had no sense of him anywhere. No danger of any kind at hand. Her thoughts drifted as she walked. Armistead, William Mark.

Simon.

He'd seemed different these last few days. Quieter, more cautious. His eyes always flickered around, as if he regarded the world as a threat. At the funeral he'd been subdued, standing with Rosie, his hands on the twins' shoulders all through the short service. Was something wrong with him?

Boys and girls came running to her, then darting away again with fresh orders, new streets to explore. They all knew how to survive; they'd learned to build that hard shell around themselves. Jane saw her own reflection in their faces, the way she had in Sally.

How many of these would last another year? Each day was a battle for them, a fight to stay alive. She looked down at the girl walking beside her. Pale, dirty hair, an eager smile. Clothes which were scarcely rags, feet and legs bare. Fine while the weather was warm, but would she be able to last through the winter?

Three hours and she could see they were beginning to flag. Jane shepherded them back across Leeds Bridge and bought all the pies on Kate's tray to feed them.

'What are you now?' the woman asked. 'A governess or a teacher?'

'We're hunters.' She glanced at the children, wolfing down the food, not a crumb wasted. A few of them had gathered round Davy Cassidy, dancing and laughing with pleasure as he played a reel. 'You heard what happened?'

'I did, pet,' Kate said. 'Poor little lad. It's terrible.'

At home, Dodson was awake, smiling as he saw her enter.

'Your name is Jane,' he said. No hesitation in his voice. His eyes were brighter and clearer.

'Yes.' She crouched by his side, studying his face. 'How do you feel?'

'I . . .' He frowned. 'A little better, I think.' The beggar cocked his head and his voice was unsure. 'Did I have a wooden leg? I seem to remember it, but I'm not certain.'

'You did, and a crutch.'

'Ah, yes. That's right.' His face brightened as he looked around the room, then clouded again. 'Where are they? I can't see them.'

'You didn't have them when you were found.'

'But how will I be able to walk?' Panic flared across his face.

'We'll take care of that once you're ready. I promise.'

NINETEEN

William Mark. Simon felt the name eating away at him. More than two weeks had passed since he'd been hired to find four stolen silver cups. He'd followed a twisted path through history, treason, and three murders to . . . exactly where had it brought him? he wondered.

Simon still hadn't recovered the cups. Instead, he'd somehow turned into a man liable to jump at the sight of his own shadow. Fear was good; it kept you aware and alive. But too much of it crippled a thief-taker.

Will Mark was still free. He was still in Leeds. He had to be, Simon felt; the man had nowhere else to go. With little money, this was the only place he might still have credit. All Simon could do was keep chasing around town to try and find him.

The name took him by surprise. He was in the Rose and Crown, caught among a press of people who'd just come in from the London coach, when a man three feet from him called out, 'Catesby! What the devil are you doing here?'

At first he wasn't sure if his mind had played a trick. But as his eyes searched the room, he spotted a young man with a wide grin, weighed down by his heavy valise as he shouldered his way through the crowd.

'Stand me a drink, James. I'm parched after that last stretch and not a farthing left to my name. The capital's a joy, but damn, it's expensive.'

Simon stayed close as they sipped brandy. Too many around for them to notice him, and they were caught up in their chatter.

'How long were you in London?'

'A fortnight. Needed to shake off this bloody place for a while and have some real pleasure.' He drank and smacked his lips with pleasure. 'Spent the last of my allowance down there. I'll tap the old man for a little more tomorrow.'

Two weeks in London. He'd left before the murders began.

'You've missed all sorts here. The Moot Hall and Middle Row have gone.'

'I saw that when we came in.'

'They found a secret room and a body when they tore it down.'

'What?'

A garbled account of it all. Simon watched Catesby's face, rapt at the tale, astonished by it. Ten minutes and he put the glass down.

'I think I'm about ready to sleep after that journey. Seen any of the crowd while I've been away?'

A few names but no mention of Will Mark. As Catesby made his farewell, Simon slipped out and crossed Briggate, standing in the shadows until the man came out.

Simple enough to follow him down the street. The night was warm, but Simon felt a chill and huddled in his coat.

He heard the dull thud of bodies, then saw Catesby topple to the ground. Two men had appeared from nowhere, standing over him, one beginning to reach for the valise.

Simon stopped, staring for a short moment. Without thinking, he drew one knife from his belt and a second from his boot and start to run.

'Thieves, thieves,' he yelled. Something, anything to halt them.

But there was hardly a soul around to help. The few people on Briggate seemed to melt away. The hobnail soles of his boots sounded like an army as he dashed across the cobbles.

The robbers hesitated long enough to glance at him. One started to lift the case, felt the weight and realized it would slow him. He dropped it again and the pair dashed away, disappearing around the corner on to Commercial Street.

He hadn't thought, he'd let his instincts take charge, and he hadn't felt a scrap of fear; it began to creep back now it was over.

Catesby was coming to his senses, groggy as he slowly sat up, resting his back against a wall.

'What happened?' he asked. A grimace as he touched the back of his head.

'Two men were trying to rob you.' The blood was still racing in his veins, every nerve on edge.

The man blinked, trying to recall. 'You stopped them?'

'Not really,' Simon answered. 'I ran and shouted, that's all.'

'I'm grateful to you.' Wincing, he pushed himself to his feet, placing one hand on the grip of the valise as if to assure himself it was still there. 'What did they do?'

'Knocked you down,' Simon answered. 'You must have hit your head.'

'I know I hurt like the devil.' He exhaled. 'At least it's not far to my rooms.'

'I'll walk with you. I doubt they'll come back . . .'

That small seed of doubt was enough.

'If you're willing, I'll be glad of your company.' He gave a rueful smile and touched the back of his head once more. 'I can't promise much of myself at the moment. Forgive me: I'm Jonas Catesby.'

'Simon Westow.'

Catesby hefted the case and began to walk down Briggate. An awkward limp, halting every few yards to shift the weight to his other hand.

'I can take that,' Simon offered.

'Thank you, but you helped enough back there. God knows what they might have done. Slit my throat, perhaps.'

'They saw the chance, nothing more. The smallest problem and they were gone.'

The man gave him a shrewd glance. 'You seem to know about things like that.'

'I'm a thief-taker.' He shrugged. 'It's my business.'

They turned on to Boar Lane and Catesby pointed.

'I live over there, across from the church. Always a devil of a lot of noise on a Sunday morning when a man's trying to rest.'

At the door they shook hands. Simon began to walk down the street, then quietly turned back to stand in the blackness cast by the heavy bulk of Holy Trinity.

Less than a minute to wait before he saw a lamp lit in one of the rooms on the other side of the road and Catesby moving around.

No sign of William Mark, and he didn't seem the kind to spend his evenings sitting in the dark. That answered one question. But Catesby might be useful to help him find the man.

Perhaps he'd call on the man in the morning to see how he was recovering.

A brief, satisfied smile as he walked away. For once at least, Lady Luck had been kind.

Then the feeling passed as the night crowded around him, and all the fears and worries returned to accompany him home.

Everything felt different now that all the terrors that roamed the dark were penned up by the daylight. It was already hot enough to leave Simon sweating inside his shirt. The air was oppressive, thick enough to cut; how long before a storm arrived to clear everything?

He'd slept, the fits and starts of a man plagued by night demons, awake at dawn. Simon had been one of the first at the coffee cart, letting the drink jolt him awake. No mention of the attempt at robbery, but he'd never expected to hear anything; thieves never advertised their failures.

Home to breakfast with Rosie and the boys. As he ate, he watched the twins. Once he'd found Mark and returned the cups to Sir Robert Foley, he'd see about a school where Richard and Amos could complete their education. They'd go into the world prepared; at least he could do that for them.

Once Jane arrived, and the boys were outside in the yard kicking a ball, he told the others about Catesby.

'I'm sure Mark isn't staying with him—'

'Which leaves us back where we began,' Rosie said, picking at a loose thread on her sleeve.

He turned to Jane. 'William Mark knows things about Mangey. That hidden room in Middle Row.'

'Yes,' she agreed, and he saw the question in her eyes.

'You read through everything Armistead had. Was there any mention of places Mangey liked to go?' The odds were against it, but with no trace of Mark, he had to chase every possibility, no matter how small.

She stayed silent for a long time, eyes narrow, trying to recall things she'd read, before shaking her head.

'I don't remember anything like that, but most of Armistead's material was from his trial and evidence. It wasn't likely to be in there. All I remember is his house on Kirkgate and the workshop. There might be more, but I wasn't looking for anything like that.'

'Would you go through it once more?' He heard himself, trying to keep the brittle desperation from his voice as she nodded. 'I'll ask Porter to tell one of the watch to meet you there in an hour.'

Jane slipped away.

'Where do you want me?' Sally asked. She'd been silent, listening closely.

'Have you had any luck finding this John?'

'No.'

'There's nothing to keep him here, is there?' Rosie asked.

'We're going to keep looking until we're sure he's gone.' Her voice was like iron.

The clock at the Parish Church struck ten. Not too early to call on someone who'd endured a long journey then two men trying to rob him.

Simon presented his card to the landlady. Three minutes later she returned and directed him up the stairs. Everything was well kept, clean, smelling sweet, a pair of paintings hanging on the walls.

The door to Catesby's room stood ajar. A tap on the wood and he entered, finding a jumble of furniture. Chairs, a scattering of small tables, and a larger one by the window, where the man sat with his pot of coffee.

'Mr Westow.' He stood. 'Will you join me?'

Simon shook his head. 'I wanted to be sure you were well after last night.'

Catesby gave a smile that was full of charm. He was handsome, hair brushed in some curious London fashion. A snowy stock and linen, a well-cut coat and trousers fitted tight against his thighs. But he held himself stiffly, as if he could feel his bruises, and his hand moved cautiously as he touched the back of his head.

'Well?' The man gave a snort. 'Not when this hurts like a smith's anvil and every part of my body aches.'

He had the air of a man who'd never known much pain. Maybe it didn't intrude into his world, Simon thought.

'It'll pass in a day or two.'

'I'm grateful to you,' Catesby said. His gaze hardened. 'If you're hoping for payment, though, I have nothing to give you.'

Simon smiled. 'I wouldn't want your money for something like that.'

He saw the man's eyes narrow with suspicion. 'Then—'

'A simple call. You took quite a blow on your head.'

'Like you said, it will pass. I came back from London particularly for the assembly tomorrow night and I intend to be there.' The smile returned, broader than before. 'There's a lady I'm hoping to see.'

'I'm sure it will be a fine affair. How long were you away?'

'A fortnight.' Catesby cocked his head. 'I seem to have missed a great deal. Someone told me a few things have been happening here.'

'The Moot Hall and Middle Row gone. A body found in a secret room there that belonged to a man hanged for treason more than a hundred years ago.'

'Good for gossip.' He poured more coffee from the pot. 'Is any of that your business?'

'After a fashion,' Simon told him. The time was right, he thought. 'Tell me, do you know a man called William Mark?'

The liquid slopped over the rim of the cup. 'Will?' he asked in astonishment. 'You're not trying to tell me he's involved in this.'

'I'm not sure. I'm trying to find him.' Nothing to lose by naming the man. God knew he'd had no luck with anything else. 'Do you know where he might be?'

'I've been in London,' Catesby reminded him, but Simon could see the calculation at the back of his eyes, the way his thoughts were turning.

'You know him.'

'Of course. I have done for years.'

'Then you might have some idea where I can find him. His father disowned him at the start of the year.'

'He made sure we *all* heard about that. Where is he now? How the devil would I know, Mr Westow? You'll recall I only came back to Leeds last night.' He waved a hand at the room. 'It's early yet. I haven't had chance to see anyone.'

The man chose his words with great care. No denial. That blow to the skull certainly hadn't addled his brains.

'You have friends who'd let him stay.'

An elegant shrug. 'Perhaps. I'd need to ask.' A long pause, then the cunning smile and Simon knew exactly what he was about to say. Not an ounce of subtlety to the man. 'But why should I?'

'Your duty?'

Catesby snorted. 'Duty is for fools who follow the flag. I'm sure you understand that, sir.'

Suddenly he was weary of the man and his airs. Greed was the same, no matter what fashion it wore. All he wanted to do was make his bargain and leave with the information about Mark.

'How much?'

Dodson was awake again. His recovery was moving faster than she'd expected. Still the pain of his broken ribs, he had scabs and bruises, and Mrs Shields kept his head bandaged, but each day he was growing a little stronger. The only thing lost was the memory of John and what he'd done to him.

Each time Jane asked about it, a worried frown pebbled his face. He'd think and finally shake his head.

'I'm sorry,' he told her. 'You're doing all this for me and I can't . . .'

'It doesn't matter,' she told him.

'His memory of all that may never come back,' the old woman told her later. 'I've seen that before. Nobody seems to understand why it happens. It's as if the mind has stopped working for a while. Can you chop some herbs for me?' She showed her hands, the old fingers curled like claws. 'They're bad today.'

She did as she was asked and dropped a soft kiss on the old woman's head.

'I need to go. Simon wants me to look at Mr Armistead's books again.'

Jane pulled back the shutters from the windows and dusty light filled the library. Everything was exactly as she'd left it, as if she'd only stepped out for a minute, not days. The scent of death still hung in the air. The noises from Kirkgate were faint, somewhere in the distance she heard the sweet tones of Davy Cassidy's fiddle as she took a deep breath and began to glance through the papers, feeling Armistead's ghost watching over her shoulder.

She lost track of the time, falling into the books, the story. A tap on the door made her stop and look up.

Sally, entering warily and gazing around, looking out of place in this room full of words.

'From Simon?'

The girl shook her head. 'The children discovered where John's been sleeping.'

Along Briggate a violin played an urgent jig to hurry along their walk out to Sheepscar in the heat, before they climbed the slope from the road to a place hidden among the bushes and trees.

'Do you recognize it?' the girl asked.

She nodded. Sally had brought her here before. She'd seen something up here as she and Simon rode back to Leeds.

In the clearing, Jane gazed down at charred wood, the remains of a small fire. That hardly meant John had been here; anyone could have done that.

Sally pointed. 'Take a look up there, in the branches.'

It took her a moment to understand, then she saw it, half-hidden by the leaves. The remains of a small animal. Skin flayed and ripped off the body, strung up safe from other creatures. Pieces of flesh hacked away.

The birds had been clawing at it, the crows and the magpies; she could hear them flying and calling close by.

'It has to be him,' Jane said. Nobody else could have done that. She felt the certainty in her bones, in the fury that rose inside.

'He must have been here last night,' Sally said. She nodded towards what remained of the animal. 'Any longer and there'd be nothing left.'

Jane stared around. They were no more than a few hours behind him. She raised her head and breathed deep, as if she thought she could catch his scent.

'You can see where he went,' Sally continued. 'Those tracks through the grass right there.'

She could barely make out a thing. Something that might have been a footprint, or she simply wanted to believe it was. But Sally had grown up in the country; noticing those signs was in her blood.

'Can we follow him?'

But Jane knew the answer, even as she spoke. If they could, they'd already be moving. At least they could be certain he was still here. She kicked through the blackened wood.

'Tonight?' That was their chance. The darkness would be their friend. John would need a fire to cook his meat.

'Where?' Sally asked.

'Out here.' It was a place to begin.

'Unless Simon needs me.'

Back with the papers and the documents, her thoughts wouldn't settle. She forced herself to work. Her eyes raced over the pages, astonished that she could read it all so easily; there had never been a reason to be scared of these words. Suddenly, a passing reference stopped her, and she made a note.

Jane hurried through the rest, reining in her thoughts as soon as they began to stray. Another hour and she closed the final volume of Armistead's work on Arthur Mangey and placed it on top of the others.

One last walk around the room before she closed the shutters again and the day faded to gloom in the library. Then she was out into the street, locking the door behind her. The guard from the watch wasn't the genial man she'd come to know when she worked here before. This one was sullen, unhappy with the duty and glad to see the back of her.

At least the visit had been worthwhile. Maybe she should have spotted the detail when she was first poring over the papers. But she'd been seeking other things then. Without thinking, she stroked her forearm through the sleeve of her dress. Only the very faintest of ridges were left now, those places where she'd cut herself every time she thought she'd failed. Another thing pushed away.

A lesson, though; she'd learned that the past never let you go. You believed you were free, then it came back and took you.

It was an old building. The bricks would have been rosy once, but a dull, deep black now from the soot in the air. Simon paused, wiping his forehead. Another warm, close day.

The information had cost him five pounds. Catesby might have had a knock on the head, but his thinking was sharp enough to know he held the whip hand. Smirking as they haggled over the price. Ten pounds to begin, but that was never going to last.

The man stuck on five. Still a fortune, pure robbery, but he refused to go lower, knowing he needed money until his next allowance was paid. Frustrated, Simon had paid; it was Foley's money.

'If you're lying . . .'

'I'm not, Mr Westow,' Catesby had said. 'Call me what you like. Greedy, anything, but you ran those robbers off last night.' His eyes were serious. 'I don't believe I'd dare lie to you.'

No, he'd take advantage of him instead. All that money for an address where the windows looked lifeless. Mark was there, the man had claimed. It belonged to a friend travelling in Europe. He'd agreed to let Will Mark stay while he was gone. Full of sympathy for someone disowned by his family.

There was no good spot out of sight to keep watch; they'd need to do whatever they could. He'd already walked all around, looking for any likely place. The front door gave on to the Head Row, between Vicar Lane and Briggate. But at the back, the yard opened into the maze of courts and ginnels than ran between the streets.

'William Mark is living in rooms on the Head Row,' Simon said.

'How did you find that out?' Rosie asked. Her eyes narrowed as she spoke.

'I paid over the odds for the information,' he admitted with a bitter scowl. 'Don't worry, the man is well aware of what will happen if it's not true.'

'Have you told Porter?'

'Not yet. I want to watch the place first.' He turned to Sally. 'Nobody would notice you. There's a back way, too. He could easily use that. See if you spot him tonight.'

She nodded, saying nothing.

'I found something, too,' Jane said, and Simon watched all the eyes turn to her. 'Arthur Mangey's wife had a property in her own name. A small house just on the other side of Leeds Bridge. I walked over and it's still there. But if you're sure that Mark is in this other place—'

Simon face darkened. 'For what I paid, he'd better be.'

'I'll go tomorrow and find out,' Rosie said, and he nodded. 'Paying a call on a lady but at the wrong address.'

'Will you need me for anything tonight?' Jane asked.

'No. Thank you for finding that.'

Before she left, he noticed the disappointed look that passed between her and Sally.

TWENTY

'I've heard there's an assembly tomorrow evening,' Simon said to Rosie once they were alone.

'Is there?' she asked in surprise.

'Apparently so. I asked; it's to raise money for charity.'

Her expression turned to amusement. 'You know, Simon, in all our time together, I think that's the first time I've heard you mention an assembly.'

'Jonas Catesby, the man who told me where Mark's living, intends to go. Makes me wonder if Will Mark will, too.'

'You've decided that we ought to be there, too.' Her mouth creased into a smile.

'It will give you a chance to wear one of those good gowns of yours. Do you think someone would be willing to take the boys?'

'Very likely.'

'Then would you accompany me, Mrs Westow?'

She curtseyed. 'Even without the romance I'd be delighted, sir. Do you think you might claim a few dances with me? They even allow the waltz there now, I hear.'

He laughed. 'Only if you want a partner who's likely to tread on your toes.'

'Then perhaps I'll hope for another offer, sir.'

Her mind had been full of John. Where to try and find him. How to catch him. In the hot shank of the afternoon, Jane walked into the cottage behind Green Dragon Yard and stopped for a moment, scarcely able to believe her eyes.

Dodson was sitting up in the bed, back resting against the pillow. Freshly shaved, days of beard neatly cut away. He had a book open on his lap. She recognized it: *The Scottish Chiefs*, the one she'd borrowed from the circulating library.

The old soldier turned his head. His eyes were clear, and he gave a tentative smile.

'Jane,' he said. No tremor or quaver in his voice.

'He's much better today,' Mrs Shields said from the doorway of the kitchen. She was smiling with pleasure at her patient's improvement. 'He was complaining about the bristles on his face, so I found my husband's old razor and he stropped an edge on it.'

'You're reading, too,' Jane said. She had no idea he'd ever learned his alphabet. But she knew so little about him. Not where he was born or the kind of family he'd once had.

'Only a little. Very little.' He frowned. 'It's been a long time. After a few minutes the words begin to swim, so I keep putting it down.'

'I've never seen you with a book.'

He shrugged, sorrow in his expression. 'We didn't have room for them in our packs when we were on the march through Spain. After I lost my leg and came back, I needed my money for other things.'

It would still be days before he'd be well enough to look after himself, Mrs Shields told her. Jane sat with him while she ran her knife over the whetstone. Leaving the edge sharp enough to cut leather.

'What you're doing, will it be dangerous?' he asked.

'It might. I want to be prepared. In case.'

Dodson watched as she worked, then said: 'I remember when you lost that finger,' he said.

'Do you?' She stopped, holding out her left hand, the space when the little finger had been.

'I told you how you'd imagine you still had it.'

She remembered. Even now she still sometimes felt a phantom twinge. Mostly, it was only when she needed it or glanced down that she realized it had gone. One sharp cut, then pain. But the man who did it had paid.

'My room,' he said in a sudden panic, trying to push himself upright.

'No need to worry. I paid for it,' Jane told him. His body eased as he slumped back.

'You brought me here, you've looked after me. Now that.' He looked into her face, grateful but confused. 'I don't understand.'

She didn't try to give him an answer. Jane had found him half-alive, a good man, a gentle man. She couldn't leave him to die. There had been no need to think more about it than that. She didn't want to dig, to try and find words to explain it. She'd done it; that was enough.

Jane thrust the knife into her pocket, laced her boots up tight and pulled a thin shawl around her shoulders.

'It's time for me to go,' she said to Mrs Shields.

Simon went from inn to inn; he was doing it so often it was coming to feel like a habit. Always careful, skin prickling if anyone came too close, his knife ready. Fear had infected him; it sat in his body like an illness. He needed to break the fever, to recover, but he didn't know how.

In a far corner of the bar in the Talbot he saw Barnabas Wade trying to convince a man to buy his shares, then the way his shoulders slumped as the customer walked off.

The Rose and Crown was quiet, with no more coaches due tonight. But two arrived in the few minutes he was at the King's Arms, a rush of noise and people dazed from their journeys. A brief stop and they were on their way again, just a change of horses before they were rushing up Briggate, whips cracking and the wheels rolling over the cobbles in the darkness.

But wherever he went, there was no sign of William Mark.

Sally was watching the house where he was supposed to be staying. If he left, she'd follow. As long as she was able to spot him.

Throughout the evening, the air had grown more oppressive, tight around his chest. A storm was coming. The first drops arrived as he walked towards Swinegate, Heavy, warm as blood on his skin.

A crack of thunder. It sounded like doom as it filled the sky, close overhead, slowly rolling away. Another and another until the world was filled with noise. Lightning flashed, a moment when he could see everything. Then the deluge began, as if someone had ripped the clouds apart.

No point in running for his front door; inside a minute he was soaked. The rain bounced high off the pavement, gushing down the streets in a flood. He saw the body of a rat swirl through the water as it was carried away.

In the kitchen, he stripped off his clothes. Old coat, waistcoat, trousers, all sodden. Boots, hose, down to his linen, and he towelled his hair with an old piece of cloth. The rain hammered loud outside, barking a rough tattoo against the windows, and he hoped Sally had found somewhere dry to shelter. Mark wouldn't be out in this.

Jane felt the rain creeping closer, but she kept searching. On her own; Sally was busy with work from Simon. She started where John had made his camp. Standing, trying to catch the sense of him, where he might have gone. But there was only emptiness, nothing to lead her in any direction.

She kept the knife in her hand, turning the gold ring for luck, for safety. Moving quietly, standing in the thunder and lightning, then under cover of the trees as the rain began to pour.

John would need shelter for the night. Most of the thick woods around town had been cut down; nothing for him there.

She was soaked, but she scarcely noticed as she moved. Her gaze shifted constantly, alert for the smallest movement, but the streets were dark and deserted. At least Dodson would be dry, she thought, and suddenly stopped.

His room.

It was empty. Somewhere out of the rain. John surely knew the place well. She hadn't checked it again.

Jane hurried through town. The rain was still pouring. Not quite as heavy now and the air was cooler on her skin.

A flickering light shone through the crack at the bottom of the door.

Jane stopped. No sound from inside. She swallowed, taking breaths, waiting until her heart slowed. A long time had passed since she'd done any of this, but she was ready. Dodson, the boy called Harold; they deserved their justice. She wished Sally was with her.

She reached out, took hold of the doorknob.

Tried to ease the door open, but a shriek of rusted metal gave her away.

John turned. In the flame of a candle, she could see his face properly for the first time. Dark eyes, bottomless, cruel. Thin, colourless lips. Cheeks pitted with smallpox scars, so many that his face seemed more holes than flesh.

He was quick, pulling a knife with a long, rusted blade and darting towards her. Jane didn't move. No need, not yet. She pushed the door closed behind her. He'd need to get past her to escape.

She let him move. John tried small pushes forward, feints to her left, to her right. Jane kept her ground, grateful for those practice sessions on the moor, poised to strike as soon as the chance arrived.

Twenty seconds and he'd yet to come close. He seemed to burn with frustration. A lunge, too obvious. She slipped to one side and brought the tip of her knife up into his armpit. Not deep enough for real damage; he was already slithering away.

Another attack, rushing straight at her, trying to overwhelm her and pin her against the door. She waited until the last moment, when he had a look of triumph on his face. Then she ducked, moved to the side and brought her body up.

John grunted, caught off balance, and slammed into a wall. He turned, but Jane was quicker.

She felt her knife slide through cloth. The brief resistance of skin, then she was pushing the blade home into his side. He tried to pull away but she ground it deeper.

Dodson. Harold. Who knew how many others?

The man had madness in his eyes. His fist came from nowhere. Fast, hard, a crack on her cheek that snapped her head back. Jane stumbled. Flailing to keep her balance, trying to guard herself.

A second blow, the side of her skull this time. Sharp, hard as a hammer. She blinked, dazed, trying to see him. Jane pushed her arm forward. A quick, hopeful jab. Her knife cut him for a third time.

Good.

She needed to hurt him. If she fell, he'd kill her.

Feed on her.

Everything was blurred. Pain jolted through her head. He brought his face close. Rank, evil breath. Trying to force her back.

Jane brought her hand up. Made herself concentrate. Sliced his forehead open with her knife. A long moment of nothing, then blood began to drip into his eyes.

John howled. An animal sound that crashed against her ears.

He tried to wipe at his eyes. The blood was coming faster, blinding him. She tried to slice him again. Missed. He caught her wrist. His fingers were tighter than she could have believed. Another second and he flung her across the room. His strength had come from nowhere.

She hit the corner of the bed, winded as she sprawled across the floor. All the air slammed out of her lungs as she hit. But she'd kept hold of the knife. When he came . . .

But he didn't. She tried to watch him. To be ready. John's shape blurred and turned watery. He seemed to remain still for long seconds. Jane swallowed, waiting.

A whirl of motion and he vanished.

The door slammed. She heard his feet running down the stairs. But she couldn't make herself stand.

She lay there until she could see straight, letting the breath return to her body.

Very slowly, Jane pushed herself off the floor. Steadying herself with one hand on the bed, then the wall, stumbling a few paces until she was certain she wouldn't fall.

She'd wounded him. Hurt him badly. But still he'd escaped.

Outside, the rain was still falling. Standing in the small courtyard, she felt it like a blessing, raising her head to the skies before she carefully made her way home.

'Child, child.' Mrs Shields rubbed ointment on Jane's cheek. 'Why didn't you wake me? I could have put this on last night.'

Morning and the rain had stopped, the storm turned to memory. The blow was a dark red smear on her face. She hardly felt the tender touch of the old woman's fingers.

'I didn't want to bother you.'

Mrs Shields stopped and stared at her. 'Nothing is a bother with you. You ought to know that by now. Let me feel your head. There, that's another one, isn't it?'

She didn't ask what Jane had done, but that had always been the old woman's way. She recalled Mrs Shields's relief when she walked away from being a thief-taker, but she'd accepted the return without a word.

'Look at me. Can you see straight?'

'Yes.' Her head ached, skull tender and throbbing where John had hit her. But her sleep had been solid, her sight was clear when she looked at things. Only the bitter anger of not winning.

'Was it the man who hurt me who did that to you?' Dodson asked as Jane pulled her shawl over her hair.

She nodded. 'Yes. Not just you. Others, too.'

He stayed silent, eyes narrowed as he mulled the thought.

'Is he worth the risk?' the beggar asked finally.

'He is,' she told him. She'd done it without thought or question. Because it was the right thing.

'There were lights burning in the rooms upstairs,' Sally said as she and Simon walked back from sparring on Woodhouse Moor. 'He came to the window twice to glance at the rain. After he blew out the lamps, I waited a little while in case he left. He didn't come out of the main door, so I left.'

'Could he have seen you?' Simon asked.

'No.'

Rosie and Jane were waiting in the kitchen when they returned. It had only been a short session with the knives, but he could smell the sweat on himself. Sally was still much faster, but Simon could feel he was a little quicker and more confident. Exactly what he needed to conquer these feelings gnawing at his mind.

Simon stared at Jane, wondering about the mark just beginning to flower into a bruise on her cheek. But she shook her head and said nothing.

The storm had left deep puddles in the road and on the pavement. She dodged around them, only covering twenty yards along Swinegate before Sally caught up to her, mouth full of questions.

'Where did you find him?'

'Dodson's room.'

'Is he dead?'

Jane shook her head and looked as the ground as she walked, kicking a stone along the pavement.

'Not yet.' He'd beaten her. That hurt more than the bruises. Jane had wounded him, but he'd still managed to escape.

'Let's go and see it.'

At the door, she hesitated for a second. What if he'd returned?

But this time she had Sally with her. Knife in her hand, blood pounding, she entered.

It was empty. The bed still sat askew where she'd landed against it. A chair overturned. Blood soaked into the bare floorboards.

'It looks as if you cut him badly.' The girl squatted, running her fingertips over the stains.

'Not enough.' Her face showed nothing as she pushed everything back into its place, ready for Dodson's return. He'd need a new lock. No, perhaps not. By then, John would be dead.

She tried to put herself into his mind. Into his blur of darkness and pain. 'He's wounded. He'll have gone to ground.'

Sally nodded. 'Animals do that.'

'If someone comes across him by accident . . .'

'I'll warn the children. Make sure they keep their distance.'

TWENTY-ONE

Saturday afternoon and Simon took the boys out to kick a ball around, the three of them running, laughing, playing a game with no rules or sense. A chance not to think, to enjoy his sons. No William Mark or Arthur Mangey. No fear leaving its visiting card in his mind.

Tonight, Richard and Amos would be with one of the neighbours while he and Rosie attended the assembly. It only seemed fair to deliver a pair of boys who'd fall asleep quickly. All he needed to do was stay awake himself, he thought as he led them home, cheeks flushed and feeling old. But for once there was no fear, no worry nibbling away at his mind. For a short while, contentment.

'The house that Arthur Mangey's wife owned was sold when she died,' Rosie said. 'The grandfather of the man who lives there bought it.'

She studied herself in the mirror before starting to pin up her hair in an elaborate arrangement.

'How did you manage to discover that?' The things she could charm from people constantly amazed him.

She turned and smiled at him. 'His wife answered the door and we started talking. Honestly, Simon, you've no idea, have you?'

'No,' he agreed with a chuckle, 'maybe I haven't.'

Sally had gone to the homeless children for the evening. The house seemed empty, too large, as if every slight sound might echo around the walls.

Simon sat in the kitchen, reading the *Leeds Intelligencer* as he waited. Rosie was moving around upstairs, taking her time as she prepared for the assembly. When she finally appeared, he stood, tongue-tied for a moment.

Her gown was the deep, dense blue of a late evening, the trim pale yellow. It flowed around her, flattering and enticing. Her hair was up, showing the soft curve of her neck.

'You look wonderful.'

The blush came readily to her cheeks. 'I've had this for a long time. I had it made when the boys were young. Honestly, I'm surprised it still fits.' She twirled to show off the dress. 'You look handsome, too.'

His best coat with the long swallowtails given a hard brush, an embroidered waistcoat that barely stretched across his stomach these days. Fine, pale trousers that clung to his thighs and shoes polished brilliant black.

The assembly room by the old Cloth Hall was a bright glitter of light that burst out through the high windows. He heard the musicians as they climbed the stairs. A low murmur of male voices behind the open door of the card room.

Simon knew his wife was eager to dance; he led her straight through to the ballroom. Glass chandeliers hung from the ceiling, filling the long room with the soft light of candles. In the middle of the floor, dancers moved more or less in time with the music, men and women of all shapes and sizes and ages.

More people watched from the edges of the room. The women were seated, talking, assessing, while the men formed their own small groups, standing with wine glasses in hands.

The music finished to polite applause. Rosie tugged him out to the dance floor.

'You'll be able to look all around while we dance,' she whispered as they took their places with other couples and the tune began.

Rosie moved with a natural, flowing grace. Simon felt as if he was in a constant battle with the melody. But she was right. As the couples changed places and moved up and down the line, his eyes could wander over everyone in the room.

He spotted Jonas Catesby in a far corner, in the middle of a knot of young men. No sign of anyone resembling William Mark with him. It was early yet; he might arrive later.

Simon was warm by the time the music drew to a close; dancing was more exhausting than he remembered. At a table, Rosie introduced him to three other women, all older than her, chaperoning their daughters to the dance. He bowed, waited until they were chattering nineteen to the dozen and began to wander. Catesby saw him, raised his glass in a toast and gave a slight shake of his head: no Mark.

Simon had a plan: if he spotted Will Mark here, he'd slip away and search the man's rooms for the silver cups, then send a member of the watch to fetch Porter.

No sign of the man in the card room, either. A cloud of smoke hung below the ceiling, the air heavy with the smell of cigars and pipes. A few familiar faces and invitations, but he had no wish to lose money playing piquet.

Simon returned to the ballroom with two glasses of punch, but Rosie wasn't at the table. One of the women pointed to the dancers. There she was, standing up with old Eli Hardcastle. He watched them, admiring the lithe, easy way his wife moved, surprised at the spry fashion with which Eli partnered her. Catesby was up, too, grinning as he accompanied a young woman. No wonder, he thought as she turned and he saw her face. Miranda Robertson. A woman with a large dowry. Probably the reason he'd returned to Leeds.

Simon's eye roved across the heads. He caught someone staring at him, then turning to speak to a companion who hurried away. A rolling stride, familiar, but for a second he couldn't place it. No, he thought as he stared. It couldn't be. It simply wasn't possible.

He placed the glass on the table and left the ballroom, dashing along the corridor. The noise and laughter receded as he descended the stairs two at a time. The man selling tickets at the door gave him a curious look.

'Did someone just leave?'

'A moment or two since. Mr Hutton. A friend of yours, sir?'

'Do you know which way he went?'

The man shook his head. 'I'm sorry, sir. Are you looking for him?'

But Simon was already pushing the door open.

What in the name of God would make the captain risk coming back to Leeds? The man couldn't be that mad . . .

Simon stood, trying to listen for footfalls but hearing nothing. He felt the fast thud of his heartbeat and reached up his sleeve for the knife.

Out here in the warm darkness, fear began to tug at him. He hesitated, then forced himself on. Hutton had wanted him dead.

Kirkgate first. Plenty of life in the gin shops and alehouses. But nobody with that rolling seaman's walk.

Rushing to Vicar Lane, then Duncan Street, desperation rising, his chest growing tighter. Hutton hadn't had time to go too far. Somewhere, somewhere . . . down Call Lane, towards the river and the bridge, moving as swiftly as his fancy shoes would allow.

A shape silhouetted against the parapet. The right build and size, crossing towards Hunslet.

Simon ran. The man turned, panic on his face. Not a shred of doubt now; that was Matthew Hutton. Ten yards between them as the captain began to flee. Fright gave him speed, but Simon kept pace as revenge pushed him on.

Down past Salem Chapel, cutting over to Black Bull Street. No light here, only the sound of shoes on stone to guide him. The terrors were crowding around him. But if he gave in now, he'd never manage another thing.

He followed all the way to Hunslet Road. The captain was pulling ahead, but Simon kept going. His breathing was ragged, the muscles in his legs ached. A deep breath and he pushed harder.

Then . . . nothing. A few seconds of silence before the voices began. He slowed, approaching warily.

Hutton was trying to back away from two large men. Simon stopped five paces behind him.

'Are you looking for him?' one of the men asked.

'We have some unfinished business,' Simon told him, careful to keep his distance.

'So do we.' He glanced at the captain. 'We've been searching for you for a long time, Tommy Tyler.'

Now he knew. The men in Hull had received his letter.

'I'm not Tyler. My name's Hutton.' He turned to Simon, eyes pleading. 'You tell them, Westow. Please. You know who I am.'

'I do. I know exactly who you are,' Simon answered. 'These men are right, Mr Tyler.'

'Westow?' one of the men said. 'You're the one who wrote to us.' A small bow. 'I'm in your debt, sir. One of those who died because of this man was my brother.'

'You should never have come back to Leeds,' Simon told the captain. He stared for another moment then turned on his heel and walked back into the darkness. No need to fight for once, no need to draw blood. Maybe he'd been cheated of his revenge, but the captain would pay anyway.

'Did you find Mr Hutton, sir?' the man at the assembly room asked.

'No.' He'd seen Thomas Tyler.

Rosie was sitting at the table, talking to the other women. She was watching the room intently, relief flooding her face as soon as soon as she saw him walk in.

'Where did you go?' she hissed in his ear as he sat down beside her.

'I saw someone.'

'Mark?' She looked around.

He shook his head. Simon had glanced in the card room before returning to the ballroom, checking all the nooks and corners. Still no sign of Will Mark. Catesby was dancing a waltz with Miranda Robertson while her mother glared with disapproval from her chair.

Suddenly he felt weary, the night beginning to drain away from him.

'Would you mind if we went home?'

'Of course not.' Rosie cocked her head. 'Are you all right?'

He managed a weak smile. 'Tired, nothing more.'

They walked arm in arm. She'd danced with a few gentlemen, enough to satisfy her desire for an evening out. He told her about Hutton.

'I wonder why he came back,' Simon said.

'Ellen Burstead,' Rosie told him. 'It has to be her. He's been sweet on her for a long time. She always goes to the assemblies. I saw her tonight. He was probably hoping he could persuade her to elope with him.'

'Not any more.' Nowhere left for the captain to run.

TWENTY-TWO

John must have crawled away. The children hadn't managed to unearth any sign of him. Jane swept through Leeds, into the yards and courts, searching, asking, offering a penny here, a ha'penny there, but came out empty-handed.

The bruise on her cheek was starting to take on colour. Her head was tender where he'd hit her.

She knew she'd hurt him. Those cuts had gone deep. For a moment she wondered if he'd bled to death somewhere. No; someone would have found his body. He was still alive. She could feel him. Cowering, in pain.

He needed to pay. For Dodson. For Harold. For all the others whose names she'd never know. For beating her.

Tomorrow, she thought as she settled under the sheet.

Sunday, with the usual souls gathered around the coffee cart outside the Bull and Mouth in the early morning to mutter and talk as they drank. The storm was history and the air was thick and warm again, very still, heavy and prickly. Tempers would be short today, Simon thought, sipping from the battered tin cup.

No gossip about a body found anywhere, or anything about Matthew Hutton being seen in town. In his dreams he'd seen the hopelessness on the captain's face. But it was his due.

He shook his head, throwing the thoughts away. At least the fears hadn't returned to torment him in the night.

Another short glance at the windows. He'd gambled on Will Mark attending the assembly and lost.

The curtains were closed in his rooms. Someone was inside, sleeping. He stood, studying the front of the house, willing the man to wake and look out at the world. No luck, of course. Men like Mark never rose early.

At home, he spent half an hour questioning Richard and Amos on the things they'd learned this last week. They knew so much now.

'They need a school,' Rosie said.

'We tried that when they were younger,' he reminded her.

'I haven't forgotten. We did the right thing, hiring a tutor. But they're older now, Simon. They need more than he can give them. He said so himself. They'd be around other boys, some better discipline. It will serve them well.'

He knew it made sense; he'd simply been postponing the time.

'Which school?'

'I'll talk to some women I know. They'll be able to suggest somewhere.'

He could hear the boys upstairs, playing in their own fashion. The discipline of a good school would help them. They'd meet people from the right families. That would give them more chances in life, the opportunities that learning and friendship brought. Soon enough they'd be out in the world, needing to earn their livings.

Jane sat in the kitchen, listening quietly and saying nothing as he told her about the captain. Then a nod and she left.

'Practise with the knives?' Sally suggested to him.

They barely managed half an hour before too many people were wandering over Woodhouse Moor. Sally had youth, with all its fire and speed, but his cunning was returning, catching her by surprise a few times.

He was breathing hard by the time they were done, but he felt satisfied. She barely looked winded, eyes shining.

'Do you want me to watch Mark again?'

'No.' He'd do that himself. As soon as the man went out, Simon would slip into the rooms and look for those cups, the way he'd hoped to do last night.

'Anything at all for me?' Sally asked.

'Not today.'

The curtains were still drawn tight, even as the church clock struck eleven. He couldn't imagine lazing the day away like that.

Another hour before they were pulled back and Simon had his first glimpse of William Mark. Unprepossessing, with thick, sandy hair. None of his father's bulk; a weak chin and small eyes. Maybe he'd seem more impressive strutting in his finery.

It was well past noon before the door opened and the man

emerged on to the Head Row. Simon shrank back, but Mark never glanced around. He was wearing a good coat with a close cut and trousers almost moulded to his thighs. He strode away; Simon's eyes followed until he was out of sight.

Two more minutes, in case he returned, then Simon moved. The lock on the front door was nothing. Five seconds and he was inside the building, breathing the fresh smell of beeswax polish as he climbed the stairs.

He worked with the picks, inserting one in the keyhole, moving it slightly until he felt it catch. Gently, carefully, the second joined it. A flick of the wrist and he was inside the rooms, softly closing the door behind him.

A moment to let his breathing steady. Fear was a tingle on his skin.

A brief look around. Mark had left clothes tossed over a chair by the bed, the sheets and pillows a tangle. The landlady would be up to tidy soon enough. He needed to hurry.

Simon knew how to search; he was familiar with all the places where people hid things. They believed they'd found somewhere safe, but there was never anything new; every nook and cranny had been used before.

Mark would have the silver cups here. He'd killed three men to have them. With his own twisted reasoning, he seemed to believe they were his birthright.

It took a quarter of an hour. Steady and thorough, replacing everything exactly as it had been. Leaving no sign that anyone had been looking in the rooms.

Finally, turning the mattress, he saw the split. As simple as that. Two more minutes and the cups were sitting on the floor as he put everything back in place. He lifted one of them, the silver so smooth and beautiful. It felt perfectly balanced in his hand. Mangey had been a real craftsman.

Half a minute to secure the locks and he was back on the street, the day close and sticky around him.

'None of the children have seen him,' Sally said as they walked. Jane had stopped to tell the beggars about Dodson and ask if they'd seen John.

'No, and I'd keep my distance if I did,' Manchester Minnie

said. 'He's got death written on his face, that one has. Charlie
Dodson has too big a heart on him.'
    The others muttered agreement.
    'He could be dead,' the girl continued.
    'He's not.' She was certain. He was out there somewhere.
    'I need to make him pay for Harold.' Sally didn't say more
than that; revenge was written in her heart.

Foley stood back and stared as Simon placed the cups on the
table, wonder and joy spreading across his face.
    'How did you find them, Mr Westow?' Sir Robert picked one
up and caressed the surface. He examined each of them in turn
until he was satisfied, nodding to himself as he reverently put
them back down.
    'I was lucky.' No need to say more than that. The question
had been politeness; the man didn't want to know the full story.
He had what was taken from him, and didn't care about the
details.
    'I'm more grateful than you can imagine. I was beginning to
give up hope. They're a part of my family's history. That's very
important to me.'
    Just as it was to William Mark, he thought, but kept quiet.
    'They're back with you now.'
    'What about Will Mark? What's happened to him? He killed
people for these.'
    'He'll face justice.'
    Foley breathed slowly, smiling, satisfied. 'Can you wait here
for a minute?'
    'Of course.'
    He returned, waving a piece of paper. 'A draft on my bank.
A little more than we discussed. You've earned it. George Mudie
did well when he recommended you.'
    'Thank you.' He glanced at the amount; a very handsome
figure indeed, but the job had taken plenty of strange turns along
the way. A handshake and he was gone. One more person still
to see.

'You should have told me as soon as you knew where he was,'
the constable shouted.

'You'll find him there now. I doubt he's realized yet that the cups have gone.'

'Let's hope you're right. If he's flown . . .'

'Mark's not going to leave Leeds,' Simon told him. 'Where else does he have to go?'

'I'll send the inspector over there with some men.' He cocked his head. 'I heard some interesting gossip. It seems there was an assembly last night and someone surprising turned up.'

Simon laughed. 'Besides me, you mean?'

'I was told you were dressed in your finery. So was Matthew Hutton. Didn't you say he'd left Leeds?'

'He had.'

'Something must have pulled him back. I don't suppose you saw him?'

'Very briefly.' That much was true. 'I don't think he'll be troubling us again.'

Porter's eyes widened. He waited, but Simon said nothing more.

'We'll take care of Mark. I'll be needing your testimony at the trial.'

'Gladly.' William Mark had killed with a cold heart; he deserved to hang.

'I trust Sir Robert is pleased.'

Simon smiled as he thought of the bank draft in his pocket. 'Very.'

'That should see us set for a while.' Rosie smoothed out the draft on the table.

'We have to pay Sally and Jane.'

'It's still a very fair sum. Did you have any problems getting the cups?'

'No. He's going to have a surprise when he finds the law waiting for him.'

She shrugged. 'He brought it on his own head.'

Maybe the young man believed his father would take care of the problem, that he'd draw back from disowning him when the situation was desperate. It wouldn't happen. William Mark was on his own.

'We're done with it,' she said.

'Yes.' All the history and scandal. The secrets of the Mangey family dragged out into the daylight.

Finished.

Now he could begin to exorcize his own fears and return to the person he'd been before all this. He was beginning to forget who that man had been.

TWENTY-THREE

Dodson's eyes had a wide spark of life today, Jane decided. Although he still wore all his cuts and bruises, they were healing. The back of his head was tender, but he was definitely recovering. Mrs Shields was convinced he'd suffer no lasting damage.

He was still reading, too. No more than a few pages at a time, but he seemed to enjoy the book. For now, he remained an invalid, confined to his bed; he still often closed his eyes and slept during the day as well as all through the night.

'He's building his strength,' Mrs Shields said. 'I told you, child, sleep is the very best medicine, it gives the body time to take care of itself.' She gave one of her soft smiles. 'It probably won't be too long before he'll be wanting to leave.'

Very likely, although he'd need a new wooden leg and crutch first. Who would make those?

She talked to him for an hour. His mind was growing keener, many of the clouds parting. He could remember most of his old life, the other beggars, the people who he used to see. Kate the pie-seller, Davy Cassidy the fiddler, many of the others. Even one or two flashes of John, but he appeared more as a shadow than a person. Dodson couldn't recall anything of what had happened to him, how he'd ended up with the pain.

'Have you really kept paying for my room?' he asked.

'Yes.'

He bit his lip. 'You know I won't ever be able to pay you back. All I can do is thank you.'

'There's no need. Honestly.' She squeezed his hand. He had some strength in his grip now. Soon he'd be well again.

She left the house during the long evening, work boots laced tight, a light shawl around her shoulders. The knife lay sharp in her pocket.

Sally was waiting by the market cross. As soon as she saw

Jane, the girl shook her head. Nobody had spotted John during the day.

Maybe he'd gone off and quietly died. Jane knew she'd hurt him badly; he'd left plenty of blood on the floorboards when he ran. But in her heart, she couldn't believe that; men like him didn't die so readily. If he had, the animals and the birds would have found his corpse and somebody would have noticed.

'He's still alive,' Sally said with absolute certainty.

Jane nodded. He was. They would find him.

'Harold said he was going to marry me.'

'I remember.'

'He's never going to have the chance to marry anyone.' She drew in a breath. Jane watched the girl's face harden. Like stone.

'He's mine,' she said. 'Dodson's still alive. Harold's in the ground.'

'Yours,' Jane agreed. 'As soon as when we find him.'

'We will.' Her eyes were flat. Empty. Jane knew that Sally wasn't letting herself feel anything at all. Pushing it all down. For now.

The boys had been reading to him in their bedroom. Taking it in turns to stand, a paragraph each from the book the tutor had left with them. They were both comfortable with the words, no hesitation as they spoke.

Watching them, he was suddenly surprised to realize that they were growing into big, brawny lads, as if it had happened over-night. Soon enough the years would pass and they'd be men. A thought to make him feel old.

He wanted to stay alive to watch them as they came into their manhood, to enjoy the grandchildren they'd give him and Rosie.

Simon heard the knocking on the door. As he stood up, his wife called his name, an urgent edge in her voice.

Constable Porter was standing in the kitchen, kneading his hat between his hands.

'Will Mark,' he said. 'He's gone.'

'But—'

'My men have been there three times looking for him. I went inside, just a few minutes ago. It looks like he's taken whatever he can carry.'

For a moment, he couldn't believe it. He'd left everything the way he'd found it.

'The bed?'

'The mattress was turned over.'

Mark must have returned and sensed something was wrong. Maybe some warning sign that Simon had missed. He thought he'd been careful, but . . . damn it all to hell. The man must have been more cautious than he'd imagined. The first thing he'd have done was look to make sure the cups were still there. Once he realized they were gone, he'd have panicked.

'You should have told me about him sooner.' Porter kept his voice under control, but his face was full of anger. 'Now he's run, and we need to find him. He's going to be dangerous.' He stared. 'Do you have any idea where he is?'

'He has a friend called Jonas Catesby. He's—'

'I know Catesby.'

'He's the one who told me where Mark would be.'

'Right, let's see what other ideas he has. Coming, Westow?'

Simon looked at Rosie. He must have given himself away somehow. How else could Mark have known someone had been in his rooms? Porter was right; he should have told him where the man was living sooner.

'Yes,' he said.

But Catesby knew nothing more. All he could offer were the names of a few friends who'd always had a shine for Will Mark, and the thought he might have tried to go back to his father. He was telling the truth; the brooding presence of the constable seemed to terrify him.

Back on Boar Lane, Porter sighed. 'Now I have to keep looking for the bastard.' He glowered. 'I'll expect your help, Westow.'

'You'll have it.' He owed the constable that much.

Sir Robert Foley had the cups on display in his library.

'What do you think?' he asked. 'Where they belong, isn't it?'

'Hide them away,' Simon told him.

'What?' he asked in surprise. 'I've only just got them back.'

'Put them somewhere secure if you want to keep them. Just for now.'

'But—'

'Mark is still free. He's killed three people for those cups, Sir Robert.'

Foley took a sharp breath. 'I see. Then I suppose I must. How long before you catch him?'

'With luck, no more than a day. The watch is after him, I'll be looking, too.'

Mark wouldn't be used to this desperate kind of life, not sure where to turn. He was carrying his possessions. That would hinder him.

'Without luck?'

'I don't know. But be careful. Make sure all the doors and windows are locked.'

'I will.' A fond glance at the cups. 'Thank you for coming to tell me.'

Simon woke to rain on Monday morning. He shrugged into his coat before he left the house. Only three or four of the regular faces sheltering under the awning of the coffee cart on Briggate. For a change, the customers complained about the dampness rather than the heat. But they were men who were only happy when they could moan about something.

He smiled and nodded here and there, but he wasn't really listening to them. His eyes studied the people scurrying along Briggate. Will Mark was somewhere. He had to know that people were searching for him. Every step he took, he was going to be glancing over his shoulder.

No sign of him, but that would have been too much luck. Simon placed the tin mug on the trestle and walked to the far side of the Head Row. George Mudie was already working in the print shop.

'I heard you found the cups.'

Simon laughed. 'News travels fast.'

'Sir Robert sent me a note. Thanked me for recommending you.'

'He might not be so happy now.'

'Why, what have you done, Simon?'

He listened closely to the tale, nodding and frowning.

'You did your job,' Mudie said. 'Why does it matter now? This isn't your battle.'

Yet it felt as if it was. He should have told the constable sooner. Now the duty to right that wrong tugged at him. He had to see it through until Mark was standing trial for the murders.

'I've nothing else to do.' He tried to make the words sound light, but they didn't fool him; Mudie hardly looked convinced.

'Then I wish you success of the chase.'

Sally and Jane were waiting in the kitchen. Rosie finished feeding the boys and shepherded them through to wait for the tutor.

'Porter is hunting Will Mark, but we need to help.'

Jane nodded, grim-faced. He felt as if he could see into her thoughts. The man had killed Armistead and she could never forget that.

'He's carrying what he owns, and it's probably precious little by now. I've asked at the inns and nobody remembers him boarding a coach. I'd say he's still in town.' Sally opened her mouth, but he raised his hand. 'We had some names, people he knows, but the watch checked. He's not with any of them.'

'Has Porter sent a message to Mark's father?' Rosie asked. 'If he's desperate, he might try going home.'

'Someone from the watch is going up there today. But I think the father would just turn Will away.'

It was hard to believe any parent would do that. A brutal judgement. But Simon had spoken to the man and heard the way he felt. The young man would never be welcome there again.

'Does he have money?' Sally asked.

'I don't know,' he answered. 'A little, maybe.'

'He could have found a space in a rooming house.'

How many of those in Leeds? Dozens; it was something else for the constable's men.

'He'll go for the cups.' Jane lifted her head.

Simon nodded. 'I've warned Foley to hide them.' He turned to Rosie. 'Can you plant the word with some of the women?'

'They'll love some fresh gossip. It'll be all over town before you know it.' She glanced down at her clothes, the old dress and apron. 'I'll need to change first.' A look out at the rain. 'A good cloak, too.'

As she bustled up the stairs, he gazed at Sally and Jane.

'Have you found John yet?'

'No,' Sally answered. A single, angry word was enough.
He saw the determination that filled her eyes and remembered
the body of the boy who'd been buried. Murdered and mutilated;
she'd counted out the coins for his funeral. Simon didn't need
to ask what would happen when they found the man. He knew
Jane had her reasons to kill him, too – that old army beggar
recovering with her and Mrs Shields.
'Time to start looking,' he told them.

Jane stood at the bottom of Briggate, feeling the raindrops on
her face, cool and refreshing. Should she stay in town or across
the river? She felt as if she'd already searched everywhere, and
now they were back to the beginning, hunting two men again.
She walked over the bridge and followed the road towards
Holbeck. Foley lived there, in one of the large houses that looked
over the river.
    Mark would come here. She was completely certain of it. He'd
already killed three times for the cups that Mangey made. He
knew people were searching for him. The man had nothing to
lose.
    She walked with the shawl over her hair, just another woman
moving unnoticed in the warm weather. She covered a mile, then
returned. She didn't spot anyone who might be Mark, felt no
sense of someone waiting. But he'd come, he'd come. Jane found
a sheltered spot that let her see along the road and settled there
to wait.
    Three hours and nothing. The rain eased to a misting drizzle.
Carts and carriages rolled along Water Lane, men passed on
horses. She stretched and slowly walked back into town. The
waiting, the looking, they'd felt as natural as breathing. Maybe
she wasn't meant to leave this part of her life behind. However
much she tried to break away, it would keep tugging her back.
    Sally was talking to Kate the pie-seller. Jane paid her as Kate
selected the warmest pie on her tray. Twenty yards away, Davy
Cassidy was drawing a small crowd.
    'Fresh baked an hour ago. Should still be hot inside. I keep
telling you, you need the meat on your bones.'
    They ate as they ambled along Call Lane, past the clamour of
the warehouses and beyond Fearn's Island before returning.

They'd just reached Leeds lock, where the canal began, when a young girl dashed up to them.

'They think they've found John,' she said between gasps.

They rushed to follow her, darting through the streets back into Leeds. Past Quarry Hill, then out along the York road.

A group of children was waiting, gathered behind a tall boy who looked to be twelve or so. He had a look in his eye that Jane had often seen before. Full of knowing and pain and the grit of survival.

'Where is he?' Sally asked. She kept her voice low, staring into the wood by the side of the road.

'We found a fire that was still warm and the remains of an animal.'

'How far?'

He glanced around at the others. 'Two hundred yards.' He thought. 'A little more.'

'No sign of John?'

The children all shook their heads.

Jane drew her knife. Sally was already holding her blade. A nod and they began to walk into the undergrowth. She moved to the right, the girl went left. The bruise on her head throbbed.

Jane stood, took a breath as she looked around, but had no sense of him. One more step, two, barely making a sound as she walked. A tangle of thorny bushes, heavy with leaves and flowers. He could be anywhere in here.

Her heartbeat skittered, skin prickling as she picked her way through the long grass. Her fingers tightened around the hilt of the knife.

Jane caught a flash of something from the corner of her eye. She pivoted, ready for an attack, and stopped. Some small animal, scurrying away from her. She gasped, then waited a long moment as her breathing steadied. Her fingers touched the gold ring Mrs Shields had given her. Luck.

Three more paces. A small clearing. But no sign anyone had been here. Slowly, steadily, she kept going. He could be watching, picking his moment to attack.

A cry, Sally's voice. Jane didn't hesitate, plunging towards it, hardly feeling the brambles scratching her cheeks, the pull of branches against her dress.

A second cry, louder than the last, and she pushed harder.

Sally was lying on the ground. She had blood on her face and arms, struggling to breathe, hands pressed against her belly.

No John. Trampled grass that led deeper into the woods. Follow, or look after the girl?

Sally.

She knelt, fingers checking the girl's body. Cuts, nothing deep, nothing dangerous. Gently, Jane placed her arms around her, easing Sally to her feet. Watching, careful. He could return.

A full half minute passed before Sally was able to speak, still bent over and rubbing her stomach.

'I don't know where he came from. I found where he'd been sleeping and I could see the tracks where he'd gone. I was following them and then he was right there. Before I could do anything, he punched me.' Another gentle rub. 'It did something. I felt like I could hardly move. Then he started trying to cut me.'

'You screamed.'

'I . . .' she began, stopped and drew in air, standing straight and letting the colour come back to her face. She wiped her cheeks, smearing the blood. 'I don't remember. I was trying to fight him off.'

'Is the pain easing up now?'

A shallow nod as Sally took another breath and tried to swallow. Her eyes were bright, at the edge of tears.

'He was right in front of me,' she said. 'Then he heard you coming and . . .'

'Can you walk?'

The girl tried a few steps. 'Yes.' She looked at her hands, the bloodstains smeared across them. 'I need to wash it all off.'

'There's a cut on your shoulder. Mrs Shields will have something—'

'I don't want to put her to any trouble.'

'You won't.' She understood the feeling. She'd known it herself. Shame. John had beaten her. Sally would want to hide, to find somewhere dark until she felt strong again. But Jane knew the girl couldn't do that. The children would be waiting, anxious. They'd have heard the screams.

Who was John, she wondered. How could they kill a man who could disappear like that and then seem to arrive from nowhere?

Was he a devil? No, that was impossible, wasn't it? As they walked, she glanced at Sally. The girl's expression was set and determined. She knew she'd have to face him again and fight until one of them was dead.

The children crowded around her. She managed a wan smile, telling them she was fine. Wearing a mask. At a horse trough she washed the blood from her face and hands, sluicing the cold water over her hair.

Mrs Shields put ointment on the girl's shoulder and bound it with a clean cloth.

'No need to worry. It will heal without a problem,' she said, and handed her a mug. 'Drink this.'

She sniffed the liquid. 'What is it?' she asked, looking doubtful.

'Something to help you.' She nodded at the wound. 'It will ease the feeling when that begins to sting.'

Sally raised the cup and swallowed it in one.

Jane started to walk with her, but she shook her head.

'It's only a short distance home.'

Of course. She wanted to be alone. To think. The girl was strong. She wouldn't punish herself for failing, the way Jane used to do.

No sense in returning to where it had happened. John would be far away by now. If he'd left any clues, she didn't have the skill to read them.

TWENTY-FOUR

S ometimes she imagined Sally as a mirror of herself when she was young. The same anger, the silences. But it was only partly true. The girl had happily become part of Simon's family. She seemed to like being surrounded by people and noise. She took her responsibilities seriously, too, giving time and money to all those homeless children. Her good works. There would never be a shortage of the young needing help.

After the girl had gone, Jane read to Dodson, watching the pleasure on his face as he became a part of the story. Slowly, his eyes closed, and his breathing changed until she was certain he'd fallen asleep.

She set the book aside and went to sit outside in the late warmth with Mrs Shields.

'His recovery is very steady,' the woman said. 'If he had a new wooden leg, I think he might be ready to walk.'

'I'll find someone tomorrow,' Jane promised. 'A crutch, too.'

Mrs Shields turned to stare into her eyes. 'You know, child, I worry about you.'

'Why?' she asked. But she knew the reason: working with Simon, back to being a thief-taker after months without any of it.

'That bruise on your face is reason enough, child,' Mrs Shields said, reaching out and touching it with light fingertips. 'I'm scared that one day it will be so much more than that. You know how dangerous your job is.'

'The man who killed Mr Armistead is still free. So is the one who did all that to Dodson.' She paused for a moment. 'He did much worse to a boy.'

'You take the world on your shoulders, child.'

It had never seemed that way. She was only doing what she believed to be right.

'I'll be fine.'

'I hope so. I really do.'

They sat in silence, letting dusk surround them. Mrs Shields started to rise. Jane helped her inside the house and waited until she was settled, the small lantern glowing at her bedside.

Time to work once again.

'The women were shocked when I told them about Will Mark,' Rosie said. 'Half of them have children who know him.' She smiled. 'It's going to be all over town by now. If he hoped someone might take him in, he's going to find every door is closed.'

'Good,' Simon told her.

Sally was quiet, cradling her arm with the wounded shoulder. When he asked what had happened, she gave a curt account. Furious at herself, he decided. Jane sat beside her, staring ahead, saying nothing.

'Porter's men are asking at the hotels and the rooming houses,' he continued. 'If he's gone there, they'll find him. He might have rented a room, but he can't have much money.'

'The cups,' Jane said, and Simon nodded.

'That's where it began. Foley said he'll keep them somewhere safe. You've watched his house, so have I.'

'I'll go there again tonight,' she said.

'Remember, he's killed three people,' Simon told her.

'I haven't forgotten.'

The evening stayed warm. Jane let the hours drift by, thinking about Mrs Shields's words. Everything she'd said was true. Jane had slid back into a world where one day she might not go home again. There had been a time when that didn't matter. Now the old woman had become her family. So much to lose.

Once all this was done, when Mark was caught and John dead . . .

It was easy to say. But could she really walk away from it a second time? Or was it in her blood?

Simon visited the dramshops and the brothels, asking after Will Mark everywhere he went. Nobody had seen him since Saturday. Not long after the church bell rang eleven, he'd had enough.

A night of frustration, of creeping fear that surrounded him every moment he was on the street. He walked with one hand resting on the knife in his belt, constantly aware of the people around him.

The noise of Leeds grew muted as he reached Swinegate. He listened closely. A prickle up his spine. There was someone . . . Quietly, he eased the blade from its sheath. Ready. He couldn't let himself hesitate or think. Simply act.

Close to his own door he could still sense it. Key in his hand. In the lock. Cocking his head, glancing around. Trying to swallow when his mouth was dry. Gripping the knife tight. Then Simon was inside, hurriedly pushing the door closed before anyone could rush it. Turning the key then exhaling.

He stood, his heart beating too fast, standing as it began to slow. Looking down, he saw the knife and slid it away. No need for it.

Nobody had been following him. No one waiting to attack. It had all been in his mind. Nothing more than his own terror, snapping around his heels.

He sat in the kitchen. No need for a light. Nothing more than the darkness around him. A bottle of brandy close by, and he was tempted. One drink to soothe himself. But he'd done that the other night. It could become a very dangerous habit.

His own senses had betrayed him.

He raised his right hand. Spreading the fingers. The room was black, he couldn't see them, but they were steady. Not a single shake. He kept watching until he started to believe he could make out the shape of his hand. Curled the fingers into a fist and let it softly fall to the table.

What was he going to do?

In the early morning light Simon felt no danger. He'd managed to sleep once the fear had drained from his body, but he didn't feel rested. He rarely did these days.

Plenty of people at the coffee cart, half of them travellers who'd arrived on the coaches. Two of them had come from Hull, a rumpled businessman with an angry scowl and a pinch-cheeked clergyman.

They were talking about a body that had been found near the docks, just a few hours before they left.

'I heard he was richly dressed,' the businessman said. 'Someone said he was a criminal who'd betrayed his friends.'

'Whoever he might have been, the poor soul's at his judgement now.'

Simon wondered what the Almighty would make of the captain. Hutton or Tyler, or whatever he tried to call himself up there. At least now he knew how that story had ended.

At the courthouse, Porter shook his head.

'This Mark's a slippery bastard, I'll tell you that for nothing, Westow. All the men are keeping their eyes open. He's definitely not in a hotel and they've had no luck at the rooming houses. What do you think? Is he still here?'

'Yes.' He was sure of it, as certain as he could be about anything at the moment. For just a second, he felt last night's terror grip his chest, then it vanished again.

'Then we'll keep looking.'

He told the constable what Rosie had done, cutting Mark off from all the good families in town. The man gave an admiring nod, then another when Simon recounted what he'd heard about Hutton a few minutes earlier.

'I don't suppose you'd know more about that, would you, Westow?'

'Not a thing.' There was a degree of truth in his words.

A wheelwright. Jane woke with the idea in her head. Someone like that should be able to make a wooden leg for Dodson. He was missing the calf and the foot, everything from about an inch below the knee. Looking after him, she'd often cleaned the nub, the skin callused, as hard and thick as leather. She'd measured the distance on his other leg and cut a piece of string to the length.

The workshop she remembered was in Rockley Hall Yard, just off the Head Row, above Vicar Lane. Where John had committed his first murder in the town. The first they knew about, at least. Even on a hot, bright morning, the place still seemed dark, the ground damp and heavy, with the smell of a cesspit somewhere close.

'I've made them before,' the master said. 'It's not that different from turning a wheel spoke. Always managed a good job, if I say so myself.' He stared at her, running his tongue around the inside of his mouth. 'Who's it for?'

'Dodson. The beggar.'

'Oh, aye, I know who you mean. The soldier. Not seen him lately. Suppose that's why.'

'He was hurt,' Jane said. 'We've been looking after him. But his leg has gone.'

'Pity, that. It was a very fair piece of carving.'

'Can you do it?'

'It'll be plain,' he said as he pulled the string between his hands. 'I'll use good oak, so it'll be sturdy.' He was thinking, making the plans in his head. 'Straps to go over his shoulders that he can adjust.'

'When can you have it ready?' she asked.

'Tomorrow morning,' the wheelwright said after a few seconds of calculation. 'We're slack right now. I always liked Dodson, he fought for his country. I'll do the work myself.'

'What about a crutch? Can you make one of those?'

He shook his head. 'You want the chemist for that, miss.'

Sally found her as she made her way home. She sensed the girl before she saw her, melting out of a crowd near the crest of the Head Row. The girl's face was pale, dark shadows of sleeplessness under her eyes. She looked as if her soul was haunted, her body tight and huddled, holding her left arm pressed against her body.

'Do you want Mrs Shields? Some more of the ointment? A draught so you can sleep?'

Sally shook her head. 'Can we practise?'

Jane studied her face. As hard as iron. 'Are you sure? Why didn't you ask Simon?'

'He's off chasing Will Mark.' She raised her eyes. 'You're the one who understands.'

Sally needed to see off her devils; that was the only way she'd be able to rest.

No talking on their way to the moor. The girl kept the shadows of her thoughts pulled tight around herself until they reached the clearing.

'Ready?'

Sally threw herself into fighting, releasing all the frustration and shame and bitterness that was consuming her as Jane defended herself. Parries, blocks. For a tiny moment the pall over Leeds parted and sunlight glimmered on the blades, gone again as soon as it had appeared.

Five minutes and she was sweating hard. She had to move swiftly to counter every attack. Sally held nothing back. But it was what she needed. To force everything out until she was drained.

Finally, she stopped. Jane kept a wary distance, ready in case she started once more. But Sally put the knife in her pocket. She took a breath, looking empty but satisfied.

Jane nodded at the wounded shoulder. 'You're still fast.'

'Next time . . .'

'You'll kill him.'

She nodded. 'Soon.'

Mrs Shields examined the wound and rubbed in more salve. She looked deep into Sally's eyes, then took some herbs from a shelf in the kitchen and mixed up a drink.

'It tastes . . . I don't know. The way spring used to be when I was little.'

The old woman smiled. 'Drink it all down, then go home and rest. You'll feel better when you wake.'

Simon had nowhere else to look. He started back to the old places; maybe Mark has returned. But all he found were blank stares and men shaking their heads when he asked. None of it was bringing him any closer to the man.

'Nothing from the rooming houses?' he asked Porter.

'Not a single one of them will admit he's been there. But half of them would lie to the law just out of principle, so it doesn't mean a damn thing. My men are keeping their eyes open. But I've not heard any word.' He cocked his head. 'What about you?'

'I'm beginning to think I might be wrong.'

'Go on,' the constable said with interest.

'He's gone. He must have. One of us would have been able to find him otherwise. Leeds isn't *that* big.'

Porter snorted. 'You know as well as I do that this place can be large enough when you're hunting someone.'

'He's not a man who's a thief by trade.'

'You know better than that, Westow. Mark is bloody desperate.

He is a thief. He took those cups and arranged it carefully. He's murdered three men. You said his own father disowned him.'
'He did.'
'He has bad blood.'
Maybe that was the simple truth of it. Simon was still turning the thought over in his mind as he strode along Briggate, half-hearing some lilting fiddle music away in the distance. He paused for a second at the place where the Moot Hall and Middle Row had stood. Each day it became harder to believe they'd ever been there.

Arthur Mangey's hidden workshop. Where the story began. Less than three weeks since Armistead slipped through the hole in the wall. What had Mangey been like, he wondered? What kind of man had he been? Jane didn't believe he'd been guilty of the coin clipping, but she was generations too late to know the truth.

William Mark had grown up with the story. Taken it in from his grandmother's talk. It had infected him. Corrupted him. Turned his blood bad, exactly the way Porter said.

A shout from the market cross drew his attention. A man, ranting and yelling, drawing a crowd. Simon came closer. It was nobody he'd ever seen, his voice as raw and dry as a rasp as he harangued. Thin-faced and wild-eyed, with days of stubble on his cheeks. Broken teeth and dirty clothes. Someone with no home anywhere in the kingdom, looking like it was too long since he'd slept in a bed. The type of man who ate rage because he couldn't afford food. Carrying all the madness of God in his eyes.

The man gazed around the crowd and his eyes seemed to pick out Simon as he raised a bony hand and pointed.

'You. You have the fear inside you. I can see it. You can feel it clawing at you from the inside. You've tried to run from your sins, but they've caught up with you now.'

People turned their heads to stare. Simon smiled, as if it was nothing, but he swallowed, wondering if he was that open. It seemed as if this man could see deep into him.

Two men from the watch arrived. One urged the people to disperse. The ranter bellowed at their backs, but his words slipped into gibberish as his audience started to leave. Simon remained, watching as Porter's men approached the speaker, one on either side, ready to take his arms and escort him away. They'd had plenty of practice; Leeds was never short of folk who imagined they were filled with the spirit.

He caught a sudden movement, then one of the watch crumpled with a grunt, hands clutching his chest as a red pool spread on his clothes. The other backed off, hands fumbling as he pulled out his cudgel, eyes shifting between his friend and the preacher.

Women were screaming. A rush of panic sent people haring down the street.

Simon didn't move.

The ranter was holding a long knife, its blade shiny with blood.

'You. Your fear fills the air. You have the weight of the dying on you.'

The watchman was dragging his wounded comrade away. Everyone had scattered to a safe distance. Women were screaming, men shouting.

Only Simon stood his ground. The fear was there, just as the man said, beginning to tighten its grip on him.

'Do I?' he called.

'You know the truth.' He lifted his head to the sky. 'God sees it all.'

It only ever took a moment for life to turn to blood. He said nothing, studying the man at the market cross. A face was filled with belief. No doubts of any kind. That was what made him dangerous.

Simon felt his hand beginning to shake and clenched his fist. He wanted to turn and run, but he didn't move. Someone had to keep the man here and stop him hurting anyone else.

'Killing you would be the Lord's work. Purge your sins from you.'

His twisted God. Not the one from the Bible.

The man stood and stared with his dark, empty eyes. Simon kept his hand close to the knife in his belt, feeling the sun warm on his neck.

His terror was digging deep. But he daren't let it win. He had to stay and see this through. Just be ready . . .

He heard the sound long before he could see them. Men running up Briggate. All the traffic had stopped, people keeping a safe distance from the danger. Porter burst through, the inspector with him, two others behind.

'You know him?' he asked as he tried to catch his breath.

'Never seen him before. He attacked one of your men for no—'

'Killed him.'

'He's going to hang,' the inspector said.

Four of them with someone to avenge. The man would be lucky to make it to a courtroom.

'He's yours.'

Simon turned away. A single pace and he felt the movement, caught a sense of it at the corner of his eye. He whirled around, crouching, knife in his hand.

The man lay on the ground, the last ebb of life leaving his eyes.

'He started to come for you,' Porter said. The inspector was wiping his knife on the dead man's coat, the others ready to take the corpse away.

A nod, a final glance at the face. Maybe he had some peace now.

He drifted down Briggate. People kept their distance, as if he carried a disease they might catch.

At home, the boys were with their tutor, Rosie out. He sat in the kitchen, trying to find any grain of sense in what has just happened. There were always madmen and their words. They walked through a different world and saw it all through their strange visions. Simon *knew* it had been sheer chance that the man's gaze had rested on him. It could have been anyone in that crowd. Why didn't it feel that way?

Maybe there was something in him that the insane could see. All that death and guilt. All that fear.

He held out his arm. Absolutely steady. The tremors had passed. But they continued inside. Simon knew he'd be seeing the man for many nights to come.

Not the first one like that he'd seen in Leeds. Wouldn't be the last, the way the population was growing. This was a town to steal everything from people, even their minds.

He'd been sitting for ten minutes, going over everything the man had said, trying to pick the truth from the wildness, when

Rosie hurried in. She stopped as she saw him, dropping her basket on to the table.

'They were saying—'

'They were wrong.' He stood, raising his arms. 'See? Not a scratch.'

He tried to smile, but he knew she saw the truth on his face. Simon put his arms around her, felt her fingers clutching hard at him.

'I was scared. People said you'd been killed.'

He drew her head back, hands on either side of her face. 'Maybe some of them wished it was true.'

'Simon . . .' Her fingers dug into his back and he could see the tracks where tears had fallen down her cheeks.

By tomorrow there would be all manner of tales around town. They'd vanish as soon as people saw him.

Another lost soul for a pauper's grave.

Meanwhile, Will Mark was still out there, alive and free.

TWENTY-FIVE

J ane knew that people were staring as she walked along the Head Row, carrying the crutch and the wooden leg. She made a curious sight. But she barely paid attention, thinking of the joy that would spread over Dodson's face when he saw them.

Simon's name had been all over town the night before. One man said he'd been wounded, gushing blood as he staggered away. Someone else was insisting they'd seen his body on the ground. Another voice overrode them both, telling them he'd killed the false preacher. Heart in her mouth, she ran to his house, relieved when she found him in the kitchen.

No injuries. He told her what had happened, fingers fidgeting on the table.

'Why did he say all that?' she asked.

'I don't know. I've never seen him before.' He sighed. 'It doesn't matter. It's done now. He's dead.'

The words slipped out easily enough, she thought, but it had shaken him. In his eyes she saw he was still reliving it. Something had changed in him these last few weeks. But he was alive, unhurt; that was what was important. Ready to keep looking for Will Mark.

Dodson stared in disbelief. Mrs Shields used folded cloths to pad the stump, and with practised hands he pulled on the leg. He tied the straps over his shoulders and gathered the crutch under his arm before taking a tentative step, then looked at Jane.

'I don't . . .'

She shook her head. She didn't want to hear about debt or gratitude. For a few seconds she thought he'd try to argue; instead, he nodded and gave a smile before testing the leg and crutch again.

Down on Park Row, she spotted Simon's back as he disappeared into the courthouse. On the other side of the road, Sally drifted behind him.

'Does he know you're here?'

'I don't think so.' She didn't look as pained today, her face more open. She wasn't pulling her wounded arm so tight against her body. 'After yesterday . . .'

'We need to find John.'

'Where?' Sally asked and the fire returned to her eyes. 'He's vanished. He has to be dead. Either that or he's run off.'

No. He couldn't have cheated them of their revenge that way.

'If he's dead we'll have to find his bones.'

'Him and Mark,' the girl said. She turned her head towards the courthouse. 'Simon will be out of there soon.'

Jane went down to Kirkgate, to Dodson's room. Nobody had been inside since her last visit, a layer of dust over everything.

On the street she blinked in the light, the gritty air irritating her eyes. A flash of something dark beyond the Parish Church, moving towards Timble Bridge. Only for a second. She couldn't be certain what she'd seen. But it was enough to make her run.

The nails on her boot soles sent up sparks. People turned as she passed. On the far side of Sheepscar Beck she paused, glancing around as she tried to work out where the figure had gone. Too many little folds and courts where someone could hide. Jane knew them all, what lay inside each of them. She stood, breathing heavily, trying to feel him. John. She felt certain. He was close. Very close.

A pair of ragged boys were playing, tossing stones at a wall.

'Go and find Sally,' she told them. 'Tell her . . .' Something simple, fast. 'Tell her Jane's seen him. Bring her over here.' A ha'penny each and she watched them dash away, racing each other across the bridge.

'No word of Mark yet?' Simon asked.

Constable Porter shrugged. 'No shortage of hints. We've had plenty of those. It's never him, though.' He gave a snort of disgust as he threw the nib down on the desk, splattering ink across a piece of paper. 'It's never bloody him.'

'The man by the market cross.'

'What about him?' He wasn't in a patient mood. 'The bastard killed one of my men.'

'Did you find out who he was?'

'No. I don't really care. The only thing on him was a penny at the bottom of his pocket.' He narrowed his eyes. 'Why does it matter? You should be glad he's dead. He was coming for you.'

'I know.' He felt a small shiver inside, but it passed almost before he realized it.

'We'd have ended up hanging him, anyway. It was quicker that way.' He let the thought fade. 'Enough of that. You and me, we're both hunting Will Mark.'

'And we're both getting nowhere.'

'He's still here, Westow.' He sounded plaintive as his eyes moved to the window. 'He has to be, doesn't he?'

Jane paced along the cobbles. Up and back. Too many places he could have gone. But John was *here*; they had somewhere to begin.

Almost half an hour passed before Sally arrived, a straggle of children behind her. When Jane gave her a doubtful look, the girl smiled.

'More of us to search for him. Unless you know where he's gone.'

'I don't.'

Sally gazed at the streets and ginnels leading away up the hill. 'Then we need them to help.'

'He's dangerous.'

'They know that. They all remember Harold.'

The children moved off in pairs. Jane and Sally stayed on opposite sides of the street, pausing to study each of the old folds and yards. A slow business, but they were coming closer. A tingle on her skin, goose pimples rising on her arms, and she turned the gold ring on her finger.

Jane looked across at Sally; the girl nodded. She felt it, too.

The children came running back. More instructions and they were flying away again, as if this was a game to enjoy.

Another quarter of an hour. Jane wondered if he'd managed to escape them again. The church bell rang, followed by the piercing of child's scream. She froze, then moved her head, trying to place it.

Sally started to run. She followed, knife in her hand, feeling the heavy pounding of her heart. The children were dashing toward them, their faces contorted with panic, voices stolen by terror.

They turned to the right, boots crunching in dirt. A hundred yards away, a factory chimney threw out dark smoke that stung her throat as she breathed.

Sally stopped in front of a broken house. The windows had all gone, slates from the roof scattered and smashed on the ground. Above them, framed in a sagging opening, John held a young boy by his hair, a knife close against his throat.

A trickle of blood seeped down the boy's pale neck. Tears ran down his cheeks and he tried to hold himself very still.

Nobody spoke. Jane felt as if the world was holding its breath as she watched. John stayed in the shadows behind the boy; she could only see the outline of his head. So close. She began to edge away, a few inches at a time. There had to be a back door to the building.

A sudden movement stopped her. John lifted the boy. A scream tore open the sky. Then he threw the child down at them.

The boy landed with a soft thump that exploded the breath from him. Jane heard a bone snap – in his arms, his legs, she didn't know – and hurried towards him.

A glance up, but John had vanished.

Sally was kneeling by the boy, nodding as she felt the pulse in his neck. She turned his head. His eyes were open, the cut on his neck wasn't spurting blood.

Jane squatted and started to feel the boy's limbs.

'Go,' she shouted to Sally. 'He can't have gone far.'

Just for a second, the girl was torn between caring and revenge.

'I'll look after him,' Jane told her.

One final glance and Sally ran off.

'You.' She pointed at the tallest boy, then the one next to him. 'Go and find two men. Tell them to bring a door, something to carry him. He—'

'Ralph,' someone said.

'Ralph needs a bone setter.' Her eyes picked out a girl. 'Find a chemist. He'll be able to tell you where to find one. If anyone ask questions, tell them I'll pay. Hurry.'

The boy's left arm was broken. His hand was starting to swell. He hadn't passed out, but his face was pale with shock.

Gently, she slapped his cheeks until he was looking at
her.

'We're going to take care of you, Ralph.' She smiled at him.
He looked so young, so helpless. 'You're going to be fine. He
must have terrified you.'

A slow, tentative nod, then he turned his head slightly. Two
workmen arrived, plaster caked all over their jackets and trousers.
One of them held a battered door.

The boy looked happier with his arm set tight and resting in a
sling. His eyes were alert, the colour had come back into his
face. Jane had made sure he had some food in his belly, a drink,
and he could walk straight. She placed three shillings in the palm
of his good hand and closed his fingers around them. Enough
for food and clothes to cover his bare feet and legs, she told him,
and gave orders to the others to watch out for him.

Sally hadn't returned.

Something had happened.

Simon needed some piece of luck, some little spark of fortune
that would open the way to Mark. The man had found some
corner. But someone had to know where he was hiding.

He wandered up Briggate, past the market cross where the
ranter had stood yesterday. He could have lost his life to a madman
inflamed by God. But the man had been right. Simon did hold
the fear inside and he didn't know how to rid himself of it.

Could it be the sins of the past coming back? All the faces
from across the years returning? Christ, a weight like that would
break anyone's back.

There was still a patch of dried blood on the cobbles where
the inspector had stabbed the man. He couldn't stop himself; he
looked and shuddered. Then to the far side of the Head Row,
and into Mudie's print shop with its smells of ink and paper.

He was turning the handle of the printer, quickly studying
each sheet as it appeared.

'Sir Robert's man has been looking for you.'

'Why?' Then he understood. 'How long ago?'

'Quarter of an hour. He's searching all over, already been to
your house.'

'If he comes back—'

'I'll tell him you're on your way.'

Simon hurried back down Briggate, squeezing between people on the pavement, smelling their stink, feeling the damp heat of the day. Past Commercial Street, Kirkgate, Boar Lane, hurrying across the bridge where the water was thick and sluggish. Fewer people on the other side and he dashed along Water Lane to Foley's house.

'Here,' Sir Robert said, leading him along a corridor with a flagstone floor. He turned the key and opened a heavy door to the garden. 'See?'

Fresh marks on the wood. Someone had tried to pry it open from the outside. A poor job. No professional thief would attempt something like that.

'How did you discover it?'

'My wife saw it when she came out to cut some flowers.'

'He must have been here during the night. You didn't hear anything?'

Foley shook his head. 'We sleep at the far end of the house. The servants never mentioned it.'

Simon ran his hand over the wood. No real damage. The door was thick, made from stout, weathered oak. It would take an axe to break through this.

'Have you checked all the other doors and windows?'

Foley nodded. 'While I was waiting for you. This seems to be the only place he tried.'

Neither of them said the name. Mark was still in Leeds, desperate to have the cups back in his hands.

'Do you have them somewhere safe?'

'Yes. That was good advice, Mr Westow.'

'Keep them hidden until he's caught.'

Foley stared at him and chewed his lip thoughtfully before he spoke. 'How long will that be?'

'As soon as we can,' he answered honestly.

'What if he returns?'

Simon took a step back and gazed up at the house. It was solid stone and wood.

'You should be safe enough, Sir Robert. He doesn't know what he's doing. You need to make sure everything is closed and locked at night. But keep a pistol close, just in case. Even fools can find some fortune.'

A note for the constable and he returned to what he'd been doing. A stirring in his belly. The feeling that things were changing. It wouldn't be long now until Will Mark was in prison and waiting to hang for murder. If he was trying stupid things like trying to pry open a heavy door like that, the man was reaching the end of his tether. He was making mistakes.

He was home before dark, tired, aching, wishing he could sleep for a week. Time enough for that once Porter's men had Mark. He ate and talked of nothing important with Rosie and the boys as he tried to let the day wash away from him.

But his worries remained, swirling around his mind.

Sally wasn't waiting outside the house where they'd found John. Jane looked all around as she felt panic rising inside. She could be anywhere. John had already beaten both of them. He could do it again.

The girl could be wounded. Dead.

She closed her eyes, trying to sense which way the girl had gone and feeling nothing at all.

A start in one direction, then stopping, going back, trying another. None of them seemed right. Each moment she was more anxious, more fearful for Sally. She went inside the building, up the stairs where she held her breath, wondering if they'd hold her weight.

Into the room where John had stood with Ralph. The smell. She'd noticed it when she found him in Dodson's room, but it was much stronger here. Decay. A word from a book she'd read slipped into her mind: putrefaction. John was dying. Rotting. Maybe it had been by inches, but it was growing faster now. Perhaps the wounds she'd given him had festered.

Running only delayed his death.

As she came outside, only a memory remained of his rancid scent. But it was enough to set her moving, the shawl raised over her hair, right hand in her pocket, gripping her knife. Jane rubbed the gold ring against the handle. She needed every scrap of luck she could gather.

She kept going, steps growing more cautious as the houses

started to dwindle around her, streets turning into areas of dirt and weeds still waiting for the builders' shovels. Beyond them, open land. They were out there, Sally and John.

She opened her mouth, about to call Sally's name, but stopped; silence was safer. Jane breathed softly. Her nerves were flayed, chest tight, mouth dry.

A quarter of a mile and the town became a memory. She could still taste soot as she ran her tongue over her lips, but the constant noise had vanished. Only the stillness of the woods around her. Tall, thick trees and overgrown bushes. A track wound off to her left.

It twisted and turned as she followed it. She glanced around constantly, listening for any noise. She thought she heard a gasp, a sharp intake of breath. Jane stood and waited.

A small sob.

That was enough. She raced on, around another bend.

Sally was sitting on the ground, her head resting on knees that were drawn up against her chest. Jane approached carefully, unsure for a second whether the girl was alive. No blood on the ground, though. Then Sally gave a shudder. A low sob came out of her mouth. She turned her head.

'I lost him.'

Jane knelt, placing an arm around the girl's shoulders and saying nothing.

'I could hear him running. I could *smell* him. He'd gone. No tracks. Nothing at all.'

'He didn't hurt you?'

'I never came close enough to fight him. He was always ahead. Just out of sight.' Her eyes opened wide. 'Ralph. Is he—'

'The cut on his neck wasn't deep,' Jane told her. 'He has a broken arm. The bone setter has taken care of it.'

'Thank you.'

They stood. The girl grimaced as if every muscle in her body pained her. But no need for help; she took a few paces then was walking steadily.

'I've failed them.'

'Who?' Jane asked, although she knew the names.

'Ralph. *Harold.*' Sally's glance flickered at her as she added: 'Dodson.'

'No, you haven't.'

'He's still out there. He's still alive.'

'We'll find him.'

'How could he do that?' she asked in disbelief. 'How could he just vanish?' A quick movement as she looked back over her shoulder, as if he might be standing a few yards away, watching them.

'He's human.'

They'd all failed. Every single one of them. She had, Rosie. Even Simon, who was carrying his own demons these days. But you kept going. Sally had to go after him again. Then once more, until she won or he killed her. That was the only way to be. Inside, the girl knew it. But it was always a bitter lesson.

'We'll do it,' Jane said.

'Will we?' She sounded doubtful.

'Yes.'

Sally was good, better at a thief-taker's job than she'd ever been, but still so young. Every setback and wound would make her more careful, stop her charging blindly at the world.

In the end, it would always be better to fight and die than to give up.

TWENTY-SIX

S imon woke as he heard the front door. He groped for the
knife in its sheath on the floor, fingers finding the handle.
It was very late; he sensed that much. The dark felt
complete around him, the air too quiet.

Sally, it had to be. He knew that as he heard the key turn in
the lock; she was the only other person who had one. Yet he still
held his breath as he heard her footsteps on the stairs. His body
was tense, mind sparking and pulsing until she passed, climbing
slowly up to her room in the attic. He let go of the knife and
pulled the sheet around his shoulders.

Gossip was sparse around the coffee cart. A man who'd tried to
kill a homeless boy, not worth more than a few words in passing.
Simon heard and turned to watch Sally. She was standing on the
other side of Briggate, his bodyguard once again. Looking at
nothing, aware of everything.

He drained his cup and walked over to her.

'The boy last night, the one they're talking about: is he all
right?'

A breath, and she nodded. 'A broken arm and a cut to his
neck.'

'John's work?'

'Yes.' Her voice was flat. That and the angry flash in her eyes
told him everything he needed. His fear, her pain. Eating away
at them both.

A stop to see Porter at the courthouse. He gave the same shake
of the head as every other day.

'We've been pressing harder since you told me about the
attempt to break into Foley's house. But you know as well as I
do that we can't push too much with the people Mark knew.'

The good families, the respectable with their money and influence. It was the truth.

'You haven't forgotten he killed Armistead?'

'Or Kendall, or Green the pawnbroker.' The constable rounded on him. 'Don't be a bloody fool, Westow. Of course I remember.' He tapped his skull. 'They're all in here along with everyone else who's died since I took this job.'

Simon looked at him for a moment, wondering what to make of the outburst. Then Porter shrugged.

'It's this damned weather. The heat hasn't stopped for weeks, and you might as well eat the air. People have had enough of it. Everybody's on edge. Members of the watch are being attacked every night.'

Maybe that was the reason for his own fears, Simon thought. They'd never plagued him before the weather turned warm. Maybe it had opened the doors and let them in. Maybe.

'We still have to find him.'

'We've both doing all we can and we're nowhere.' He held up a hand before Simon could reply. 'I know my men made a mistake. Don't you dare go telling me you never have.'

'We need luck.'

Porter snorted. 'When was the last time you saw some of that round here? I think it packed its bags and took a seat on a London coach.'

Another minute and Simon left. Porter was prickly with his troubles; for him, Mark was just one more among many.

But the idea about the heat . . .that was interesting.

He stopped at the post office on Call Lane. A letter was waiting for him, the frank paid by the sender. Walking home, he tore it open and stopped in the middle of the pavement. People bumped against him, but he barely noticed them as he read the words again.

'That's payment of a debt,' Rosie said in admiration when she read it. 'Do you know who he is?'

'No.'

Sally stared at the page, studying the shapes of the words, then stared from face to face. 'What does it say?'

No need to look again; the words were clear in his mind.

You gave us Tyler. You've been looking for a man named Mark. If you find Weak-Arm Andrew, he can point you in the right direction. Hull

'Have you heard of him?' he asked Sally. She shook her head and he turned to Jane. She was gazing down into her lap. 'You?'

'No.'

'Then let's find him. We've been banging our heads against a wall. It's strange that none of us know him, but somebody must.' He tapped the paper. 'This is gratitude for the captain, there's no reason for them to lie. We have to take advantage of it.'

'Are you going to tell Porter?' Jane asked.

'Not yet,' he replied. 'I'll wait until we have more.'

'I can't see the good wives knowing anyone with a name like that,' Rosie said when the others had gone.

He laughed; the sound took him by surprise. 'He doesn't sound as if he'd be welcome in the best drawing rooms in Leeds, does he? But I thought I knew most people on the edge of the law here.'

'With a name like that, he should be easy to find.'

'Let's hope so.' One more glance at the letter. Maybe luck had decided against taking the London coach, after all. 'I hadn't expected this. I don't want to waste it.'

Sally marched, forceful, determined strides. She kept her fists clenched, a dark, serious expression on her face. Not speaking, yesterday still burning in her brain. Jane glanced at the girl's forearms in case she'd tried to cut herself, the way she used to do herself. But Sally was much stronger than she'd been at that age. Failure hurt, but it couldn't crush her.

'Weak-Arm Andrew.'

'None of the children have ever mentioned him.'

'I'll ask the whores later.'

'John.' The girl spat the name.

'He's going to be very careful now.'

'We have to find him.' Desperation crept into her voice. 'He's going to leave before we can kill him. I know he is.'

'We'll catch him,' Jane said. Now she had to hope her promise was true.

Without a hint of some kind, a sighting of John, they'd have as much luck chasing a ghost. He made his camps in the woods, he had the skill to trap animals. Jane didn't have the ability to track him out there; the streets of the town were her territory.

Sally did, but she couldn't blunder into all the areas outside Leeds.

For now, it was hopeless.

Weak-Arm Andrew. By the end of the day she felt as if she'd spoken the name a hundred times. To the women who ran the small shops, a few maids out shopping for their mistresses. Kate the pie-seller shook her head.

Home, defeated; she'd go out after dark to talk to the whores. Some joy was waiting, though. Dodson was wearing his new leg, using his crutch to get around the small garden. He beamed as he saw her, hobbling across, moving with a kind of confidence and pleasure she'd never seen in him before, standing to attention as he approached her.

'Thank you,' he said.

'I haven't done that much.'

'You have.' He looked over his shoulder at the house. 'Both of you. I'd have died if I'd stayed out there, wouldn't I?'

'Maybe. Who knows?' She didn't want his gratitude. It was enough to see him up and moving like this. 'In a few days you might be ready to go home.'

A new lock for his door, she thought. A sturdy one.

'I feel as if I could leave now. You've both been so kind. I've been a burden on you.'

'You haven't,' she told him, then: 'One more night. Then Mrs Shields can be sure you're fine.'

He nodded agreement, not unwilling, and she saw the faint worry in his eyes. Being out there alone, imagining the return of things that could hurt him. But he was ready to go.

Maybe they'd find John before Dodson left. Inside, she knew the truth: he'd still be out there.

She watched the locksmith do his work. A lantern was burning, the last of the daylight almost faded. The man packed his tools into a sailcloth bag, nodding as she paid him, then handing over the key.

'You'll be safe in there now, Miss. Nobody's going to break that. Nor pick it, neither.'

A final nod and she heard his boots on the stairs.

The mechanism turned easily, the lock smooth and solid. Jane smiled. She'd give Dodson the key in the morning. A final present.

Tonight, she had other business. Asking the whores about a man named Weak-Arm Andrew.

'What kind of a name is that?' Mudie asked. He shook his head. 'I've lived in Leeds all my life and never heard of him.'

The same with Barnabas Wade and others he tried. Finally, standing outside the courthouse, he decided to go in and ask Constable Porter. He'd wanted to keep this from the watch, but maybe the man would know . . .

Instead, it was the same as all the others.

'Are you sure that's right?'

'Positive.' He had it written in ink, right there in his pocket.

'You want to know what I think? Somebody's playing tricks on you, Westow. I thought you were too clever for that.'

'He's real.' The men in Hull wouldn't lie. This was their payment.

Who the hell was he?

'Someone called Andrew used to come around, didn't he, Cassie?' Jane watched as a pox-scarred woman named Elizabeth turned to her companion leaning against the wall. 'You remember him?'

The words came out slurred, stinking of gin: 'With the arm? Was that him?'

'Arm?' Jane pounced on the word and passed over three silver coins 'What do you mean?'

'He had . . .' Elizabeth groped for the words, deep in her mind. She touched her left arm. 'It wouldn't work properly.'

Withered? Crippled somehow? Her blood was racing. Jane tried to keep the eagerness out of her voice.

'How long ago since you saw him?'

The pair looked at each other before Elizabeth said, 'I don't know. A month, maybe? He never come often, just every few weeks. He likes Cassie, you see, and I look after her. Sometimes she's not well enough . . .' The words trailed away as a man approached, then moved on. Longingly, the woman watched him go.

'Andrew,' Jane prompted. She took out three more coins

and put them in Elizabeth's hand. 'What do you know about him?'

'He's always polite, you know, like a proper gentleman should. Not pushy, doesn't get nasty like some of them.' She thought. 'Never haggles over the price. Looks neat and proper. Clean.' She thought. 'He's old—'

'How old?'

She frowned as she tried to think. 'I don't know. What do you reckon, Cassie?'

'Fifty?' The word seemed to be an effort. She shrugged.

'Fifty.' It seemed to satisfy Elizabeth. 'Yes, fifty. Maybe.'

'Where does he live? Did he say?'

'No. Why would he?' She gave a short, rough laugh. 'What do you think we do, ask for their address and a reference?' Another pause and a pout. 'I have seen him twice on Briggate, walking with a woman. Not a young one, mind. Just . . .' She shook her head when she couldn't find the word.

'Do you have a nip, miss. Me and Cassie, we could both do with a nip.' She gave a hopeful smile. 'Makes me thirsty, all this talking.'

'No, I don't.' Jane needed to press them while they were still here. 'What does he look like?'

'I know he's taller than me, but I suppose that dun't mean much.' She pursed her lips as she thought. 'Not really tall. Just normal. He doesn't have much hair, what's there is white. Spectacles. He wears spectacles, you know, for his eyes.'

Jane tried a few more questions, but Elizabeth had nothing to add. No matter. She'd had the first sense of the man. Two of the other women remembered him. He wasn't a regular, no rhythm to his visits, always courteous, paying what they asked or moving on. One thought he might be sixty, another wondered if he was forty. A hint of him, just out of reach.

'Someone ordinary,' Jane said as she sat in Simon's kitchen the next morning. He'd listened carefully, trying to build a picture of the man.

'It could explain why nobody seems to recognize him.' Rosie pressed her lips together into a tight line.

'But why would someone like that know Will Mark?' Simon

asked. He'd been tracing circles on the table with a drop of water. Now he raised his head and looked at the faces. 'Anyone have any ideas?'

'Mark might be a lodger in the house,' Sally said.

Letting out a room or two to help with the bills; it happened all the time. But how would the men from Hull know about that, Simon wondered? There had to be some kind of connection.

'Trade,' he said suddenly. 'Someone doing business between here and Hull.'

Nothing to mark him him out, not a person criminals would know; just trying to live his life.

'Barges,' Rosie said. 'Most of the trade with Hull is on the canals.'

He nodded, feeling his excitement begin to rise, the sense of hope, that they were on the right path.

'I'll go down on the Calls. The warehouses and the wharves.'

'I can try the shops,' Rosie told him. 'If he's been in any with his wife, someone should remember that arm.'

'What about us?' Sally asked as she glanced at Jane.

'Later,' Simon told her. 'Once we know where he lives.'

'Here.' Jane handed Dodson the new key to his room. He stared at it as if he'd never seen anything like it before.

'But I already have one,' he told her, holding it up, then lowering his head as she explained what she'd done.

'This will make sure John can't get in.'

The beggar's eyes were shiny when he looked at her.

'You hardly know me,' he said.

'That doesn't matter.'

The walk from Green Dragon Yard had taken three-quarters of an hour. Farther than he'd been since before the attack, and the strain showed; he kept needing to stop and rest for a minute. Then to greet the people who were happy to see him return. More of them than he'd expected from the look on his face. Finally, the slow, painful climb up the stairs to stand here.

He opened the door and entered, gazing around the small space. She darted in behind him, suddenly terrified that John might have somehow found a way into the place. But it was empty.

He spotted the small pile of money on the table and turned to her.

'You . . .?'

'You need something to start you off. You're going to have to buy things.'

'Thank you. Not just for that, but . . .' He swept his arm around as if it could take in the whole world.

Jane gave him a tight smile and slipped away while he walked around the room.

TWENTY-SEVEN

'Course I know him,' the barge captain laughed. 'Everyone down here knows Andrew Bishop.'

Simon couldn't believe it was this simple. The first man he'd asked.

'With the bad arm?'

'That's the one. I heard he was born that way. Never stopped him working the boats, though. Not until he bought one. Owns a pair of them now. Run down the Humber to Hull and up to Skipton.' He cast an eye along the wharves by Leeds Bridge. 'No, neither of them are tied up now.' The man turned his head to the boatyard on the other side of the river. 'There's one of them. Over there. See it, with the red trim? It must have had some damage.'

Simon could feel the eagerness rising in his belly, crowding out any small flickers of worry. 'Any idea where I might find him now?'

The man shrugged. 'Could be watching the work, I don't know. He has a little office at the back of Hunter's warehouse, but he's not there most of the time. Always out and about is old Andrew. Trying to drum up business.' He turned his head and spat in the water.

Simon hurried across Leeds Bridge, the hobnails on his boot soles sparking on the cobbles along Dock Street, then into the boatyard. A carpenter was working to patch a hole in the barge, a small cauldron of pitch bubbling on a stove.

'Is the owner of this one around?'

'Not seen him today,' the man answered as he fitted a plank of thick oak perfectly into place, tapping it home with his hammer. 'Meant to meet him here, are you?'

'No,' Simon replied, but the carpenter was already concentrating on driving long, dangerous nails into the wood.

The yard owner expected Bishop to arrive before dinner.

'He'll be wanting to see how the work's progressing. Every day that thing's not working is costing him.'

'That must be expensive.'

The man eyed him up and down, then said: 'You don't know
the half of it, mister. Bidding for a cargo to take, then another
to bring back. A crew, horse to pull the damned thing, fees for
the locks. Hard to make a penny in that business.' He chuckled.
'Then there's the repairs when the boats grow old and end up
with a problem. Better money in owning a yard.'

'You don't know where Bishop lives, do you?'

He shook his head. 'Never asked. Not my business, as long
as he pays his bill here.'

The door to the man's small office behind Hunter's warehouse
was locked. Somebody said he'd seen Bishop an hour before,
but he'd glanced at his watch and dashed off.

'He's bound to be back. It's Friday. His barge always comes
in from Hull then, during the afternoon.'

That was still a few hours away. The sooner he found Andrew
Bishop, the quicker he could hunt down Will Mark.

Nobody who resembled him in the dram shops and alehouses
close to the wharves. He had time to fill. Might as well go and
see George Mudie; he hadn't known Weak-Arm Andrew, but he
might have heard of Andrew Bishop.

'No,' Mudie answered slowly. 'But it's a whole different world
down on the river.'

'Someone who owns a pair of barges must have money.'

'Depends how good business is, Simon. People can go broke
in any trade, take it from me.'

'Is everything fine here?' he asked.

'Don't worry. You're not about to lose your money. I can't
help you with Bishop, though.'

Jane stood on the bridge, Sally beside her, staring down at the
sluggish water. A slick of oil caught rainbow light, then a patch
of blue, red, colours from the dyeworks drifted downstream.

'Did you smell it?' she asked. 'The stink of death on him.
Like it's eating him up from inside.'

'But he's still here.' Sally turned to watch the traffic passing.
Horses, carriages, carts. A boy struggling with a loaded barrow.

'Where?' Jane asked, but neither had an answer.

*   *   *

Three o'clock. The church bell had just finished ringing the hour and Simon strode along the wharf. A tangle of boats, two and three deep, men loading and unloading heavy sacks. A crane winched up a load from a hold. He stopped, not moving as it turned and gently deposited everything on land. Quick, skilful.

He spotted Bishop. A stout figure in a black coat and low-crowned hat, left arm pressed tight against his body as he gestured with the other. He was standing by a barge with red trim, the twin of the one in the yard, speaking to the captain. An argument, from the looks on their faces.

Simon waited until they'd finished and Bishop stalked away. Simon approached. The man assessed him.

'You don't look like you're after a job. What do you want?' He had a quick, abrasive tone, the colour still high in his cheeks.

'My name's Simon Westow. I'm a thief-taker. You know some people in Hull, I believe.'

'I do. My boats go there all the time. If you're not aware of that—'

'Some people call you Weak-Arm Andrew.' Politeness wasn't about to work with Bishop.

'Maybe one or two,' the man admitted slowly. 'Why? Who are you?'

'They told me to find you. Said you might know where to find William Mark.'

Bishop cleared his throat. 'Did they now?' He took a breath. 'What's it worth?'

'I did them a favour. I led them to a man named Thomas Tyler. Do you know him?' The man's eyes widened a little. 'Telling me about you was their payment. Should I let them know you were asking for money?'

A gamble, but Bishop hesitated for a long time before answering.

'Of course not.' He attempted a smile. 'Forgive me, it was a joke. I didn't mean it seriously. But I have to tell you, there's some kind of mistake.'

'Oh? How's that?'

'I don't know anyone named William Mark. I've never heard the name before.'

'No?' Simon gave a quick description of Mark. 'You don't know anybody who looks like that?'

He shook his head. 'I told you: not with that name.'

'Some people change their name more often than their clothes. What name is he using?'

'He introduced himself to me as Walter Marsden.' Bishop was looking uncomfortable, moving from foot to foot. 'But I don't see how he can have done anything to attract your attention. He's a gentleman. You can see he was raised well.'

'He's murdered three people. I'm surprised you haven't heard about it, Mr Bishop. One of them was a gentleman too, name of Armistead. There's been plenty of gossip going around. Now, where can I find him?'

The man pushed his lips together and stared down at the ground.

'Of course I've heard the news, Mr . . . Westow? But I told you, I don't know anybody called William Mark. I give you my word on that.'

How much was that worth, Simon wondered.

'William Mark to Walter Marsden. It's hardly a great leap, is it?'

'No,' he admitted. The man seemed to have shrunk as they talked. His shoulders had hunched in on themselves, as if the truth had squeezed all the pride from him. 'No, it's not. I'll tell you something, but I need to rely on you not to spread it.'

'No,' Simon said, and Bishop looked up sharply. 'I can't make that promise without knowing what it is.'

'Times have been very difficult,' the man said after a moment. 'It happens in business, I'm sure you're aware of that. But of course nobody wants their competitors to find out. Do you understand?'

The man was erecting a fence of words around the truth. 'I do.'

'My wife and I have had to take in lodgers. Walter Marsden is living with us at the moment. We provide his meals and clean linen, all found. He's only been with us for a short time.'

True enough; since he'd been forced to run from the rooms his friend had lent him.

'I had no idea about . . .' Bishop continued.

'There was no reason you should,' Simon said. 'However, now you do.'

'He paid us for a fortnight,' the man said wistfully.

'Has he been out much?'

'Hardly at all, according to my wife. When he does, it's at night.'

Yes, going to Holbeck and trying to break into Sir Robert's house.

'I know he's growing a beard.'

A disguise to see him on his way. Completing the transformation from Will Mark to Walter Marsden.

He needed to stand trial, to hang for his crimes. But Simon knew he couldn't storm into Bishop's house and drag Mark out into the light. He'd have to tell Porter; the constable had the authority and the men to do it.

'You wanted my discretion,' Simon said to the man. 'Now I need to rely on yours. Constable Porter has been looking for William Mark, too. Once you give me your address, I'll tell him. The watch will come and arrest him. Everything done quietly.'

'Do I have any choice?' Bishop asked.

'I'm afraid not. I'm sure you have no wish to keep a murderer in your house, do you?'

'Of course I don't.' He sounded horrified by the idea.

'Then warn your wife, and not a word from either of you to Mark. I'll go and see the constable.'

But no sign of Porter or the inspector at the courthouse. Nobody knew where they'd gone. Simon scribbled a note and left it on the constable's desk: *I know where to find Wm. Mark. Westow.*

Nothing to do but wait.

Friday evening. Leeds was busy, alive with noise. Laughter, arguments, singing. Jane and Sally kept to the shadows as they walked down Briggate, then turned on to Kirkgate.

She brushed her hand against Armistead's front door, remembering the gentle man. Soon. Soon they'd find Mark and reap some revenge for the murder.

Not tonight, though. The next few hours were for hunting John. Make him pay his debts, for Harold and Dodson and Charlie and all the others he'd hurt or killed. But no matter where they tried, they found no hint of his decay in the air. As the church clock struck ten, they turned. Jane's feet ached and her bones were weary. One final look around the burial ground, then the far side of Timble Bridge. After that home, keeping out of sight of the boisterous men who still filled the streets.

'I've arranged everything,' Constable Porter said. After ten at night and the man looked dead on his feet. He'd come earlier, after he returned from a killing in Hunslet, listening to Simon's thoughts before going to talk to Andrew Bishop.

'He likes the idea?'

The constable snorted. 'He likes the idea that he and his wife won't be there. We'll be waiting as they leave. They'll let us in. Mr and Mrs Bishop will go out early. The plan makes sense. Less chance of anyone being hurt.'

'What about the servants? They'll still be in the house.'

A shrug. 'I doubt he gave them a thought. We'll make certain they're out of the way. Mark will still be asleep. I have someone keeping watch, in case he suspects something and tries to slip away during the night. It should be simple enough.'

Should be. How often had he heard those words in the past, only for everything to go wrong?

'You found the information, Westow, and I appreciate you passing it on. Do you want to come along and see the ending?'

Porter had been the one to invite him to Middle Row, when they discovered Arthur Mangey's secret workshop with Thomas Kendall's body inside. Where this tale had begun. There would be a balance in being there for the end, too. For a second, a shiver of fear stopped him. A sense that something would happen. Something bad. No. If he let the terrors rule his life, he'd never do anything. Simon smiled and breathed in.

'Thank you,' he replied. 'Yes.'

The constable nodded and stood, picking up his hat. 'Seven tomorrow, around the corner from Bishop's house.'

'I'll be there.'

'You don't have to go,' Rosie told him once they were alone. 'There's no need. You don't have anything to prove.'

'I want to. I'd like to see it end.'

'I was watching your face, Simon. It changed for a moment.'
Her eyes were filled with sadness. 'It's not the first time.'

'No,' he admitted after a long pause. 'It's not.'

'Then . . .'

He didn't know what to tell her. How to begin. What words
to use. He knew he had to say something, to answer the pleading
in her eyes. But how could a man admit to fear? Especially
someone in his trade.

'You know where all the money is. That secret drawer under
the stair and in the bank.'

'Of course.' Her eyes widened. 'What—?'

'I'm frightened all the time. Every day I'm scared of what's
going to happen.' He blurted out the truth, letting it come in a
torrent. He didn't try to control the words. It was the only way:
to sit like an observer and listen to everything as if it was
happening to someone else.

It all slowed to a trickle. Then the shame arrived. Shame at
having these weaknesses. At not keeping them hidden and out
of the light. Then having to admit it all to his wife. Especially
to her. A man was supposed to be strong for his spouse, not fall
apart in front of her like a coward.

Rosie took his hands in her and kneaded them gently.

'What did you think? That I'd stop loving you?'

'I . . .' He didn't know. He'd been gripped by the terrors, not
thinking clearly.

'Go if you feel you must, Simon. Just be very careful. Make
sure you stay alive and come home to us. None of these people
are worth dying over.' She smiled and tugged his arm. 'Come
on, let's go to bed.'

TWENTY-EIGHT

The small house behind Green Dragon Yard felt empty without Dodson; they'd grown used to his quiet presence in the place. There seemed to be more space than they'd known, and a deeper, softer silence. Jane picked up *The Scottish Chiefs* and the old soldier slipped from her mind as she became caught up in the tale again. Mrs Shields read and dozed until it was time for bed. So easy to slip back into their old routine.

She rose early, washed and dressed. A slice of bread and honey in the kitchen and a drink of one of the old woman's cordials before she slid a light cotton shawl over her shoulders. Outside, the day was already warm and heavy, not a hint of freshness in the air. Her clothes started to stick to her skin as she walked down the Head Row.

The debris of a Friday night was strewn over the pavement. Broken glass, vomit, an old pair of men's boots tucked up against a building. She turned on to Briggate, surprised once again not to see Middle Row or the old Moot Hall.

For a second she felt a twinge in her little finger. The phantom, long gone now. She could still hear her scream and smell the room where it happened. She rubbed the nub and the memory vanished into the morning.

The beggars were already out, looking for early alms from the people on their way to worship. Davy Cassidy's music flowed, and people rewarded him for the beauty. Dodson was settled near the entrance to the Parish Church yard by the bottom of Kirkgate, wooden leg extended in front of him. A prime place; she knew it was a gift from the others to welcome him back.

Plenty of coins in his cup already. When she stooped to add another, he placed his hand over it.

'No. Please.' He gave her a contented smile. 'You've already done enough for a lifetime.'

'You're going to need a new coat.' John had ripped the old army greatcoat to shreds. Dodson had always worn it, even on the hottest days.

He glanced at the silver glinting in the cup. 'I'll be able to afford one. Thank you.'

Back on Briggate she saw Simon with Sally at his side, talking to Porter as the inspector and two men from the watch stood close. The girl waved her over.

'Mark's in a house round the corner. The owners are going to let us in when they leave.'

She looked at the faces of the men. 'All of us?'

'Just the constable and his men. We're going to stay out here.'

A chance to end one story. Sally hadn't mentioned John; her silence meant nobody had spotted him.

Porter pulled out his watch, checking the time. He began to move, the men falling in behind him. A minute passed. She heard a few low voices, then a man appeared, one arm tight against his body. A woman at his side, two younger ones meekly following. He nodded at Simon as he went by.

'Weak-Arm Andrew,' he explained when the family had gone and started to move to a ginnel. 'I managed to track him down yesterday. Mark's his lodger. He's calling himself Walter Marsden now. Growing a beard, too.'

Jane nodded as she listened, then looked up and said: 'Where are we going to be? Should we watch the back of the house?'

Simon nodded. 'One of Porter's men is supposed to be covering it. But it's a good idea, in case Mark tries to escape.'

She drew a knife from the pocket of her dress. 'He killed Mr Armistead.'

Nobody was waiting in the ginnel. Only the three of them, standing outside a head-high wall that enclosed the rear of the garden. Still, together they'd be able to stop a man like Mark. For a full minute the world was quiet. Then Jane heard the insistent beat of fists hammering inside the house. Voices bellowed, Porter louder than the rest, angry and impatient.

Jane glanced up as a window opened. Her body tensed as a man appeared, carefully lowering himself until he hung by his fingertips, then dropping softly to the ground. She hissed a warning.

Simon nodded, watching her move off to his left, Sally away on his right. Both of them ready. He stood by the tall gate, a knife in each hand, waiting for Mark to come out. Fear pulsed through him, taunting him. He tried to ignore it. To listen, to only think about what was happening. A key turned in the lock of the gate and the handle began to turn. Simon drew in a breath and tightened his grip on the blades.

Mark appeared in a blur, glancing back as he dashed into the ginnel, then seeing Simon tall and broad, blocking his way. No surprise, not a moment's hesitation before a knife appeared in his hand and he charged.

Stop him? Wound him? Kill him? The thoughts slid around his brain as William Mark lowered his head and ran. Step to the side and avoid the thrust or block him head on? A dozen questions flew through his mind in under a second.

Too slow.

Mark didn't hesitate. He ran straight into Simon, knocking him off balance. Before he could find his feet, the man lunged. He parried it, knives sending up sparks that caught the morning light.

Then Mark was on him, desperate, fighting for his life. Simon stabbed his arm and heard him grunt, but he was moving fast, trying to squirm past, to run for his freedom. More shouting from inside the house. Simon could make out Porter's voice as he directed his men and wondered why he'd noticed it.

The man tried to bring the knife down in a killing blow, but Simon pushed back and it sliced through space. No harm. Not this time. He was still coming, relentless. If he could make it out of the ginnel, Mark might stay alive. Caught, he'd certainly hang.

Simon took a short step back. It bought him a moment. Mark had to come to him. He sensed that Sally and Jane were close, ready if he needed them. But he had to do this alone. To prove himself. The only way to conquer everything that was consuming him.

His mind was racing far ahead of his body. He saw Mark's arm move and wondered how to react. Weighed the possibilities. Done before he could blink, but still a hesitation. Long enough for Mark to slip inside his guard and slide the knife deep into his leg.

At first, he barely felt it. Nothing more than a pinprick in his flesh. Then the man was on him again, pushing, punching, fingers trying to gouge his eyes. Wild, urgent as Simon tried to fend him off. Then suddenly his leg started to give way and he began to buckle to the ground, helpless. Mark could kill him now. But the man just pushed him out of the way and ran on.

He looked down. His leg was gushing blood, starting to pool under him on the ground, trousers already bright red. He turned his head, searching for faces. Jane was there, already tearing a strip from her petticoat. She was yelling at Sally, 'Get Porter. Simon needs a doctor.'

He wanted to speak. He *needed* to speak, but he couldn't find the strength. All he could manage was to watch her work, and even that felt like an effort. She had deft, quick, capable hands. Tying the cloth around his thigh, tightening the knot to stop the flow of blood.

Simon gazed at her face. No emotion, only concentration as she worked. His eyes closed, then the constable was gazing down, speaking quickly to Jane. They were right by him, but their voices seemed muffled; they could have been miles away.

'You, you, find something to carry him to the infirmary. Get a bloody move on, he's in a bad way. The rest of you, after Mark. He can't have gone far.'

Jane watched as the two men lifted Simon on to the shed door and hurried away, carrying him. The wound on his leg was bad. Dangerous. She'd managed to stop the bleeding before he'd lost too much.

But she'd seen enough to understand that didn't mean he'd survive.

'Go and tell Rosie. She needs to go to the hospital.'

Sally started to run as if the devil was at her heels.

Jane stared at the ground. Simon's blood had already soaked into the dry earth. There was nothing she could do here. Sitting at the hospital and waiting for news wouldn't change whatever was going to happen. She turned and walked off.

Simon had to live. He had Rosie, the boys. Without him, she and Sally would still be living on the streets. Probably dead themselves by now. She'd seen people with wounds like his who'd recovered without a problem. But she knew the other side, too: plenty who'd died.

What she could do was search for Mark. She wanted him for what he'd done to Mr Armistead. Now she had an even closer reason to find him.

The man had a good start on her. But Jane had a weapon to help her: the street children, Sally's small army. Many of them knew her.

Her eyes were searching. They kept out of sight, but she knew how to spot them.

Less than five minutes before she found one. A coin, a mention of Sally's name, and the boy raced off to pass the word. She stood by the market cross, hearing the low, distant drone of the preacher in St John's as he began his sermon. The day was hot and drowsy. A wasp settled on her sleeve. As she looked down, she saw the bloodstains on her dress.

Simon would fight. He had to do it. Before, he'd been slow. Too cautious. He'd hesitated a heartbeat longer than he should.

Jane shivered. She needed him back, not another hole in her life.

A girl came dashing up, another just a few yards behind. Jane listened to their voices, both breathless from running, then stood and marched off behind them. She touched the gold ring on her finger. Luck, she thought, plenty of luck. Then her hand gripped the hilt of her knife.

He'd never felt so weak. Scarcely able to lift his hand. Simon understood he must be drifting in and out of consciousness; the moments all seemed disconnected. He recognized Dr Hey, silent, hands busy. Pain burned deep in his body, so hard he wanted to scream. But his mouth was clamped down on a strip of leather.

Panicking, his gaze shifted around, hoping to see Rosie. Hands kept his head still. Simon closed his eyes again, body lifting under a jolt of agony. Then blackness took over his mind.

Over the bridge and into Holbeck. Suddenly Jane realized where they were going. She should have guessed. It was the only place left. For a second she thought about sending one of the girls to fetch Sally. But she'd be with Rosie and the boys, frantic with worry for Simon. She was a part of the family.

She'd need to do this on her own.

Two more children arrived. They'd seen the man Jane described. Farthings for each of them before they left. She didn't want any of them close for the ending. No risks.

Foley's house was quiet, the front door closed. She tried the handle; it turned silently in her hand. Quietly, she stepped into the hall, scarcely daring to breathe. She stopped, ear cocked for any sound.

A small noise from somewhere near the back of the house. She started towards it, treading carefully. Slowly. No sense in giving Mark any warning.

Her heart was running wild in her chest, her breathing quick and ragged. Jane stopped for a few seconds, until her breathing calmed. She wasn't as good a fighter as she'd once been, but she was improving. She had all the reasons in the world to beat Mark.

The last door on the left.

Should she go in quietly or not? A final moment to decide.

She threw the door back, letting it crash hard against the wall as Mark quickly turned his head. He was standing behind a woman, his knife against her neck. Foley's wife; it had to be.

Sir Robert Foley stood with the servants on the other side of the room. In the middle, sitting on a table, the four silver cups Arthur Mangey had made. Where this all began. The reason Will Mark had come here.

'Stand over there,' he ordered her, nodding towards the knot of people. No power in his voice. No command. Nothing more than a very frightened man who was far out of his depth and flailing.

She didn't move.

He tugged hard on the woman's hair, making her cry out, and brandished his knife.

'I told you to go.'

Jane stood, staring into his eyes. William Mark had a weak, pale face. A man, just a few years older than her. With an education. Supposed to be a gentleman. Once upon a time. Instead he looked like a petrified little boy trying to summon up his bravado. He was lost. He didn't know what to do.

She strode to the table and picked up one of the cups. The metal was cool against her skin, touching the nub of her little finger.

She knew Mark was watching, wondering what she intended to do. Too scared to say anything, to try and use words to stop her.

Jane placed the cup in front of her. She could almost feel Mangey's hand working, smoothing them. Tenderly, lovingly. Back before his own life shattered. One by one, she moved the other three to join it, then looked at Mark. His gaze was fixed on them.

'Are these why you're here?'

'Give them to me or I'll kill her.' He ran the flat of the blade along the woman's neck.

Jane shrugged. 'She doesn't mean anything to me.' His eyes widened; her answer took him by surprise. 'You killed Mr Armistead. You might have killed Simon Westow.' She heard the quick intake of breath from Foley. 'If the watch catch you, you're dead.'

'They won't. I have her.'

'If anything happens to her, you won't leave here alive.' She said it quietly, but with no room for doubt. Not a threat, a promise.

'What if I let her go?' A pale voice filled with trepidation and hope. She knew she had him.

'Then you can leave.' A pause, just long enough to raise his sights to the future. 'Without the cups.'

She'd never been like this. Her anger had always burned bright in the past. It had consumed her. This time it sat cold and hard in the pit of her stomach. From the moment she walked into the room, she'd known what to do. How to stop him. As if something was guiding her.

'Do you give your word?'

'Yes,' Jane told him. Flickers of indecision moved across his face. She needed to stay silent, to give him time to persuade himself, to realize this was the only chance he'd have to escape. He needed to believe, to crave it.

She waited. Ready.

The pain didn't stop, but they lifted his head and made him drink something. Tipped it into his mouth, something cool and welcome, and he sank into a blessed rest. He hurt, his leg was on fire, but he could cope with it for now. He wanted to put his arms around the sleep, to caress it, love it. He wished he could feel like this forever. In some distant part of his mind he could hear the voices of the surgeon and Rosie. They were faint and comforting as he drifted far from the world.

TWENTY-NINE

The man was torn. Jane could see that. He wanted his life. But he craved the cups. Something for all he'd done. His birthright.

Her eyes never left his face, watching the expression change with his thoughts. Nothing hidden. No mask. Finally, he tensed. He'd made up his mind. Jane's fingers tightened around the knife hilt.

He moved. Pushed the woman so hard that she tumbled to the ground with a sharp cry of pain. By then he was running towards the door, legs pumping, knife out, pointing at her.

Jane kept her word. She let him pass. Foley was scrambling to help his wife, yelling orders to the servants.

Nobody looking at her as she hurried out, following Mark. He was already halfway down the path to the road. He glanced over his shoulder, saw her and ran harder. Fear spurred him.

But she was quicker. Younger, faster. She let her footsteps ring out, gaining on him with every yard. Jane knew how to do this. She wanted him to hear her coming. To know she wouldn't stop. That she was relentless. Let his terror overwhelm him as he moved. Closer, closer, until she could feel it coming off him. Armistead, she thought. Simon. The other men Mark had killed.

Now the bill had come due.

As he passed the Friends' Meeting House, she was still behind him. He swerved away into Camp Hall Court, thinking he might find an escape. Jane smiled. He'd led her to the perfect place.

He halted, shoes no longer drumming on the ground. He'd wanted to evade her. But this ginnel ended in a brick wall at the back of the dressing mill. He'd trapped himself. Signed his own death warrant.

She moved slowly. No rush now she had him here.

'You gave your word.' His voice was shaking.

'I let you leave. What did you think, that was the end of it?

You kill, you pay for it.' A word from a book came into her head. 'Retribution.'

'Are you going to kill me?'

'Unless you can stop me,' Jane told him and took two more paces.

Mark was dangerous. He'd beaten Simon. He'd probably had a fencing master when he was young. But he'd never had to fight the way she had.

He raised his hand. She could see the blade shaking in his fist. 'Come on,' he said. 'You want to kill me. Come and do it.'

She didn't answer. No need. The air was heavy and warm around them. A thought came to her: Simon could be dead.

Jane darted forward, up against him before he could react. She stabbed once, twice, three times, all in his belly. Mark's eyes widened. He gasped. He dropped his blade as his hands groped to cover the holes in his stomach.

The man opened his mouth, but he didn't beg. No tears or regrets. She stayed with him until the last light vanished from his eyes and his breathing stopped.

Revenge. She whispered the names, let them loose on the air.

In the end, he'd proved so easy to kill. All that effort to find him, and over so quickly. No battle, no real fight left in him. He hadn't even tested her. Three blows and it was done. No resistance. But if it hadn't been her, the watch would have found him. This way, she could make sure the dead had their justice. She'd kept the promise she'd made in Armistead's library.

Jane bent, wiped her knife on his coat and walked away. No regrets. She didn't look back. That story had ended; time to put him out of her mind. His face wouldn't torture her dreams.

Simon. She hurried across the bridge and down Swinegate. Nobody in the house. Up Bishopgate and Infirmary Street until she was at the doors of the hospital, gasping for breath and her heart in her mouth, suddenly terrified by what she might find.

She waited with Sally as Rosie finished talking to the surgeon, a man with a rough stony face. He ambled away, hands in the pockets of a bloody jacket. Rosie came to the two of them, body shuddering and shivering as if she couldn't control it. Her face was red, streaked from all the tears she'd cried since Sally had come running for her.

'Simon's going to live. They didn't have to take his leg.'

Jane felt the rush of relief flow through her. Without thinking, she hugged Rosie tight, then Sally.

'The surgeon said that putting the tourniquet on so quickly saved it.'

'Jane did that,' Sally told her.

'Thank you.' Her tears were cascading again, dabbing at her eyes with a handkerchief. 'Thank you.'

She didn't know how to answer, so she kept her mouth closed, just a flicker of smile that vanished almost before it appeared.

'He should be fine unless there's an infection.' Rosie drew in a breath, looking as if she needed something, anything at all to stop her thinking of Simon in a bed inside the echoing building. 'That man. Mark. The watch must be searching for him.'

'No need.'

Short and plain. Two words, that was enough. Someone would find his body. Maybe Foley would say more. But silence would be simpler.

'I'll tell Simon once he's awake. Dr Hey said I can sit by him.'

'Where did you find him?' Sally asked as they followed the street towards Swinegate.

Jane shook her head to try and clear the tangled thoughts inside. The day had an unreal quality, as if she could put her hand through it and gather up all the fragments into a basket. Davy Cassidy's playing carried over the town, a sober, noble tune; a hymn for Sunday, perhaps.

'Foley's house. I got the children to look for him.'

'Did you kill him there?'

'No.' She could see it all, let the images play in her mind. But it felt as if it had happened to someone else. 'I had to let him go. I found him in an alley.'

The girl knew not to ask too many questions, even though her eyes were eager to know it all.

They stopped outside the door of Simon's house.

'Is he going to be all right, do you think?' This was the question Sally had waited to ask her. The vital one.

But she didn't know. The doctor had told Rosie that Simon would be fine. They all had to trust that. She glanced up at the windows. The girl had built a life here. She'd found her home. If something happened, it could come crashing down around her. 'I'm sure he will.' She'd seen how bad the wound was. It would take time. Weeks, maybe months. It was time to change the subject. 'Where are the boys?' she asked.

Sally nodded towards the next house. 'The neighbour. I'll bring them home and tell them. They must be scared.'

A nod and she started to walk away. Behind her, Sally's voice was low and clear: 'John.'

Simon opened his eyes. Everything was a blur, faint outlines of light and shadow. A moment, then the pain arrived, searing through him.

His leg. He remembered. A knife. The blood. William Mark. 'I'm here, Simon.' He turned towards the voice. Rosie. Thank God. She told him. Only a few words. He was going to survive. Simon could feel himself fading away from the world again. That bliss of floating, leaving the pain for a while. But he would survive. He wasn't going to lose the leg. That was enough. He tried to squeeze his wife's hand, but he had no strength.

Sleep, he thought, and let himself drift.

A man's voice called her name as she walked slowly up Albion Street. Hand on her knife, Jane turned. Constable Porter, hurrying across the road to reach her. His face was haggard, the lines around his eyes and mouth deep as crags.

'Westow?' he asked.

She kept her distance. He'd taken her for questioning once. She still remembered the hand of one of the questioners grabbing her breast then slapping her so hard that she fell. In the past, but not forgotten. It kept her wary around him and the watch.

'He's going to recover. The doctor says he'll keep his leg.'

Porter nodded as he listened. 'That's good news.' Then he raised his eyes and stared. 'Sir Robert Foley sent me a note. He said that you went after Mark.'

Suddenly, she felt as if the day had come tumbling down on top of her. Her body was heavy, her mind dull and slow. All she wanted was the peace of home with Mrs Shields, to close the door behind herself and sleep. No dreams. The dead could rest.

'My men haven't found him yet,' the constable continued.

'They will,' she told him and walked on. For a moment, she expected him to say more, but he stayed silent. Suddenly, she was back in that library room, smelling the old paper and the bindings and hearing Armistead's voice, his quicksilver enthusiasm for the Mangey case. She shook her head and it disappeared.

His body was hot, as if a fire was coursing through it. He heard fragments of conversations in his head, unsure if they were real or half-remembered from years before. Rosie was there. He knew that much beyond question. He sensed her, felt her hand when she touched his.

Simon woke, peering through a haze into the early light. Somewhere in the distance, the rattle of hooves and wheels of a cart on Infirmary Street. He needed to push himself out of bed, to go down to the coffee cart on Briggate.

Suddenly, he knew where he was. A surge of pain in his leg that made him bite his lip to stop crying out.

It came back, rushing around him. William Mark stabbing him, the way he felt himself slipping to the ground. The blood. Jane, calm, in control.

'You're going to be fine.' The voice sounded real. He turned his head towards it and blinked his eyes open again. Rosie. But her face seemed different. Contorted by something. Fear? Relief? He didn't know and he was too tired to think about it.

'Mark . . .' The word struggled out of his mouth, a lump of sound.

'He's dead.'

He exhaled and closed his eyes again. Something was right in the world, at least.

Jane was still surprised by the emptiness of the small house without Dodson. He'd barely moved as he recovered, but he still seemed to fill the place. Now there was space, more room to breathe as she made porridge for Mrs Shields. The old woman nodded approvingly as she ate. Jane was dressed in the patterned muslin, the one she'd worn every day at Armistead's house. Her work dress was only fit for rags now, too badly stained with Simon's blood.

Last night Catherine Shields had listened to the whole story. She was the only person who'd ever hear everything. Once it was finished, the old woman looked at her with that gentle face.

'Was there anything else you could have done?'

'No.' Mark would have died by her hand, the watch, or a hangman's noose. This way Foley's wife was still alive.

The front door was open, inviting the small breeze that cooled the air inside the house a little. Jane heard footsteps crossing the flagstones and turned her head. Without thinking, her hand moved towards the knife in her pocket.

Sally, standing, uncertain until Mrs Shields spoke.

'Child, there's no need to stay out there. Come in and let me see how that shoulder's healing.'

A brief inspection, a final application of ointment, and the woman was satisfied.

'You'll have a small scar. But it will fade,' A smile. 'Nobody will ever notice it.'

Out in the world, with the soot from the chimneys filling the air and the noise of the week all around, Sally began to talk about Simon.

'Rosie told him about Mark when he came round yesterday. I saw her afterwards. It made him smile, she said.'

'Has the surgeon said anything more about Simon?'

'He's doing well. He has a fever, though.' She looked at Jane, seeking some hope. 'He'll live, won't he?'

As they walked down the Head Row, turning on to Briggate, Jane realized her dreams had been empty. No William Mark. Just as she'd desired; a calm, deep, satisfying rest.

The bells were ringing for Sunday service.

Dodson's crutch leaned against the wall as he sat on the pavement, wooden leg stretched out. Jane paused for a long minute, watching as people on their way to church stopped to talk to the beggar, then bend over and put a coin or two in his cup. Most had probably never noticed he'd gone, but now they were pleased to see him. Maybe there was some kindness in the world.

She didn't try to give him money, just a few moments of talk as Sally watched.

Simon. The name ran through her. Everything would be well, she felt sure of it. She *knew*. He'd always been there.

They were close enough to the water to smell the stink and hear the voices of the bargemen as they worked on the wharves. She saw Sally open her mouth to speak.

Before any words, a scream came. Shrill. Petrified.

They started to run towards it.

THIRTY

'Where?'

'It can't be far.'

On the Calls, feeling as if they were dashing through a world that had slowed down around them. Past Pitfall. Eyes searching, straining to hear another scream, or any noise at all, so they'd know where to go.

Jane glanced down. She held the knife in her hand, no memory of drawing it. Sally had her blade ready. People cowed away from them, terrified.

Her heart was thudding. Beating so hard it seemed to bruise her ribs.

John.

Another scream, paler, weaker than the first.

'There.' Up Call Lane, close now. She could feel it, taste it like iron in her mouth.

One more sound. Weaker, hopeless. Down into Queen's Court. The passageway was dark, barely wide enough for one person.

John.

Jane stopped to take a breath. Sally squeezed ahead of her. Just enough time to see her face. Set. Hard. Deadly. Then she was moving. Three yards and the ground widened. More light around them. Wrecks of buildings on either side.

There, in the deep shadows at the far end. A figure on the ground, with another above it, kneeling, arm raised.

John.

The smell of decay filled the air.

She stopped, touched the gold ring. For luck. To stay alive. To hope for Simon.

Sally plunged down the court. She shouted his name, letting it hammer down off the walls. He turned his head and she was on him.

Jane stood. She was there if the girl needed her. But this was Sally's fight. It had burned in her since she saw Harold's body. He'd beaten her before. Now the flame roared.

Sally's knife flashed as she brought it down. John grunted and
rolled away. Trying to find space to fight. He was bleeding; it
was smeared and shiny on his clothes.

As he squirmed, Jane saw the face of his victim. Manchester
Minnie, the beggar. She was dying, it was there on her face. But
she couldn't get close enough to pull the old woman free.

Sally lunged again, then parried a desperate blow. Brought her
foot up and kicked his knee. Another grunt as he stumbled. It
was enough. She pressed, forcing him back against the wall,
stabbing, cutting as he tried to fight her off.

Jane watched the girl's eyes, seeing the hate flare.

Sally moved fast. A feint. A shift. To the left. The right.
Confusing him. Going low, bring the knife up hard between his
legs. He howled. He tried to hit her, but Sally had already pulled
back. She was panting with blood lust. Eyes alert for any small
movement John made.

This was her revenge.

It was for every pain and hurt she'd ever known. For all her
terror about Simon.

Carefully, Jane squatted and took Minnie's hand. A small
squeeze to let her know someone was with her while metal
clashed on metal. A soft, peaceful sound as she gave her final
breath and her feeble grip was gone.

One more John had killed. Another name on the bill for him
to pay.

She stood and took a pace towards him. Dodson, Minnie. He owed
the world for all his evil. John's eyes flickered towards the girl.

For a moment, he wasn't watching Sally. That was all she
needed to drive her blade home in his belly. All the way to the
hilt. As she pulled it out, dripping with blood, he made a feeble
cut that only sliced through air.

He'd long ago put himself beyond mercy.

Sally was lashing out again. Knife, fists, feet. John's fingers
opened and let go of his blade. With the toe of her boot, she
kicked it beyond his reach.

He looked at her. The anger could only flicker in his eyes.

'It's time to stop,' Jane said quietly.

'Why?' Sally turned on her. 'He killed Harold. He might have
killed Simon.'

She nodded at the woman's body in the dirt. 'He's killed Minnie, too. But look at him.'

The girl stared down at John. His breathing was ragged, whistling in his chest, scarcely there. 'What about him? Do you think he deserves to live?'

'He's already dead. You see all that blood? There's hardly any left in his body. Two minutes and he'll be gone. He can't crawl away from this.' She stared down at him, no expression on her face. 'He was dead before he ever came to Leeds.' She placed her left hand on Sally's arm. Fingers splayed, the small one missing. 'You've killed him.'

With a reluctant nod, the girl wiped the knife on her dress and slid it away. A final glance as they pulled shawls over their hair and left through the other end of Queen's Court. John's eyes were empty. It was over.

Finally. The hunt was done. It had loomed so large. Consumed them, then finished so quickly.

Over. It seemed hard to believe.

But it wasn't all finished. Not with Simon lying in the infirmary.

All the noise, the people on Briggate was overwhelming. Every one of them going about their lives, not knowing what had happened just a few yards away.

Sally looked dazed.

'Come on,' Jane urged her.

'Wait.' She stopped over a horse trough and sluiced cold water over her face and hands to wash away John's blood. There was plenty of it across her dress, for anyone who looked. The water seemed to wake her. 'It's done,' she said.

The story was over. No need to talk about it as they made their way to the infirmary. Jane felt her heart pounding and heard the thud of her boots on the pavements as they hurried along the streets.

Alive and whole. The words ran over and over through her head as they passed the Mixed Cloth Hall, all the way to the infirmary.

Simon. The fever during the night.

A hand reached for hers. Sally, looking young and frightened. 'Simon? Will he . . .'

'Yes,' Jane told her as she looked at the doors in front of her. 'He will.'

She took a breath. It was time.

It was easier to keep his eyes closed. Opening them was too much of an effort. The light of the day was too bright, too intense.

The night had been a battle. There had been times he'd thought his body would give up. Hours when he'd believed it would be easier to let go of life. But he couldn't. He had too many things holding him here.

Each time he breathed, pain sliced through his body. It felt normal now; he'd forgotten what life might be like without it. It was deepest in his leg. In his wound, he felt as if a furnace was roaring.

Rosie was sitting by the side of his bed. Not saying a word, but he felt her. Hour after hour. With him through it all. Tethering him to home.

The scrape of chair legs, then a man's short cough. The surgeon; Simon smelled the tobacco and brandy on him. Fingers probed the cut and examined the skin on his thigh. Each push was another stab, searing him.

Finally he was done. Now the verdict.

They stood in the heavy air outside the hospital.

'The surgeon said Simon's fever has broken. He's through the worst. Now he needs to mend.' Rosie was crying, her face filled with joy and relief. Sally embraced her, clutching tight like a daughter.

Jane closed her eyes and let the joy flood through her. The world felt right again.

'Will he be able to walk?' she asked.

Rosie breathed in, then gave a slow nod. 'It might take a long time. He'll probably always need a stick.' Her eyes were shining, and bright. 'But he's alive. That's the important thing. The surgeon says he's strong. He should make a complete recovery. As long as there's no infection . . .'

Jane listened, but she was off in her own thoughts. Grateful that Simon was going to survive, that there wouldn't be that hole in her life. A long time before he was walking, Rosie said. What would happen then?

THIRTY-ONE

Leeds, October 1825

Simon leaned on the stick. He'd walked from Swinegate all the way up Briggate to the market cross near the Head Row, the furthest he'd managed since he was stabbed more than three months before. Still no great distance, but each step felt like a victory. He was growing stronger. Quicker. In August walking one hundred yards from his house to the corner had taken him a quarter of an hour, and left him pale and drained.

He was tired now, but a short rest and he moved on. Limping, favouring his left leg. The scar on his right thigh was livid, but gradually fading. Still some pain, especially if he tried to do too much.

Hard work, but he was learning. A few yards further and he opened the door of Mudie's printing works. His first time here since spring, but as he looked around, nothing had changed.

'About the only difference is that I'm older and poorer,' George Mudie told him as they sat.

He sighed, feeling the relief as he eased the weight from his legs.

'How's your business?' Simon asked.

'It's business.' He shrugged. 'I've been putting money aside, towards what I owe you.'

'Thank you.' Every penny was welcome. He hadn't been able to work since the knife had entered his body. Foley had visited him, telling him what Jane had done, then adding more to the fee he'd paid. Simon had passed over half of it to the girl; she was the one who'd earned it.

There was money in the bank; they were a long way from starving. But it wouldn't last forever. The itch to work was finally back after so long simply thinking about recovering. Finding the strength to keep going through another day. This last fortnight, things had changed. All those fears that had snapped at him even before Will Mark's appearance had finally vanished. He'd begun

to look out at the world and be ready to be a thief-taker in it
again.

'You have colour in your cheeks, Simon.' Mudie raised a bottle
of brandy, but he shook his head. Too early. Too dangerous to
start drinking.

'It's about all I do have.' Each time he studied himself in the
mirror, he saw the change. He'd lost weight, his clothes hung
loose where they'd once fitted well. He face was gaunt. More
grey in his hair. Right before his own eyes, Simon Westow was
turning into an old man.

'You're alive. That's better than many.'

He was right. But it was none of his own doing that he was
still breathing. That was Jane and Sally, the surgeon and Rosie.
All he'd done was give in to his fear in that last fight. He'd
hesitated, waited a moment too long and come close to paying
everything for it.

Jane had visited. He'd questioned her until she told him
everything about Mark's end. No mention of the other man, John.
Sally had said nothing, either. They'd built a wall of silence. If
a body had ever been found, he'd been too ill to hear about it.

Simon made his slow way back down Briggate. Autumn in
the air, with a swirling wind blowing the soot and smoke all
around. He paused for a moment, realizing he was a few yards
from where Middle Row had once stood. Where the business
with William Mark had really begun. Such a small thing, so
ordinary: find and return a set of silver cups that had been stolen.
It had turned into something more than he ever expected. He'd
done his job, but in the end, had it been worth the cost?

He rested his weight on the stick, grateful to Rosie. She'd
bought it for him. The wood was a deep, dense ebony, the handle
a textured knob of shining silver. It looked elegant and it definitely
made walking easier.

'Turn the top,' she said while he tested the balance in his hands.

Curious, he twisted it, feeling something click. Looking at it,
he began to pull. A long, thin blade. A sword. Simon stared at
it in disbelief.

'It belonged to the husband of a woman I know,' she explained.
'He decided to stop carrying it.'

'I'm not a swordsman—'

'I know. But in case someone attacks you. It'll scare them.'

He'd never be a knife man again. He only carried one these days, not the three he used to strap on his body. No point; the agility had vanished, and it was never going to return; Dr Hey had been emphatic on that. Perhaps it was for the best. But with this he had an unexpected weapon to defend himself. If he returned to work, he might be grateful to have it.

'Remembering, Westow?'

He turned at the sound. Constable Porter, people moving out of the way around him. With a flourish of noise, a coach came out of the Rose and Crown Yard and thundered over the cobbles, on its way to some other town.

'Difficult to believe anything once stood there, isn't it?'

The man snorted. 'Good bloody riddance to it.' A moment, then a nod. 'I'm glad he didn't kill you.'

Simon chuckled. 'So am I.'

'I heard it was that lass who did for him.'

Safer for Jane if he admitted nothing. 'I was a patient in the infirmary, remember, wondering whether to die. Does it matter?'

'No, I don't suppose it does.' He glanced up at the sky, then lowered his gaze to Simon face. 'You're out and about. Planning on starting back to work soon, Westow?'

'If I can find a way.'

'Still a pretty penny to be made in your trade. Plenty of people know you in this town. They ask me about you. Maybe you should think about it.'

'We'll see.' A tip of the hat and he limped along the street.

Finally he was home, sitting weary but satisfied at the kitchen table.

Work. Work . . .

Almost a week later, on a Monday morning, he sat and listened to the stillness of the house. The boys had just left, chattering as they went to their classes at the grammar school. At first he'd wondered if it was the right choice; now he was pleased with it. They seemed happier, tested every day with learning. They'd stay long enough to put a polish on their education.

Footsteps on the stairs, then Sally came into the kitchen, settling at the other end of the table. Over the last months, she'd spent most of her time with the homeless children, over there almost every day and evening. Good work, but it was hardly a living. Simon knew she spent money on them; her savings had to be growing threadbare.

Rosie was rubbing a finger over the worn embroidery on her dress. An old one that she only wore around the house and for going out shopping. She'd been patient and loving, looking after him while he fumbled his way back to . . . to wherever he was now. Firm when he needed it. But he knew she craved more than that, especially with Richard and Amos now gone each day. Years before, they'd worked together in the thief-taker's trade. She'd helped him at times since then, and he'd seen the hunger in her eyes to do more.

Simon heard the front door open. A moment later, Jane entered. He'd sent her a note, asking her to come. A glance around, then she slid on to the bench, next to Sally.

'It's been a long time,' he began, glancing at their faces. 'It certainly feels that way. But I'm stronger now. Ready to look at working again. I've spent the last few days talking to people. There's business out there, those who'd be happy to employ us. Things are still being stolen and plenty are willing to pay a fee to someone who'll return them.' He paused and tapped his leg. 'I can't do what I used to do. Probably not even a quarter of it. That's obvious. But I know people, and I understand how Leeds works.' He could see them all watching him: Rosie's eyes wide with curiosity, Sally's filled with hope, Jane's showing nothing at all. 'It will be different, but some of it will be the same. No client is going to want to deal with a woman.' He shrugged. 'That's the way of the world. They feel they can trust a man. I can talk to them, soothe them. None of you can go into the inns and alehouses to ask questions. I can. I can talk to lawyers, people in authority. I know plenty of criminals. I'll still be here. Very much a part of it.' Simon halted, giving them time to take in what he'd said.

'It wouldn't be too much of a change from the way things have been. You can see the big difference.' His expression soured. 'I wouldn't wager on myself to win a fight. It's time to work again. But you'd be doing a lot more. I'm going to need you.' He stared at Jane. 'All of you.'

No hesitation from Sally or Rosie. His wife's eyes were alive, shining, eager to have the opportunity. The girl immediately said yes, but he'd been certain she would.

Jane looked down at her lap. Before the Mangey silver and the hidden room, she'd stayed away from this life for months. He'd had to coax her back to it, offer her something different to interest her. From there she'd picked up her old ways. She'd saved his life, and he'd never forget that. He'd barely seen her since the stabbing. Now he was asking her to be a part of this again.

Jane listened. When Sally delivered the message, she'd expected something like this. What other reason could there be for asking her to visit? She sat and talked about it with Mrs Shields, wondering whether to gently refuse the invitation.

She liked her life. Back into a rhythm of reading, walking. The old woman was passing on her knowledge of herbs and fruits. Jane was learning different things. Useful things.

She bought food at the market, saw Kate the pie-seller and Dodson. A chance to listen to Davy Cassidy playing his fiddle and drop a penny or two in his cup. A visit every week to the circulating library to change her book. A small life, but she was content to let it wrap around her.

'Go and see what he has to say,' Mrs Shields told her. 'Listening costs nothing but time, and you have enough of that. I've seen your face sometimes, child.'

'What?' She didn't understand.

'You have a hunger for something more than this.'

The words took her by surprise and made her think.

Now she turned them over in her mind yet again. It was true enough that last time Simon had drawn her back she'd slipped so easily into a thief-taker's life. Was this who she was meant to be? It wasn't too late to stand up and walk out. To leave it all behind again. If she did that, she knew that sooner or later the dreams would return.

From under her lashes, she watched the others. All of them gazing at her, waiting. They would be fine without her. Yet . . .

Jane raised her head. Ready to speak, but still not quite certain what she was going to say.

'I'll do it.'

AFTERWORD

A rthur Mangey really existed. He was a gold and silver-smith in Leeds, and made the Leeds mace. He was also found guilty of the treasonable offence of coin clipping and hung in York. His son joined the clergy and went on to marry the Archbishop of York's daughter.

The evidence against Mangey was flimsy at best, and the shoemaker who accused him had been in jail himself, and did accuse other upright men. He did also vanish for seventeen years after the verdict. I'm grateful to Lee Catton who'd looked into the trial and generously let me have his research. The hidden room was mentioned during the trial, but apparently never investigated. It only came to light when the old Moot Hall and Middle Row were torn down in 1825. Shears and an Elizabethan coin were found in the room.

It's a story that's too good for any crime writer to ignore, and I can't avoid temptation like that. Everything else is my own invention.

I'm grateful, as ever, to all the folk at Severn House, especially my editor, Sara Porter, Mary Karayel, and Shayna Holmes. Lynne Patrick helps improve my writing with her work, as she's done for a long time now. I'm thankful, too, to all who review and read these books. And, above all, Penny Lomas, for her love, support and critique.